The Missing

The Missing Husband

Vijay Medtia

ISBN 9780946745340
Crocus

Copyright © Vijay Medtia 2019

The right of Vijay Medtia to be identified as the author of this work has been asserted in accordance with section 77 of the Copyright, Designs and Patents Act 1988.

The characters, institutions and situations in this book are entirely imaginary and bear no relation to real persons, institutions or actual happenings.

First published in 2019 by Crocus

Crocus books are published by Commonword, 3 Planetree House, 21-31 Oldham Street, Manchester, M1 1JG

A CIP catalogue for this book is available from the British Library.

No part of this publication may be reproduced without written permission except in the case of very brief extracts embodied in critical articles, reviews or lectures. For further information contact Commonword.

admin@cultureword.org.uk

Crocus books are distributed by Turnaround Publisher Services Ltd, Unit 3, Olympia Trading Estate, Coburg Rd, Wood Green, London N22 6TZ UK

Cover design by tymedesign
Cover image by Naomi Kalu
Printed by biddles.co.uk

CROCUS

Acknowledgements

Dedicated to my family, without whom nothing would have been possible.

Thank you, with kind regards to my publisher, Crocus Books, U.K., for believing in my novel.

Finally, my heartfelt gratitude to my kind and demanding editor, Peter Kalu, who didn't allow a single line to escape.

1

THERE ARE some cases that are more trouble than they're worth. This thought occurred to me as Gautam, a public prosecutor, invited me for a drink. He said he had a delicate case that required discretion. The party was a multi-millionaire, Joseph Fernandez and his daughter. He explained the details and yes, this sounded dangerous and embarrassing for Fernandez. We were sitting outside the Oberoi Hotel looking out at the Arabian Sea. In the distance, you could see the lights of cargo ships. A cool sea breeze touched my face, bringing with it the smell of seaweed. He cut me short when I asked about the daughter and slapped his thigh,

–Well, well, talk of the bloody devil. Look across the road, see that woman with the clown on her arm, the one everyone's staring at? Well there she is.

Even from a distance, her face fascinated. It combined a glassy stare, accentuated by pencil line eyebrows, a petite nose and a mouth formed of quick thin lips. She held that snub nose as if she sailed some inches above the ordinary scent of humanity. A loud laugh and a few wayward steps broke the illusion.

She pulled at the muscular man by her side and steadied herself. People continued staring at her, guessing she was drunk. I couldn't tell whether the inebriation was feigned or real. The man whose job it was to hold her, whispered in her ear almost on cue and she laughed again. Then she stumbled in a way that made her emerald, three quarter wrap dress shimmer under the bright lights. They turned the corner and sailed out of sight.

–She's the wild bundle of trouble we've been discussing. Anita Fernandez, the daughter. And she's out on the town again. I'm so glad my daughters didn't turn out like that.

–She likes to party, it's not a crime. What's the racket? I asked and took a sip from my glass of whisky.

–On the surface, small-time blackmail, but I'm not so sure. Her father will explain the details. He's a prickly old man and if he doesn't like you in the first five minutes then he isn't going to play. He's asked me to be discreet. I've already told you too much. This requires discretion, not your usual blunt and forceful methods.

–In that case, I'd better turn on the charm.

Gautam nodded with a slight smile.

–I've done the setting up and put in a good word. You don't see him otherwise. You'll be meeting him tomorrow afternoon. He leaned into me, –Look, this might be straightforward, but I doubt it. It has a nasty feel to it. These people have the nerve to squeeze someone of Fernandez's standing. So, you need to be careful, but the fees will be generous if you come through.

He had my attention, business had been quiet and I was low on my rupees. The kind of low that makes your stomach grumble.

–You only call me when you have such nice jobs, I said, and finished the drink, –okay, I'll see Fernandez and take my chances.

–You be careful.

–I'll try not to get killed, if that's what you mean.

Next afternoon I headed down to Malabar Hill, the most exclusive residential area of South Mumbai where even a wooden bench costs an arm and a leg. I drove through the small fishing villages scattered along the coastline. These people were the original inhabitants of Mumbai. They had small shack-like houses and their fishing boats were anchored in the sea. Then I skimmed by the large skyscrapers that dominated the Mumbai skyline, and entered the maw of noisy road traffic. It grew every day in equal measure to the pedestrians, people out shopping and heading to work as well as the street traders and the migrants who entered the city of dreams in their hundreds, daily.

The roads grew wider as I entered the richer part of town, driving past the flash houses in Malabar Hill. I slowed and turned left just past the newspaper stand. A peacock stood on the pavement. It spread its deep blue and green feathers with the false eyes, and showed itself in full flirtatious glory before a peahen. She didn't seem too interested however, jumped onto a wall and flew away. The feathers swiftly came down. Brother, I thought, we all know that feeling. I drove straight towards the circle.

I had made an effort today to wear a good dark cotton suit, white shirt, black shoes and socks. I was clean-shaven for a change and feeling good, everything a well-dressed private detective should be. This was no ordinary client. He was my ticket to a richer clientele and hopefully some good square meals. Maybe that's what the blackmailers had in mind too. I parked my dark blue Hindustan Contessa near a hedge, careful not to scrape the bodywork, and walked through the side gate to the house.

The house had a clear view of the Arabian Sea and the mansion must have been worth a fortune. I thought to revise my low fees. The sun bounced off the white garden walls as I knocked on the door. A man with horse teeth showed me into the lounge and asked me to wait. Rich people always ask you to wait, it must make them feel even more pompous; a power play they have perfected down the centuries.

The spacious room had Italian bespoke furniture; a family of ten could live here happily. The cream coloured walls matched a rose and cream marble floor with a black border. Sunlight shone through the tall windows and two sets of French doors opened onto a well-kept side garden. I sat in a gold-painted chaise longue and thought I could get used to a place like this. A cool breeze touched my face from the open French doors. The smell of freshly cut grass drifted in, mingled with the scent of roses. I got up and glanced outside. A chauffeur in a grey uniform polished a new 1995-imported Mercedes-Benz. All his attention was on the car and I didn't blame him.

I turned around and studied the oil painting above the stone mantelpiece. A large portrait of a couple in a gold-plated frame. The woman rocked a red evening dress while sitting primly on a gilded chair, her imperious eyes seemed to survey the flaws in me. Behind her stood a man of medium height in a grey suit, a receding hairline, an aristocratic nose and black eyes that stared out. He too was trying to find my inadequacies and it seemed as if he had found them. Mr Fernandez perhaps, when he was younger. He was sixty-six now according to Gautam. His first wife had passed away and he had married a younger woman as men tend to do, some thirty years younger. He had a son and a daughter from his first marriage.

I checked my watch, two-fifteen in the afternoon. A door opened and a woman strode in with an owner's confidence. She was twenty-five or so, held a black purse and looked ready to leave. She wore an ochre coloured top with the word *Hippy* written across the front. Her green cotton trousers matched her dreamy eyes, eyes that will you to write poetry. When she came closer however, I could see the eyes were more drunk than dreamy. I had seen her yesterday.

–Hello, you are tall, she said.

–You have good observation skills.

She tilted her head with a puzzled look. I noticed the Portuguese bloodline in her features.

–Handsome too. We call men like you TDH.

–You make me sound like a phone company.

–Tall, dark and handsome. She smiled and shifted feet at

the same time, –What's your name?

–Subramanyam Saraswati Narayana.

–A very long name.

–You should hear my uncle's, I said.

–I don't care about your uncle's, but you don't look like a South Indian.

–I'm not. My parents just didn't like short names.

She bit her lower lip and tilted her head. Most men would have folded right there and then. Some would have folded even before that. She looked me up and down, the feet squaring up.

–What are you doing in my house?

–I help people with delicate problems. I'm a private detective.

Her eyes narrowed a fraction. –You're not really a detective, but it sounds fun.

–I'm not sure about fun but it has its moments.

–You're teasing me, Narayana indeed. Are you married? I'm guessing you are. That shouldn't stop you enjoying life to the full.

–You have it all figured out, why don't you become a detective?

–Maybe I will.

She moved closer, shook my hand and looked at me. Her breath smelt of whisky. She was trouble all right, the kind of trouble that made fools take out a second mortgage and blow it on a wild weekend in Goa.

–What are you doing this evening? I promise not to tell your wife.

–I don't think that far ahead and I'm not married.

As much as she tried to hide it, there was an edge of nervousness when she spoke.

–I'm at a party at Rubies tonight. I'm bored and you would be a nice change.

–You make me sound like a vacation.

She squeezed my hand. Her eyes promised that holiday

right now. She almost had me. A man chose that moment to enter. He looked like a wrestler, black crew cut hair, medium height, and the grim face of a man passed over for promotion repeatedly because he had the habit of entering rooms at the wrong time. He wore a tight-fitting grey suit with a black tie and moved towards us like a tank.

–Don't forget me tonight, she said, moving away from me. She turned to the man, –MD, I'll be home late tonight. Tell Papa not to wait up, though I know he won't. She smiled, gave me a little wave, and bounced out of the room.

–Sir will see you now, Mr Abhay Chauhan.

He gave me the hard look of a jealous boyfriend.

–Are you the butler?

The look got worse.

–No, I'm Mr Fernandez's personal secretary. Everyone calls me MD, it stands for Manoj Das.

–Is her name Anita Fernandez?

He nodded and frowned.

–She knows how to make a man feel welcome. You could pick up some tips from her.

He pulled his lips tight against his teeth. We left the lounge through the French doors without a word. Talking wasn't his strong point, I guessed. That was okay with me.

2

WE WALKED down the steps, parrots flew from one Neem tree to another calling with their shrill cries. The chauffeur ignored us as we headed to the rear garden. At one end, across the lawn, stood a man spraying red roses. An apartment block was under construction to our far right. The faint sound of cement mixers cut across and spoilt the idyllic setting a little.

MD's heavy tread led me across the lawn. We reached the main man. He wore a beige cotton shirt, trousers and a grey scarf. He stood with a slight stoop and his silver-grey hair was short. When he turned, the aristocratic nose was intact, and a grey moustache and goatee beard added to his gravitas. The man in the oil painting, Joseph Fernandez. He placed a red glove on the side table along with an ant spray.

–This is Abhay Chauhan, Sir. The private detective.

Fernandez stared as a bank manager might, wondering about my income and suitability. He stared a good while and looked as if he thought I didn't have two rupees to rub together. And I had made an effort to dress well today. He didn't offer to shake my hand.

–Thank you for coming. What would you like to drink?

–Anything with a kick will do.

–MD, send two Bacardis, it's early, and place some lemon inside.

–I'll have it freshly cut, Manoj.

–It is always freshly cut Mr Chauhan, said MD, his jaw line hardening.

Then he ignored me.

–I will tell the butler Sir. Will there be anything else? I need to take a file to Madam.

–Is my dear wife back?

–No Sir, Madam is at the office. Would you like me to call her?

–Not yet, thank you. Where would I be without Maya.

The tank moved back across the lawn and Fernandez half turned to spray the roses.

–Do you mind if we talk whilst I finish this? The ants and mosquitoes have been very bad this year. They have been causing me all kinds of problems.

–Don't mind me.

Three gardeners were trimming a hedge to our far right.

–I know what you're thinking young man, but it keeps me active. It gives me joy. Do you like gardening?

–I don't think I'd mind it, if I had a garden. I have a one-bedroom apartment in Boriwali.

–Oh, I see. You must have been an honest Police Inspector.

–We all make mistakes.

He had my background information, Gautam had filled him in. A butler hurried across the lawn and placed a silver tray on the table. Two expensive looking glasses, with freshly cut lemon, Bacardi and soda. Fernandez nodded and the man left. He finished spraying the roses. We took our glasses.

–To your health, he said.

I raised the glass. It was a fine tasting Bacardi. The finest I'd tasted in a while.

–Tell me about yourself Mr Chauhan, I'd like to know with whom I'm dealing.

–I'll keep it brief. I'm a licensed, Private Detective. I don't do divorces or run after unfaithful spouses. I'm thirty-four, single and nowhere near rich. I'm good with secrets and if you're on the level, I'll be with you all the way. Cross me, and you won't like me.

Fernandez shook his head slightly and a faint smile

appeared at the corner of his mouth.

–You don't say.

–I used to be an idealistic Police Inspector, but five years on the Mumbai force sorted that out. I was born on the poor tracks of the city. I've had to fight hard for everything I've achieved, nothing was given to me on a silver plate.

–I was told you were different.

–I'm different all right. I live in Boriwali, the Sanjay Gandhi National Park just behind. About four years ago, I set up in this line of work. It pays the bills most of the time, and I actually like working for myself. I took a couple of cases for Gautam. He explained your problem and one more thing, I don't like authority figures interfering in my work.

–Is that why you left the force?

–I suppose so. I didn't like working for donkeys, and some of my seniors gave donkeys a bad name.

–What do you know so far?

–I have some details but it's better if you explain it.

He took a long drink and looked as if he still hadn't decided about my suitability.

–My dear wife Sandria passed away when I was fifty-five. A year or so later, I met and married Maya. She is, he coughed and took another sip. –She's younger than I am and that's why my children drifted away, I think. I wouldn't say they hate me exactly but it's not far from the truth. Maya was a breath of fresh air though, she helped me overcome the loss of Sandria. Now she's busy running the company and socialising.

He stared at the table.

–We might as well be living in two separate houses. I don't blame her, you see she was twenty-five when we met, an age difference for sure, but she has been good to me.

I resisted from saying anything on the age difference.

–What about your son?

–He's about your age and a wastrel. I had high hopes, but he's a playboy and drunkard in Europe somewhere. I haven't seen him in five years, imagine. My daughter isn't much better. She's a little wild. It's my fault, I neglected them whilst I built my business.

I took a sip from the glass.

–Any ideas about who might be causing you this trouble?

–I'm coming to that. I've cut down on company affairs now. Board directors, Maya and my secretary oversee things. After the way my children turned out, the motivation has gone. I don't want this embarrassment at my age. I'm only glad that Sandria never lived to see it. It would have killed her.

I tried again, –About your problem.

He narrowed his eyes as he looked up at me.

–You're impatient. Prem Nath is the same. You wouldn't know him, but Anita married him earlier this year. A good man and they were happy for a while. It lasted only six months and even that was an achievement for Anita. He used to be in the army you know and he's tough too. Then they decided to divorce against my wishes, but before it could be finalised Prem disappeared. It's five weeks ago now, yes, the start of October. No sign or word, nothing. I'll be frank, it's really worrying me. It's not like Prem to just disappear.

This took me by surprise, Gautam hadn't mentioned anything about the son-in-law.

–I met Anita just now. You wouldn't have guessed she's missing her husband.

–She's hiding her feelings and has gone off the rails a little. I spoilt her I'm afraid. She says he will turn up soon. Prem used to brighten up the place. He had so many Army stories, funny too, liked his drink. Then he just disappears. I don't blame him, Anita could test the patience of a saint.

–Anyone looking for Prem Nath?

He nodded slowly.

–The Missing Persons Bureau. However, they are incompetent. No leads in five weeks. I would have been better finding him myself. Do you know what they said?

Fernandez narrowed his eyes and a little anger flashed inside.

–They think he's committed suicide. Prem was tougher than that.

–He might turn up, I said.

He nodded again.

–I hope so, perhaps he's blowing off some steam. He did that one time for two weeks and returned. He stopped Anita's excesses but now she's out of control. She drove him away. A stupid marriage of course but if anyone could save my girl from ruin, it was Prem. I hope I can trust you Mr Chauhan.

–You can trust me Joseph. Do you mind if we drop the formalities, you can call me Abhay.

The wrinkles deepened around his eyes.

–Yes, I do mind. Address me as Mr Fernandez until I say so.

I let it be; you don't become a multi-millionaire by being easy-going, I guess.

–India has been good to us. I bought this place thirty years ago. Mumbai wasn't crowded then, clean, and beautiful. Sandria loved India, it was her decision to move here from Goa, a good financial decision. The business expanded tenfold. Now however, my second wife wants to sell and move to America. I've been offered a fortune by developers, but you can't keep selling everything Mr Chauhan, then there is no sense of belonging, and besides Sandria died here, in my arms. No, I cannot sell this house at any price.

He stared at the grass.

I waited before saying, –We could do with discussing your problem.

He rubbed his forehead and said, –Sorry, I haven't spoken like this in weeks. Anyway, there are people demanding money. It's left a bitter taste. I would have put the rascals straight myself if I'd been younger.

He put his glass down, took out a red envelope from his

trouser pocket and passed it to me. I finished the Bacardi, placed the glass on the table and took the envelope.

–They want ten lakh rupees in cash, he said, –They have... well they say they have compromising photos of Anita.

His voice grew weak with embarrassment as he said that, and he couldn't meet my eyes.

–Have you asked her?

–Yes. She thought it was funny. No shame, I tell you. She can't remember and said she was probably drunk at the time.

I straightened a little.

–Do you believe her?

–No, I don't. She would sell me if she could. It's not a nice thing to have to say about one's daughter.

There was an awkward silence and I could feel his great disappointment.

–When did you receive this letter?

–A few days ago.

I waited a moment, looked at him and said,

–Do you think Prem is involved?

–Good God, no, not Prem, this is small change. I gave him more than that as a wedding gift.

I raised my eyebrows. It was more than a year's salary for most hard-working people. I opened the envelope, pulled out a typed letter on a blank piece of paper. I turned it over. Everything was on one side, typed in bold black letters. The signature at the bottom was hand-written with a blue pen. It was addressed to Fernandez.

Dear Sir,

We have intimate photos of your daughter. We don't wish to send them to the Society magazines for publication. We understand your esteemed reputation. The photos will cause you extreme embarrassment. You ignored the first request for five lakhs three weeks ago, and now these people want ten lakhs in cash, next Thursday. We work as intermediaries and wish to help keep your good name. On prompt payment, the photos and negatives will be returned. Any POLICE involvement, will mean publication.

Well-wisher,

A.S. Santana

Santana Ladies Boutique. Marina Road, Mumbai.

I read it twice.
–What do you think?
–I'm not sure Mr Fernandez. Have you contacted this Santana? Does Anita know him?
–She says she doesn't remember but I think she does. I sent MD to speak to this Santana. He was arrogant and told MD the people behind this want payment or there will be consequences. MD said we had better pay or call the police.
– Did you speak to the police?
He shook his head side to side.
–Not yet, I don't trust them. It would leak out and the magazines would be at my front door, not to mention the newspapers. It would be a disaster. I can't afford this humiliation at my age. It took me a long time to build my reputation. This would make me a laughing stock.
–Do you think Anita might have spoken to your wife. Explained what's happened?
–No, she hasn't. She hates Maya even more than me. This isn't what you would call a home. It's the envy of people but it's a cold unwelcoming hotel. We are strangers living under the same roof. I see more of my servants than I do my family.
–I'm sorry to hear that, but it is your house.
–It's not been a home since my dear Sandria...
 He looked melancholic.

–Okay, this is a blackmail demand with intimidation thrown in. It's not a problem if you pay them. You said ten lakhs was peanuts. If they're your well-wishers, then they'll hand over the prints and let the matter rest.

–Don't you wish to earn money, Mr Chauhan?

–I do and things have been quiet lately, but I don't like to rob people.

He straightened. His eyes gleamed with irritation.

–You're right, I can pay them. But I have pride. I won't stand for it.

–I'd feel the same way. Santana could be an ex-boyfriend trying to cash in on Anita. I'm hoping that's the case, then it wouldn't be difficult. However, if he's part of a blackmail gang, then it could be a bigger problem. You have to be vigilant, people get shot when they become careless. Does Anita have money in her own right?

Fernandez looked at me and stroked his moustache.

–I give her a generous allowance each month but it's never enough. Since Maya took control however, money has tightened. They have shouting matches, but Maya is right, you have to be strict.

–Who else knows about this problem?

–Maya, and she wants to pay and settle the matter.

He took a deep breath.

–Well, Mr Chauhan, are you going to help me or not?

I closed my fist and placed the envelope in my pocket. This could be more trouble than it was worth but I liked Fernandez. Dare I say it, I felt sorry for him. Besides, business had been quiet.

–All right, I'll get Santana off your back. It may cost you, besides what you pay me. It's better to deal with this now before the demands get higher. They think you're an easy touch.

–Thank you, he said, –What are your fees?

–Fifteen hundred rupees per day plus expenses.

He raised his eyebrows.

–You're joking. I pay the gardeners more than that.

–In that case, I might have to look into gardening work.

He smiled. –Okay, we have a deal Abhay Chauhan. If this is completed successfully, allow me to pay what I think is appropriate.

–I can live with that.

We shook hands. A gentleman's agreement. They are stronger than legally binding contracts, or at least they used to be.

–I'll need to speak with Anita and your wife sometime.

–If it helps.

–Where can I find your wife?

–At the office, and Mr Chauhan, he said, looking me straight in the eye, –I wish you luck.

He passed me two cards, one with his address, the other with Maya Fernandez on it and the company address. I turned, walked out through the plush gardens towards my dark blue Hindustan Contessa. It had double headlamps to either side of a metal grill with the small HM logo. It looked older after glimpsing the world of the rich but at least it was mine. I wasn't sure about the sound of this creep Santana and the whole thing had a nasty feel about it.

3

MARINA ROAD fell outside of Malabar Hill, and Santana had a small frontage store there. A man pushed a trolley cart of empty red gas containers, as I drove past. It looked as if the weight of the world was on his shoulders. I parked the car across the street to go and check it out. Above the glass front, it read in bold red capitals A. S. SANTANA LADIES BOUTIQUE. If this was the man, he wasn't hiding it. I crossed the road, dodging some scooters and bicycles. There was a mannequin in the window wearing a red dress, with a nice smile. I almost smiled back. Several stores ran along the front; one was shining with gold jewellery, and next to that a men's barbers. The barber stood at the entrance smoking, a man with short black hair, a quiff and wearing a black apron. He stared at me strangely as I entered the boutique.

The store was bigger inside, a long rectangular-shaped shop with women's clothes packed on shelves. It was hardly a boutique, more a case of cheap dresses sold at the highest prices. The place smelled nice however, and the perfume drifted from a woman who sat behind the counter. At the far end, there was a closed door. It crossed my mind that Santana could be behind it, another office where he wrote out those nasty little notes.

The woman walked towards me with a cool indifference, in a tight blue skirt and a faint orange coloured blouse. Thirtyish, sharp black eyes that measured me with every step, and they had made a quick judgement: I represented trouble, even though I smiled. She stood erect and folded her arms across her chest. This was one tough lady. You couldn't charm her

quickly, she'd probably heard all the lines before.
 –You don't look like a man who buys women's clothes.
 –Cross-dressing is all the rage in the West, I said.
 –The men are funny over there.
 I smiled, –Some definitely are.
 –How can I help?
 –I'm looking for a birthday dress for my sister.
 Her eyes became cooler and she looked impatient.
 –What size?
 –A tricky question. I have no idea, what about this yellow dress, here?
 She raised her left eyebrow.
 –If you don't know her size, you're wasting your time. That dress is 7,000 rupees.
 –What's it made of, gold?
 –If the price is too high, we have some cheaper ones at the back, she said it tartly and raised her head a little.
 –I'd like to discuss a good discount. Is Santana in? Perhaps he can help.
 She touched her nose.
 –I'm sorry he isn't in, and we don't give discounts. You can try the mall where you can haggle as much as you like, she said, her voice brusque.
 –You're missing a trick, I might have bought two if you gave discounts.
 She shifted her weight to her left leg.
 –Are you really looking for a dress?
 –My sister won't speak to me if I don't buy her one. She doesn't speak to me much as it is.
 She gave me a cool stare, wondering how much truth I was speaking. I looked back, smiled, and then glanced at the back door.
 –I'd like to meet Santana, some of these dresses belong in the mall not in a boutique.
 –He isn't in, I told you that already.

I felt the material of the yellow dress, it was soft and of good quality.

–I can wait. Santana might be able to help. My sister will kill me if I don't buy her a dress.

–She'll have to kill you then, she said, –He will be out *all* day. Anything else?

–I guess that covers it. You're going to break my sister's heart.

She looked as if she couldn't care less, pushed her nose in the air and walked back to the counter. Outside, the barber was still leaning on the doorframe and he had finished his cigarette. He straightened when I walked over.

He was slim and of medium height, but the energy was in his quick eyes.

–Find what you were looking for?

–No, they don't have a size 20.

–It would look good on you.

He had a barber's easy chatting manner.

–It might at that, but before you propose to me, the dress is for my sister.

–Isn't that what they all say?

I let him have that and smiled.

–Can I help, saab?

–She's a cold fish in there.

–Ice Baby? She's arrogant and won't even look at me.

–For a boutique, they don't have many dresses.

–No surprise. Santana's hardly ever there.

I glanced around and said,

–Who's he?

–The owner, saab. There's a man with all the luck. He attracts women as a dog attracts fleas. A different girl every week. He isn't even good looking. And I think he has some mental issues you know saab, he's not all there, there's something bad about him, but I didn't tell you this. He just gives me a bad vibe.

–So, he doesn't pay attention to the store?

−I don't know how he makes it run. I work six days a week and I still can't afford the car he has. He bought a new white Tata Sumo SUV.

−I have a mind to complain about Ice Baby, she doesn't give discounts. Where can I find the owner?

He looked up:

−Your best bet is the Rubies nightclub. He's there most evenings.

−What does he look like?

He shrugged his small shoulders.

−What's in it for me?

−You're standing up for all the sisters. I'm going to make a complaint.

−My memory isn't so good, he said and rubbed his hands together.

I took out my wallet and slipped him a fifty-rupee note.

−Yes saab, it's coming back, he said with more cheer on his face. −Santana's a gym bunny. He likes to act tough, thirty tops, and he won't care less for your complaint. He won't give you a discount either, really tight with his money. He has never given me a tip yet for a shave or a haircut.

−Thanks, I said, and took a step away.

−I'm sure you're not looking for a dress.

−You're smart.

−You have to be in today's world, saab. Are you a police inspector?

−Not a bad guess.

I nodded and was about to move, when he added.

−If you need a haircut, I'm the best, and I only use A grade blades.

What would a lightweight like Santana be doing blackmailing Joseph Fernandez? I thought, as I walked across to my car. He was way out of his league, unless he was working an angle with Anita Fernandez. Santana was too careless to be part of the underworld; they didn't operate in the open like this. No, it looked like Santana was a Romeo-boy making easy money from worried parents. That could explain his new car, and the disinterest in his business. I could wait here for him but I was also curious about Maya Fernandez, a young wife taking control of the business, because the children were wastrels.

I imagined her as a sharp operator, someone with charm and persuasive powers. Perhaps a striking looking woman too, for she had won over Fernandez. Big businessmen aren't won over too easily. Yes, I was curious about her, and she could be my biggest challenge. She ran his business and that required a level of smart beyond most men. I could try and catch Santana at Rubies. The club would be expensive, and my fees didn't seem enough. I decided I wanted to meet Maya Fernandez first.

4

AT THE first set of lights, two little boys tapped on the window, stretched out their hands and called, *–rupiya, rupiya*. I gave them ten rupees, they smiled, ran and knocked on the next car. Mumbai was a tough city to make a living. It took a little longer to reach the offices because two motorbikes had collided, and the riders were shouting and swearing as if they were in my part of town. The FT, as Fernandez Towers was known around here, was a high-rise building of fifty floors or so, a rectangular block, several storeys higher than the other ones around it. It had a blue glass front, and the half-full car park was to three sides. I drove in and parked my Contessa, the exhaust coughing more than was healthy. I headed into the spacious foyer.

The signboard told me most of the floors were rented to various businesses and the middle section were apartments; the top five floors however were taken up by Fernandez Enterprises. The receptionist was chatting to the security guards in black uniforms with pistols fastened to their sides. None of them seemed interested in me. The lift doors opened. Two men and a woman in glasses stepped out.

–But by God Jyoti, Lakha shares are trading at one-ninety, it's a steal, have you bought any?

–I'm thinking about it.

–Don't think, buy.

I ignored them, and sailed up in the spacious lift, which stopped several times as people came in and out again with a bell sounding each time. The lift reached the top floor and I hoped Mrs Fernandez was in her office. I hadn't had much luck with Ice Baby. The smell of paint filled the corridor, and workers in blue overalls were in the lobby. Flowerpots were spaced evenly along the hallway and the scent of the flowers was competing with the paint.

The office doors had half-glass panels with dozens of people sitting in front of computers and telephones. They looked as if the taxman had called, maybe he had. No wonder Fernandez thought ten lakhs was peanuts, with this many employees. I walked along the corridor, glanced out of the tall windows; we were high in the sky all right. The receptionist was a sturdy no-nonsense woman and her eyes were staring at a pencil case in front of her. She was trying to kill it, I thought, just with her eyes. She sat behind a wide desk and had a square face that said, flirting won't work. She glanced at me, while speaking on the telephone.

–No, you listen Yousef bhai, this is no good. The delivery should have been here this morning, Mrs Fernandez is very strict about that. If you can't bring it today, the order will be cancelled... I beg your pardon, be reasonable? I'm being reasonable, goodbye.

She put the phone down, noted something in her diary and glanced up with the frustration of the last call on her face. When I smiled, she looked like she wanted to slap my face.

–You can't find reliable people these days, I said.

–You certainly cannot. And you are?

–Abhay Chauhan. I have an appointment to see Mrs Fernandez.

Her eyebrows knitted together as she flicked through the thick diary with chubby short fingers. I knew what she was going to say. I moved towards a door that had a name upon it. Mrs Maya Fernandez, Chief Executive Officer. The door was slightly ajar and I heard a woman say.

–The old fool, why doesn't he leave all this to me?

–I suggested the same, said a voice that sounded like MD.

–He's become stubborn of late and I don't know what to

do, Manoj...

A tap on my shoulder forced me to turn around just as it was becoming interesting. The receptionist held her thick diary as if she meant to slam it over my head.

–There's no appointment for you. You lied to me and now you need to leave. I knew I hadn't heard of you before.

–There must be some mistake.

–I don't make mistakes, Mr Chauhan.

–I believe you, sister, I said and tried to smile.

–And I'm not your sister.

–Thank God.

–Do you want me to call Security?

–Call them if you like.

She sighed and held the diary tighter. She looked as if she wanted to grab my arm, twist it and slam me to the floor. And she looked very capable of it. Luckily, the office door opened and another wrestler stood before me.

–MD, this person is being very difficult. He doesn't have an appointment. We should call Security at once.

–I thought we were getting along, I said.

–My foot!

–It's all right, Mrs Patil, I will handle this, said MD.

She turned and marched back to the desk with a look that would stop an Alsatian in his tracks.

– I think you saved me, MD.

–I might regret it, he said dryly. –You're a man of surprises Mr Chauhan.

–You have no idea. I'd like to speak to Mrs Fernandez.

A sharp voice called from behind: –Manoj, who is it?

–Madam, I was telling you about the detective...

–Oh, let him in, if he's here.

The voice that must belong to Mrs Fernandez had a seductive quality. I walked inside the office. I had never seen one like it; an open plan apartment would be more accurate, with white walls and space everywhere I looked. Large windows showed blue skies and the marble floor gleamed in the light. A cool breeze entered the windows, and there were panoramic views of Malabar Hill; tall and medium white tower blocks intermingled with greenery and the sea in the distance.

It beat my office hands down but that wasn't difficult. A big mahogany desk was to my left with a black leather chair. It had a computer upon it and a printer on a side table. There was a row of new steel cabinets behind the desk and some family photos, but only of Mrs Fernandez and her husband. Anita and her brother were not in a single picture.

She sat to my right on a beige coloured three-piece leather suite. Mrs Fernandez was a striking looking woman with dark eyes that had brains behind them. She wasn't ordinary by a long shot. Maybe there was love involved but I decided it was probably from Fernandez's side. I didn't blame him an inch. I tried to gather my senses, but they were having none of it. She lay on the sofa with her shoes off and made no attempt to rise when she saw me.

She smoothed out her dark red skirt and adjusted her peach coloured blouse. Her black hair curled to her shoulders and she looked at me with a haughty air. Her eyes gave away nothing of her thoughts. At last, she pulled her legs down from the sofa, and slipped her feet into a pair of red heels. She sipped from her glass of orange juice on the glass table. Her eyes took me in, but she had made me wait, to make it clear what she thought of my importance.

–Take a seat.

I sat to her side on an armchair. MD hovered near the desk and picked up a file he had no interest in.

–*Achha*, so you're the private detective. I didn't know they existed in India. I thought they only appeared in films, nosy men snooping around dirty little hotels.

I didn't say anything, and she took another sip; a diamond bracelet shimmered on her right wrist.

–You're Abhay Chauhan?
–Yes, in person.
She looked down at her glass.
–MD said you met Joseph earlier.
–News travels fast.
–He must have liked you, he doesn't like many people these days. You're the third detective he has interviewed recently. He's become stubborn and so hassled these days, so you must have said the right things.
–I guess so.
–There was no need to hire you, actually. We're handling this tricky situation. We don't need an outsider.
–Your husband thought differently.
She looked up.
–No, no, it must have been something more. He wouldn't have hired you for such a trifling matter.
–Ten lakhs isn't trifling.
She gave a superior smile and raised her nose,
–Yes, I understand now, that would be a large amount to you. This bracelet is worth more.
She shook her wrist. The diamonds gleamed in the late afternoon light.
–You paid too much, Mrs Fernandez.
The superior smile disappeared.
–Oh, I can see the similarity, that's exactly what Prem would say. He gave Joseph good company and Prem really shouldn't have disappeared like that. Joseph took it personally you know, although he won't say, or did he?
–He mentioned him, yes, but Anita seemed fine with it.
–Anita's headstrong, she acts first and thinks later. She drove Prem away. If I understand this correctly, you have been hired to find him?
I looked at her, shrugged my shoulders and remained silent.
–What does that mean? she asked.

–It means, I don't know.
–You're not much of talker are you, Mr Chauhan?
–I'm not applying to be a radio host.
–That's good, you wouldn't get the job by a long mile.
I raised my eyebrows and smiled slightly.
–If you're worried about Prem, then the Missing Persons Bureau would be a good place to start. They're a big organisation and finding Prem isn't a one-person job.
–Do you think we're stupid? It's been with the police for the past five weeks and they still haven't any leads.
She glanced at MD. He hadn't opened the file and was looking at me. There was something between the two of them, but I couldn't guess what it was. He hadn't been asked to leave, and she obviously trusted him.
–Don't dismiss the police just yet, they're not all bad, I added.
–Oh, but how in heavens will you find Prem? Joseph wants to feel like he's doing something by hiring you. He's missing Prem, but this time I don't think Prem will return. He's had enough of Anita. They were about to get divorced.
–When did Prem leave?
–Didn't Joseph tell you?
I remained silent.
–Hmm, I expect answers to my questions Abhay Chauhan. I don't think I like your manners very much, she said, and her black eyes narrowed and then she didn't look so nice.
–It's all right, I'm not crazy about yours either Mrs Fernandez, but we're not on a date.
She took a deep breath and gripped the glass in her hand.
–No one talks to me like that. No one! If I snap my fingers, you will be off this case in one second. Do you understand?
The sudden ice in her voice threw me for a moment.
–I have other cases, Mrs Fernandez. And before you start snapping your little fingers, I work for Mr Fernandez and not for you.

–I told you he was rude, Madam, said MD, coming around from the desk and tensing his jaw line.

I looked at him.

–I'll get over my manners MD, but what are you going to do about your face?

He grimaced and hate flew in my direction.

–It's all right MD, she said, –I can handle this.

–Look, I don't mind you becoming angry or not liking my manners, but don't waste your time trying to cross-examine me. I'm supposed to be asking the questions here.

–You don't tell me what to do!

She slammed her glass on the table, some of the orange juice spilled over. MD moved with muscular menace and stood behind taking quick short breaths.

–Shall I take him out of the building, Madam?

MD looked as if nothing would give him greater pleasure. He flexed his arms, and his suit stretched so that it didn't look good on him at all, one of those men who always buy a suit one size too small.

–I can find a dozen such detectives with one phone call, said MD.

–You won't, I'm one in a million.

–You're really something Chauhan, she said, –too confident, I hate arrogant men, they're too sure of themselves and always cause trouble.

–I'm hardly arrogant, I can't afford to be on my fees Mrs Fernandez. But you don't have to hate me, I'm on your side.

–Really? I don't think I can trust you.

–So many compliments in one day, I might faint.

She glanced back at MD, before looking at me.

–Did Joseph hire you to find Prem?

–Why don't you ask him, he's your husband?

She flared up again.

–Get out! You are a very rude man, I don't know what Joseph saw in you.

I stood with a slight smile, as she clenched her hands into little fists. Her eyes were glaring into mine but she looked more confused than angry.

–Sit down! I'm not finished yet.

I remained standing and so she stood, shaking a little. She was above medium height and irritation shone on her face.

–You make me angry. She sighed, –Can you find Prem if you wanted to? Anita, deep down, wants him back. About five weeks ago Prem drove away, depressed. He wanted a divorce, but then they found his car near the beach and we haven't heard from him since. We are all worried about him. I mean, anything could have happened to him.

–They?

She smiled, a cunning satisfied smile, and looked relieved as if she had outsmarted me. Maybe she had.

–Joseph didn't tell you anything, did he?

–He mentioned Prem, yes. Is that your worry?

She sat down again.

–I don't care what you say. You pretend to know things Chauhan that you obviously don't. For a while, you had me worried, and for no good reason at all.

–All right, someone is blackmailing your husband for ten lakh rupees in cash. Do you have any ideas about that?

She looked at her red fingernails.

–Anita's playing silly games. She's devious, trying to find ways to suck more money from us. I'm surprised Joseph hired you for such a trifling matter. He's becoming stubborn isn't he, MD? Abhay Chauhan, I've decided we won't be requiring your cheap services any more.

She stared with triumph.

–Yes, I've decided I don't like your manners either. MD, arrange to find another detective, if that's what Joseph really wants.

–Madam, I'll do it at once.

–Before you start with the phone calls, I said, –I work for

Mr Fernandez. Until he says so, I'll be seeing you both around.

She laughed.

–He's funny isn't he, MD? Tell him, that Joseph doesn't even sneeze without me telling him to.

MD grinned and rubbed his shovel-like hands together.

–I wonder how you pulled that trick?

–It's not a trick Chauhan, it's called charm and brains.

–Oh, and for a moment I thought you were going to mention love.

She stopped smiling.

–Anyway, time is money, as you rich folks like to say, I said, and turned before she could open her mouth again and left the office.

Outside, the sea breeze touched my face. This might be my shortest case yet. Hired in the afternoon and fired by the evening. Fernandez would probably call me, but I hoped he had some guts left and could stand up to his wife. Maybe I was hoping for too much. Still, while I wasn't fired, it was time to find Santana and see what kind of compromising photos of Anita Fernandez he possessed.

5

AS I drove back towards the boutique, a man was riding a Honda motorbike with a woman in a pink shalwar kameez wrapped behind him. Her black hair blew in the afternoon breeze and she laughed, the kind of carefree laugh that said she had no worries in the world. The sunlight reflected off the glass front of Santana's boutique and two women in yellow hats left with bags. People did shop there and they had more money than sense. It was contrary to what the barber had said. I was in the wrong business.

I parked the car diagonally across from the boutique and sat with a paperback in the passenger seat. The local constable might show initiative and ask what I was doing hanging around. No need to lose sleep over that. A man pushing a cart with green coconuts passed by. I signalled for him to stop and bought one. The man sliced the top of the coconut and placed a straw inside. The coconut water tasted sweet, cool and fine. It was perhaps best to catch Santana before the evening at Rubies. And before I was fired. I didn't know how strong Maya's influence over Fernandez was, but chances were she could turn on the style in the blink of an eye, and easily have her way. Fernandez however had hired me without consulting her and that gave me hope.

Santana showed around five-thirty, as I was reading a good plot angle in the novel. A worldly woman was seducing the inexperienced Russian hero, and he was swaying between his young love and her. I put the book down reluctantly. Santana drove a new white Tata Sumo SUV, as the barber had said. He stepped out, came around the front and kissed a young woman in the passenger seat. Romeo boy led a charmed life. I didn't hold that against him. What I did hold, was the sonofabitch worrying good people for money.

The woman sat looking at her nails as Santana strolled into the boutique without a care in the world. He was muscular, of medium height, in a black t-shirt and blue jeans.

He walked with a swagger, trying to copy the style of rap artists and not managing it. After fifteen minutes, he hurried out, looking less carefree. Ice Baby followed, he passed her an envelope and a bag. He seemed to give her strict orders, then she returned inside with a subdued face. Although she hadn't been much of a smiling personality in the first place.

The Tata Sumo drove out as I started the Contessa, swung it around and followed, four cars behind. I hoped he was meeting his boss; he seemed too wet behind the ears to be running this racket. There again, there was no age limit to bastards. He drove past a shopping mall and stopped at a cafe. He was alert now. I pulled over to one side after driving past him. The woman shook her head and hurried inside the cafe. Trouble in paradise for Romeo boy. She left without looking back, even though he called out to her.

Tyres screeched as he hit the gas. The old police training kicked in as I followed. Traffic grew. Office workers joined the roads, varied horns blew, and diesel fumes spread. Santana turned left at the lights and drove by a high concrete fence with the trees hanging over. Stacks of wheat bags were placed against one garden wall and two men were carrying them inside. Then we passed a metal railing that had been painted with the Indian tricolour flag, orange on top, then a band of white and the green at the bottom. We went under the bridge just as the train, the carriages painted red with a yellow band on top, passed overhead, commuters hanging out of the doors. One or two always looked as if they were about to fall out. A lot did.

He turned left again into an expensive looking colony of

bungalows and two-storied houses. It had wide roads, tall trees planted along the pavements, with trimmed hedges in front of several bungalows. A new development and the prices were not worth thinking about, not for me anyway.

He was either meeting his boss or going home. I hoped it was the former but I didn't think I'd be so lucky so quickly. He parked in front of a white bungalow, with a red tiled roof. Along the front, there was a three-foot hedge. He walked inside without looking back. I drove around the back of the bungalow and parked. I reached under the seat and pulled out my Glock semi-automatic pistol and put it inside my jacket. I didn't think I'd need it for this idiot but you never knew.

Some physical persuasion might be enough, though he didn't look a pushover. If he had built that muscle with protein shakes then he wouldn't be that tough, and if not, I had a fight on my hands. Banging his nose into a wall might help him forget about harassing Fernandez ever again. Pretty boys didn't like having their faces busted, I doubted the ugly ones did either. I waited a few minutes before stepping out and heading towards the bungalow. The wooden gate was open.

I rapped my knuckles on the wood. The door opened and Santana stared at me with a cigarette in his hand. He was unshaven, wore a diamond stud in his left ear, and the eyes were hard and suspicious.

–Santana?
–Who wants to know?
–I've come to talk business.
–Oh yeah, like what?
–Are we going to stand here and talk?

He didn't move, blew out the smoke from the side of his nasty mouth.

–Fernandez sent me to make a payment.
–I don't know your name mister, and I haven't seen you before.
–Abhay Chauhan. If you want me to leave, then I have

better things to do.

I half turned to go.

–Wait, all right, come in.

From close up he looked over thirty, hard eyes, going all out for the bad boy look that some women went crazy for. I walked into the front room, it was clean and had a good sofa suite. Cigarette smoke however didn't hide the smell of weed coming from the passage. A Kodak camera lay in the corner with a big lens. This clown was careless. The type of idiot I didn't like. They acted tougher than they were and caused trouble of the worst kind. He was involved in this racket, no doubt.

I sat on a sofa with my back to the window; he sat opposite on the main sofa, legs spread wide and arms stretched out on top of the sofa. He enjoyed feeling important and had a wide smirk on his small mouth. He blew the smoke in my direction to show he wasn't scared, and his biceps were impressive.

–I bet it was you asking about me at the boutique, you weren't after a dress, *sala*.

–Actually, I was looking for a dress for my sister.

–Oh yeah, sure you were... send your sister to me, I'll help her find one.

He grinned with a challenge in his eyes.

–I'm not here about my sister. Do you have Anita Fernandez's photos?

–Not me, man, they're with the other guys and let me tell you, good girls shouldn't have such photos taken.

–How did you get hold of them?

–That's for me to know.

–Did Anita put you up to this cheap little trick?

–A stupid question man, are you drunk or what?

–Look Santana, if that's even your real name. Fernandez hired me, and if I find out you're involved then I'll be back. I'll wipe that stupid smirk off your face.

–You don't scare me, Chauhan, or whatever your name is. I

have nothing to hide. I'm only trying to help a friend, that's all. If this is your attitude, the price is going to go up, these people don't fuck around. Anita is a friend, okay, she got drunk at a party and careless. Some bastard took pictures of her in her underclothes, dancing. It wouldn't look good in the society magazines. Now, I'm a reasonable man, this could have been settled for five lakhs. The old man ignored me, and now these people want ten lakhs in cash.

He rubbed the stubble on his chin.

–The police won't like the sound of this, I said.

–Look, I'm trying to protect Anita. Ten lakhs isn't much for those people but it will save them embarrassment. You should see the photos man, not good.

–If I pay, will the problem go away? Fernandez is worried about this, you understand.

The smirk came back. –I promise, have you brought the money?

–Do you have the photos and negatives?

–I'll hand them over as soon as you pay and listen, no funny business. These people don't mess around, I mean that. You pay tomorrow morning at ten-thirty, sharp. The problem goes away.

The smirk suggested he felt close to getting the cash with his grubby hands. Slamming his face into the table was an option, but I didn't think it would help right now. Romeo boy was in way over his head, he lacked credibility. It was possible Anita the dopey head was involved, or Santana was using her.

–Tell them Chauhan, they have to pay tomorrow. This is their last chance. I'll hand over the prints and no funny business or the deal's off.

–You're way over your head, Santana. It's best you hand over the prints to me, now.

–Oh yeah, let me make the jokes. You bring the cash like a good girl and I'll take care of the rest.

A sound alerted me from behind, quick footsteps. Then

something metallic touched the glass window. I dived off the sofa. The glass broke and a fast zipping sound flew through the room, twice. The sound of a gun with a silencer. It's always deadly. I pulled out my Glock, aimed at the window, and then rushed to the side. A stocky man ran out the gate and jumped into the back of a black Maruti 1000, with tinted glass. Tyres screeched out of sight, down the road.

I turned around. Santana had one bullet in the middle of his forehead and another in his heart. The back wall was splattered red with fragments of skull and brains. His mouth was wide open. Blood trickled down his face. There was another patch around his heart. The shooter had been professional. Romeo boy wasn't grinning anymore. The man would probably have shot me as well if I hadn't dived.

Santana hadn't understood who he was dealing with, if you ran with the devil, then Hell wasn't far away. The shooting could be a lucky break. It dealt with Fernandez's problem in the short term, but I didn't think this was the end. If anything, it had probably gotten worse. Anita was mixing with the wrong crowd, and if these were her friends, then God help her. I looked at Santana again. He had seen better days for sure, and he wouldn't be saying oh yeah anymore.

Looking out the window, there was no one around and no one seemed interested. It was unlikely anyone heard two shots fired with a silencer. Someone groaned, I looked back at Santana, but he was still dead.

I left the room and checked in the passage. A small neat kitchen was at one end with a separate backroom. It had gym equipment, bench press, dumbbells and weights. I opened the last door. It was a large bedroom with low lights and dark curtains. Under the red silk bed sheets, lay Anita Fernandez. She was in a black bra, a pair of silver earrings and nothing much else. She stared at the white ceiling, mouth open, groaning as if she had a headache. Her eyes had the dreamy look I associated with heavy drinking. I was wrong. She half

turned and looked at me without recognition.
 –Santana...
 She seemed a long way away, and a near empty vodka bottle lay on the table. I smelt the powder beside it. Heroin. I had to get her out before the first *policewalla* ran through the door.

6

ANITA FERNANDEZ'S green trousers and ochre top were hung on the back of a chair, and her shoes had fallen to the side of the bed. The smell of heroin and alcohol were combined in the air. She lay on her side with her smooth skin contrasting with her black underclothes. I tried to hide my surprise. It seemed Santana was her lover. Payments would have been a waste, he could have taken more pictures whenever he liked. I should have felt sorry, another rich young woman going to pot, but I didn't. She turned her head.

–Hello cutie, is that you... where's Santana? I need him...
–He's taking a long rest.

I went to the ceramic sink in the corner, filled a nearby glass with water and poured it over her head. She giggled. I refilled the glass and splashed the water harder on her face. She sat up, took quick breaths, and wiped her face with the bed sheet.

–What the bloody hell, is this?
–We have to leave.
–Why?

I helped her on with her trousers and 'hippy' top. She stared at the wall opposite and shook her hair. I took out a pair of plastic gloves I carried and put them on.

–Where am I? she said, then fell sideways on the bed and closed her eyes.

I opened the cupboard. Santana's clothes were stacked neatly, an expensive collection of brand names. I opened and closed several drawers. One at the bottom was locked.

I hurried to Santana, found keys in his trouser pocket. I

tried several, before one opened the bottom drawer. Cash, jewellery and a little red book. I took the book out, flicked through it and saw names and initials, codes and telephone numbers. The writing was the same as the signature Santana had written at the bottom of the typed letter to Fernandez. I placed the notebook in my pocket and locked the drawer.

Some names had ticks, others had question marks and a few crosses. I walked back to Santana, pushed the keys in his pocket. He didn't look very well. I returned to Anita. I had to protect my employer's interests. I helped her to her feet.

–Where are we going, cutie?

–For a walk.

–I, I don't want to go.

–The police are coming and you'd better hurry.

Something registered in her head. She fell sideways and held me close as I grabbed the white purse, then we moved towards the kitchen. I pulled back the metal stopper and opened the door. A narrow path led out, I walked her to my Contessa and sat her inside. She just about stayed upright, eyes bloodshot and staring like a drunk. A middle-aged woman in a pink sari glanced at us from across the road, she was sitting on a swing on her verandah; a reliable witness no doubt.

She might come forward, but people don't like to be involved in a police *lafda*, not if they can help it. I put my foot on the gas and left the pretty looking estate with Santana dead. I had a doped-up Anita Fernandez in my passenger seat and a hundred questions forming in my head. None of them had easy answers.

There was a stupid van driver in front of us, you meet these often; he kept braking, beeping, trying to overtake the car in front and failing. This caused me to brake more than once. I was about to overtake the clown and call him a choice name when my sleepy passenger widened her eyes with a start. She jerked forward and placed her hands on the black dashboard. She stared with knit eyebrows, rubbed her head with her left hand in a way that indicated a headache or a hangover or both.

–Oh, cutie, hi, where are you taking me?

–Home.

She banged the dashboard with her fists.

–No! I can't return like this.

–I'm sure they've seen you worse.

The lights turned green and luckily, the van turned left. I drove straight on but slower now, thinking that I might have to change directions. Two women in orange saris walked along the pavement carrying baskets on their heads filled with vegetables. They walked easily as if the weight on their heads was as light as cotton.

–I, I can't go home like this, she said, rubbing her thighs.

–Okay okay, where can I take you?

–To my apartment, it's the second left down here, do you have a cigarette?

I passed her one and she lit it with shaking hands; took a deep drag and blew out the smoke. This brought her back to life and she looked around to gather where she was.

–God, what a hangover, Santana always makes me drink too much.

–I bet he does.

A recollection came to her, as smoke filled the car. I wound down the glass.

–But I was at Santana's house, with him.

–Is he a good friend of yours?

–He is, keeps the boredom away cutie. How is he?

–He's seen better days.

I didn't want to break the bad news in her state, I had no idea how she might react.

–You have nice friends.

–I certainly do, they make me laugh and forget all my worries. Oh, what a headache but this helps.

–Well, Santana won't be worrying you for a while. Did he take the photos of you?

39

–Oh no, you're very wrong there. Santana isn't like that. He's my friend and trying to help, and he will. Why didn't we stay at his house? You said something about the police, didn't you?

She scratched her head with the cigarette in her hand.

I didn't answer. She took another deep intake of smoke. I turned left and drove down a wide road with new white apartment blocks on both sides. I slowed until she pointed right to a sign that read Eden Gardens. A new block, some thirty floors high, with car parking space and trees all around the edges. I turned inside and parked. I got out and went to help her, though she was now stronger on her legs. She could walk by herself but still held me for support as we entered the foyer. She led me to the elevators and pushed the button for the twenty-first floor. A bell sounded as the new elevator went up smoothly. She smoked and looked up now and again.

We walked out onto her floor, along a wide corridor with granite floor tiles, and stopped in front of apartment 221. She fumbled in her purse, took out the keys and entered the apartment. She hurried to the kitchen, pulled out a half bottle of whisky and poured a drink, neat. She drank it fast and made another one.

The apartment was new, shiny and a mess. Clothes were scattered across the floor and on top of the red three-piece sofa suite. Glasses and ashtrays lay on the table with cigarette ends. A layer of dust covered everything. I walked towards the tall window and opened it. The breeze swept inside. Another apartment block was across the road, which rather blocked the view from this side. I lit a cigarette and turned around. Daddy had bought her an expensive place, but she didn't care for it. If she carried on this way, it wouldn't be long before her good friends took it off her. She put the glass down.

–This helps a hangover. Thanks for bringing me here. You understand that I couldn't return to Papa's house in this state.

–Yeah sure.

She walked towards me, placed her hands on my shoulders, and kissed me on the mouth. When she tried again, I held her back.

–You're a good kisser, I said, –But, what's that for?

–For bringing me here, cutie.

She glanced towards the bedroom.

–Don't tell me you're shy?

–I'd like to know you first Anita, I know that might seem old-fashioned these days.

She blinked several times and moved slowly towards the sofa, sudden anger radiating towards me.

–I know your game. Now get out!

When I didn't move, she grit her teeth.

–Get out and close the door behind you!

–That's gratitude for you.

–You're no longer so cute, either.

–Now for a few questions Anita, then I'll leave you in peace. Were you involved with Santana in blackmailing your father? A simple yes or no will do.

–Go to Hell! I don't even know what you're talking about.

–Santana had nice pictures of you. Does that ring a bell?

–Who cares, I do as I please.

–Your father for one, your friend asked ten lakhs for their return.

–I hate him, Maya, and you, I want all of you to leave me alone.

–Are you involved or not?

–I'm telling you nothing, cop.

–Okay, have it your way. Try to stay away from your nice friends. There's trouble coming, big trouble.

Something registered, she tilted her head to her left and rubbed her nose.

–I have no idea what you are talking about, I'll see Santana whenever I want.

–It might be difficult.

–What do you mean by that?

–Nothing, only your friend has gone on a long journey. Not many return from there.

–You can't scare Santana, not you or anyone else. Now, leave my apartment. You're no longer welcome, and I have a very big headache.

She turned into her bedroom and slammed the door shut. I couldn't make head nor tail of her varied facial expressions, and I was supposed to be good at reading people. I walked out of the apartment and closed the door.

I sat in the car and thought things through. A dead body lay back at the bungalow. Two things could have happened whilst Anita Fernandez offered me the best present of my life. One, the neighbour might have phoned the police and there's cops all over the place. Two, no one had bothered with civic duty, and the poor sucker was lying there with a bullet in his head. I couldn't leave him in that sorry state. I drove out thinking, who could have shot him, and why. I came to the lights and turned right, overtaking a green truck filled with goods, the top covered by a large sheet of blue tarpaulin, tied down with ropes. It was a wonder the traffic police hadn't pulled him over.

Plenty of people might have wanted such a blood-sucking leech off their backs. This might have had nothing to do with Anita's pictures. If there were no more demands, then lady luck has smiled, but things never worked that easy for me. Ten lakhs might be nothing to Fernandez, but it was a big amount in the outside world. People were shot for less than a lakh these days. If a new demand came, then there would be more menace attached to it. Santana had been careless, showy, and the people running this racket had come to the same conclusion.

They meant business, and Fernandez was going to need me more than ever. I turned right at the Hanging Gardens, past a line of black and yellow roofed taxis. Someone had murdered

Romeo Boy and it annoyed me. He could have given some real answers. The information that I had been hired must have leaked from the Fernandez household. I didn't like that thought either. I pulled over at a STD telephone booth. I picked up the phone, placed a handkerchief over it and dialled the number. The Police needed to wake up. It was one thing trying to find a blackmailer, and another dealing with a dead body.

–Yes, Head Constable Salim speaking.

–I heard some glass breaking, I said, and gave him the address.

–What's your name?

–A concerned citizen. There aren't many of us around in Mumbai.

–What?

–It doesn't matter, I think there's been a murder.

–How do you know?

–Because there's a dead body inside.

–Is this a joke? Who are you? What's your name?

I put the phone down and decided to head home, shower and have a drink. It took an hour through the traffic north to Boriwali, back to the crowds, pollution and noise. My apartment was in a packed colony of several apartment blocks.

I parked the Contessa to the rear and stepped outside. An alley cat was ready to pounce on a rat near the steel dustbins. Kebab time. The block rose in the night, lights on in about half the block. The sound of a Hindi song drifted out towards me in the cool night air, the latest Jackie Shroff film song. It was upbeat but I didn't feel that way. I took the lift that sounded as if it would break down anytime, walked across the tiled corridor and opened the door. It was good to reach home, and I was lucky to have my one-bedroom apartment, because it was mine. I didn't have to share it with another six people like so many Mumbaikars did. Space was always at a premium in Mumbai. It didn't have spectacular views from level eight, I could only see the lighted buildings across the street.

I switched on the lights and drew the curtains. Maybe I would be fired before the night was out. Maya Fernandez might be trying to persuade Fernandez right now with her considerable charms. I wasn't going to lose sleep over it. I had a shower, rubbed down with a towel, changed into loose fitting cotton pyjamas, and finally felt clean, after meeting the people I had today.

I checked the red book on the bed. There were over three to four hundred names. I didn't envy the police their job when the book was passed over to them. At the back of the book, there were initials, A.K. R. D.B S. There were a few more, a lot of phone numbers and more initials. There were ticks against names as well as crosses and a few question marks. I tried to find Fernandez name, nothing.

I stretched out and drank a glass of Royal Stag whisky. Anita Fernandez was high maintenance. Maybe Prem Nath had bailed out because of it. No one else seemed to care either. Tomorrow, I would inform Fernandez about Santana. If there were no further demands then this would be my quickest case to date. I tried to hold onto that thought without too much success. Anita Fernandez had wriggled back inside my head. I fell asleep with that happy thought.

7

THURSDAY MORNING brought grey clouds and a scattering of rain. I washed my face, drank coffee with toast and listened to the answer machine. No new messages and I'm not even sure why I checked it, it's not like I was expecting a call from my mother. Someone had kindly left me outside an orphanage, aged one. That someone was probably my mother. She must have had her reasons. The only scrap of information the orphanage manager told me was that he had seen a young woman leave me outside the gate. She had hurried away before he could reach her. Something like that could make a man bitter, but that's life. And no, I hadn't tried to find her yet.

The recorded messages would be at the office. I expected the gloating voice of MD informing me that I had been fired. I had finished the toast and coffee when the phone rang. It was Gautam. I had made the mistake of giving him my number, when business was slow. He had, however, come through with a nice few earners.

–Chauhan, how's the clever sleuth?

He sounded like a man who had just had a big breakfast.

–I've had better days, that's for sure.

–Yes, I can imagine. Did you meet Fernandez?

–I had the pleasure yes. He hired me but I guess I'll be fired today, his wife didn't like me.

–I thought you were a charmer, he laughed. –But yes, she can be bloody hard work. They're an odd family, but Fernandez helped me when I was coming through the ranks and so I owe him, regardless of what his wife says.

–She's hard to ignore.

–Listen, we've found a car stuck in the Sagar Front inlet.

I held the telephone tight.

–A new car, dirtied with sand and seawater and oh the interesting part, there's a man inside.

–What does that have to do with me?

–It's related to your job, and his name... well, I'll tell you there. Can you come out and see me?

–Yes.

–Okay hurry up. That's one less worry for Fernandez. He'll thank us for our good work.

–Why, what have you done?

–Ha, ha, nothing gets past you hey, Chauhan. But I like to take credit and I did send you to him. Now hurry along before the fish eat the poor man.

I was wearing a pair of black corduroys, a white shirt and my short black leather jacket. I slipped the Glock inside my coat pocket and headed out. Sagar Front was an inlet of the Arabian Sea, cutting into the north side of Malabar Hill. It had been turned into a beauty spot for boating, fishing and restaurants, so this wouldn't be a sight people wanted to see over breakfast.

Driving south, I reached there in an hour-ten. I parked across the road, away from the police cars and jeeps. I moved out and lit a cigarette. The rain had eased but a breeze blew across the bay. Gautam saw me and walked across; he wore a black lawyer's jacket, white shirt and black trousers; a big burly man, pushing fifty-seven. He had short grey hair and he smiled as he reached me. A yellow crane had pulled out the car behind him. People gathered in groups, pointed and stared. All the boats were anchored to the right, no boat rides this morning.

–You look well, said Gautam.

He shook my hand and glanced over his shoulder.

–See him over there. That's Inspector Dhanwan. He's in charge and he's a suspicious officer, so be careful.

–You said there was a man in the car. Anyone you know?

–Yes, but you have a look at him first. They found Santana at his bungalow last night by the way, with a bullet between his eyebrows. You were looking for him, right?

–I was. Looks like someone got to him first and didn't like what they found.

–You don't look too surprised. Did you meet him?

–Not yet, I was trying to find him.

–Dhanwan won't be so easy to convince, if there is anything you want to tell me, I suggest you tell me now. It's not Prem Nath either. This man is smaller, and Prem was almost as tall as you. This man is in his mid-twenties.

–Why are you talking about Prem Nath? He doesn't concern me.

–No reason, but keep your eyes open. Fernandez really likes Prem, and I like him too, but then he just disappears. We haven't heard a word in weeks.

–Maybe he didn't like being married to Anita Fernandez. She's a handful.

–From what I've heard, she's a crazy fireball. If you come across any information on Prem, you let me know first thing. I owe Fernandez and this is my chance to pay back.

–I haven't been hired to look for Prem. Santana yes, and you said he's dead, so that doesn't help. I need those photos. Did the police find any at the house?

–A few but none of Anita Fernandez.

Inspector Dhanwan waved his arms at someone as we crossed the road. Water dripped out from the side of the vehicle and underneath the doors. The seawater smell mixed with the strong smell of weeds hung in the air and it wasn't pleasant.

People stared from one end shaking their heads, and at the far side two constables stood near their motorbikes to divert traffic down a side road. A metal portable fence had been placed to create a roadblock. The rain came gently, with the smell of damp soil strong in the air. Gautam shook hands with the inspector and the man gave me an unfriendly glance, then we ducked underneath the police cordon.

A wooden barrier was broken, where the car had gone through and down into the water. The yellow crane with the long metal chains was backing away. Several men stood around the Tata Sumo taking pictures and making notes. We walked down the stone steps and onto the gravelly sand. The front bumper was bent and the headlights smashed. The bonnet had a big dent, the upholstery was sodden and black. None of the tyres seemed damaged.

The man was crushed against the steering wheel, dull eyes with his tongue sticking out of his ugly mouth. He had an unnatural look. He was a slim, dark haired man of twenty-four or so, who had been alive not so long ago. He didn't have a bullet in the middle of his forehead. His face was puffed up with a dull light brown skin colour. His eyes stared, lifeless. On the side of his head, a big lump stood out from the rest of his skull. He too had seen better days. I tapped the cigarette.

–This is Abhay Chauhan, a private detective.

Inspector Dhanwan glanced at me as if I was something the cat had dragged in.

–A friend of yours, Gautam?

–He works for me sometimes, yes.

–When are you going to trust us, instead of these people?

–You have to win trust, Inspector.

Dhanwan half turned towards me.

–Abhay Chauhan. I remember you. You used to be a Police Inspector in zone 10. What happened, find the work too tough?

–I just didn't like working with donkeys, I said.

A sneer appeared on Dhanwan's face.

–Is that right? I heard you were fired for insubordination. In this profession, you must have discipline.

–Honesty helps as well but that's another matter.

–What are you doing here? This is strictly police business.
–He asked me to come along.

Dhanwan shook his head and his shrewd eyes looked irritated.

–Any reason Gautam?
–Chauhan helped me with a few cases in the past, the man's good and gets results. I thought we could use him, said Gautam.

–I don't like snoopers on my cases, they get on my nerves. I also don't like people keeping information from me and these people always keep information back. They get in the way. Cause more trouble than they're worth.

–Now, don't give me the third-degree Inspector, Chauhan's a good man to have around.

Dhanwan looked about forty, with short black hair and a clipped moustache. He was muscular, of medium height, and when he stared at you, you knew about it. He looked at another officer, older and pot bellied.

–What's the story?

The man rubbed the back of his head and pointed at the broken fence.

–Sir, the car went through there, must have hit it hard. The rain stopped early here, around two a.m. The broken wood is dry inside and that places it after the rain stopped. Water filled quickly, otherwise the car would have drifted out to sea. We had the first call this morning, a jogger saw the top of the car, phoned in. A check on the number plate said the car belonged to A.S. Santana. This isn't Santana.

–I know, but he could be a friend or a partner. Any witnesses from last night?

–Sir, you know how it is, no one is coming forward.

–*Sala*, bloody frightened bastards. And they blame us all the time. When is the public going to stand up to these criminals?

No one said anything to that.

–Have you found Santana? asked Gautam.

–We found him last night. Shot dead at his bungalow. I think it's an underworld hit, very professional.

Gautam turned to me. I blew out the smoke and tapped the cigarette. I didn't like to hear that but that's how I had figured it too.

–Do you think this man killed him? asked Gautam.

–Unlikely, said Dhanwan. –But anything is possible. Forensics will tell me how this man died. I don't like the bruise on the side of his head. He was scared, running from someone. The car was going at speed. If only some witnesses came forward.

Another man, wearing white plastic gloves, turned around from the door.

–He could be a drunk or had boyfriend trouble with Santana. Gay people are very emotional, he said with a grin.

–Do you know many gay men, Pandey?

–I was just saying.

–Come up with intelligent suggestions. Do you think we're on a picnic here? I have two dead men on my hands, and if you can't take it seriously, I'll transfer you to traffic control.

Pandey looked at me and raised his eyebrows, before staring at the dead man. Dhanwan put everyone on edge. A man with a tired round face and a black bag came around the car. He had been taking photos and he looked at Gautam.

–A new customer, Doc, said Gautam.

–Yes, he took the car for a swim and discovered the hard way that cars are not good swimmers.

Pandey smiled, whilst Dhanwan narrowed his eyes again. Doc looked at the dead man without expression, rubbed his grey temples, then looked closer at the man's bruise and at the steering wheel. He took out a notebook and wrote something, then looked up.

–He was hit with a hammer or metal bar, the blow occurring before he reached the water. You had better take

him out before he goes stiff, you won't like doing it afterwards.
–You don't think it's a suicide, Doc?
–No.
–Then how did he manage to drive here with a blow to his head?
–He didn't. He drove off the bend and crashed into the water and someone has followed through and swung at his head to make sure. The rain has washed out the footprints.

As he was speaking, Potbelly came around.
–Saab, we found a wallet. His name is Raja, a photographer.

Dhanwan looked at the wet wallet with interest.
–Phone through to find out where he lived. We have to inform his next of kin. That will be a nice job for you Pandey.
–Not me saab, I did it the last time.
–No Pandey, you will do it, since you find this so amusing.

Pandey's smile disappeared.
–It should come from you, said Gautam.
–You're telling me how to do my job? Stick to the law. It's my case and I know how to handle it. I'm sick of all these wild suggestions.

Everyone stared at one another with a look that said, *the new Inspector is a pain in the backside*. As the silence grew, I said,
–I used to like suggestions. Sometimes they helped to break a case open.

Dhanwan squared up to me.
–That's why you were fired, for taking too many wrong suggestions.
–I wasn't fired. Listen Dhanwan, you're going to need all the help you can get with this case. This isn't straightforward.
–Why? Do you hold some special information? If you do, I'd like to hear it.

Dhanwan jabbed a finger in my chest. I took a step back.
–You sound like a man who's all talk, Chauhan. Leave the real work to us. Go find a cheating wife or husband, that's

appropriate work for a snooper like you.

–You're not funny or clever Dhanwan. I'll be surprised if you solve this case.

–Why you...

Dhanwan came within a few inches of my face. I could smell his cigarette breath. When I didn't back up, Gautam pushed an arm between us.

–Gentlemen, please not here.

–You take him away from this murder scene, said Dhanwan. –He has no business here and I don't trust these people at all.

He was glaring at me. Everyone had stopped what they were doing.

–I wouldn't stay here if you paid me, Dhanwan.

–It's Inspector Dhanwan, and if I find that you've been withholding vital information, I'll throw you in jail.

–That'll be the day.

I took a step back. This seemed to satisfy his ego. He turned around.

–Let's move! he shouted. –We have work to do.

Gautam walked back to the car with me.

–I'm sorry about that Chauhan. I didn't know he was such an arsehole. I'd heard he was hard to work with, but I also heard he gets results.

–He's an idiot. As for results, we'll see.

–What do you think? Did your job have anything to do with him?

–No, I've not even seen him before. I thought you'd called me to look at Santana, but you said he was shot in the house yesterday evening.

–That's right, they found him last night.

We stopped near my Contessa, turned around and looked at Dhanwan. He was shouting and waving his arms at Pandey and Potbelly.

–I knew Raja, said Gautam. –As soon as I saw him in that car. I don't forget faces. He'd been arrested several times for burglary, then about six months ago for attempted blackmail. We didn't have sufficient evidence that time. It's possible he teamed up with Santana and because of Dhanwan's attitude, I'm going to let him spend time finding out about Raja. A bad attitude makes your work harder.

–Yeah, but that doesn't explain why they're both dead and how they're connected to Fernandez. This doesn't look so good now.

–No, it doesn't. But Raja had served six months at Thane last year, before showing up here. He'd decided to move up market. Perhaps he should have stayed small-time. Anyway, does Fernandez know about last night?

–I doubt it. I have to check whether I'm still working for him or not. I might have been fired.

–Fernandez is unhappy about many things right now, so no I doubt he'll fire you. He wants answers. Don't underestimate him, he likes results. Did he mention Prem Nath?

I remained silent.

–I know he wants Prem found. He's upset about him going missing.

–I'm not looking for Prem, just the unflattering pictures of his daughter.

–Okay, okay, I'm thinking aloud. Dhanwan got under my skin. He's not going to be easy to deal with. Let me know if Joseph has fired you. I'll try to change his mind.

I nodded, sat back in the car and drove out.

One shouldn't be feeling hungry after seeing that poor sap being pulled out of the water, but I was. At a small eatery near a Honda motorbike showroom, I ordered lunch. The waiter, a teenager with too much oil in his black hair, brought a masala chicken curry with naan, salad and yogurt chutney. The price on the receipt here in Malabar Hill made me blink twice. I could have eaten a full three-course meal in a good restaurant in my part of town. The food tasted good. There was a middle-aged man opposite me eating vada pav with his gums. It was a funny sight and I wondered why he didn't have some dentures fitted. Then he smiled and half scared me to death. He had the look of a ghost about him.

Lunch finished, with my wallet a lot lighter, I drove to the office. I wondered about Raja and why he'd been killed. It looked like they were partners. Both dead within hours of each another. Someone killing Santana could be understood but why Raja? There were numerous possibilities. I whittled it down to one, maybe two. It could be that the bosses had decided to clear the deck and take charge. Or it could be the work of an aggrieved boyfriend or father.

It would be better if it wasn't some underworld psycho, because they were tougher to deal with. Dhanwan was going to make this case difficult and try to have me removed. He looked like a man who'd want to take all the credit. Time was running short and if I didn't make progress, the leads would go cold. Dhanwan and maybe Mrs Fernandez might have turned Fernandez's head by then, and I would be off this case before I could empty a glass of whisky.

8

I REACHED the front of the eight-storey office building, named unaptly as Rising Towers, and parked the car. The plan had been to add another twenty floors but the owner of R.T Enterprises had lost on another project, and so this building wasn't rising higher any time soon. Rumours of an underworld protection racket also hovered in the air like dark secrets. It wasn't my concern for now.

The light rain touched my skin as I stepped out and looked up at my office. It was on the sixth floor, where small businesses with big ambitions rented half the floor. The first three floors were retail space, the next two apartments, and half of these still hadn't been sold and were gathering construction dust. Rising Towers wouldn't be finished in the next ten years. Developers were often just as incompetent as the contractors they employed.

I caught the lift, exited at the sixth floor and walked across the wide tiled corridor. The sign on the clear glass panel read, *Abhay Chauhan, Private Detective Agency.*

A new client might be waiting, I hoped, then I pushed the door. You could always hope. No new client, only the small table, a few wooden chairs and some film magazines I had spread about so that the client wouldn't get bored. I kept this door open. The agency had been started four years ago by renting this office. A year later, I split it into two, to make a waiting area and an office. The grand plan had been to hire a secretary and she would work from the spare room.

The secretary hadn't arrived yet, not on my fees, but I'd been getting along pretty fine without one; the answer machine was reliable. It came in on time every day and didn't take sick leave. The conversation wasn't great, it tended to be repetitive.

I unlocked the office door that had a solid wooden bottom panel and a frosted glass panel above. Everything was the same apart from the fine layer of dust. I opened the window, fresh air sucked out the stale air. A billboard across the road showed a woman with pouting lips. I called her Rekha. She was smiling with shoulder length curly hair and enticing me to buy a sun cream. She could sell me anything. I sat down on the swivel chair behind the wooden desk and was about to listen to my secretary on the answer machine, when the phone rang.

I picked it up on the third ring, expecting it to be from the stiff MD, and to listen to the pleasure in his voice as he fired me. It was a woman's voice instead.

–*Hellooo*, is this the Abhay Chauhan Detective agency?
–It certainly is, the last time I checked.
–*Oh goodness me.* I've been trying since yesterday you know, and I left two messages, don't you like to work?
–Well...
–Don't you keep a secretary at least?
–Not on my rates...
–No, but you should answer your phone, how will you find new clients if you don't answer the phone?
–I was busy, I said, and placed a finger in my ear.
–Busy wizzy nothing, I don't like leaving messages on such delicate matters, no I don't.

I rubbed the side of my forehead. Then rubbed it some more.

–Thanks for the advice. How can I help you?
–My name is Mrs Chatterjee and I want to discuss something very important.
–Mrs Chatterbox?
–No, Chatter...jee, don't you hear very well?
–There's a lot of loud noise coming from your side.

–I'll get to the point.
–That's a good idea.
–I expect complete secrecy on this Abhay Chauhan. You see, I think my husband's having an affair, she said, in a low conspiring voice.
–What can I do about that?
–Is it not obvious? You seem *very slow* on the uptake.
–Some people are just slow, it can't be helped.

I waved a fly away from the corner of the table. It flew to the other side, as stubborn flies tend to do. It was laughing at me and staying here without contributing to the rent.

–What are your rates? I heard you're quite cheap, she added.
–Depends on the job, but the standard rate is fifteen hundred per day, plus expenses.
–Oh I heard right, you are cheap.
–I can double it if you like.

She cleared her throat.

–We will discuss that later. First, I want you to find out if my husband is cheating. I want the answer in three days, maximum.
–How long have you been married?
–Thirty years. And only I know how I've suffered.
–Why do you think he's cheating, Mrs Chatterjee?
–A woman's instinct.

I smiled and leaned back in the chair.

–Have you tried to find out with your woman's intuition?
–Yes, I certainly did, and found nothing so far.
–Then I doubt I'll find anything either.

She took a long pause, I heard several deep breaths and I imagined her shaking her head.

–Really, I thought you were a detective? she said, with her voice betraying a flash of anger.
–I wonder about that myself sometimes.
–You don't seem very interested in my personal and difficult matter.

–Probably because I'm not, I said.

–I think you have poor manners.

–I'll live with my manners, but anyway, there are detectives who'll jump at the opportunity to discover if your husband's having an affair. My guess listening to you, is that your husband's probably cheating and good luck to the poor fellow.

–How dare you! Oh goodness me! I'll never be phoning you ever again!

–It's a real shame.

She slammed the phone down. I felt its vibration up my arm. I was losing a steady income stream, and this would be repeat business. There was no cure for *vehem*, a suspicious mind would ever remain suspicious. But it was no good, I knew I wouldn't be able to expose a cheating spouse. The feeling would be just lousy and leave a bitter taste in the mouth. No, it was better to live on fresh air until a proper case came along.

I checked the answer machine. She was right. There were two impatient messages from her, left with heavy sighs. Two more from R.T. Enterprises, reminders for rent. If I could stay on the Fernandez case, then that would buy me breathing space for a few months. Hell, I might even be able to feed myself. Still, I breathed easier as there was nothing from the Fernandez household and this surprised me. I was sure Mrs Fernandez would have convinced her husband to fire me. He was holding firm against her sweet smiles and charms, and she wouldn't like that.

I stared at the two steel cabinets to my left, at the empty chair across the table and the small coffee table. Maybe I should put my ego to one side and take the infidelity cases. I'd have a full waiting list and I could hire a good secretary and make her a partner later on. I was getting ahead of myself again, dreaming too much and doing too little. The hell with becoming a businessman. Bad cases were like a grumpy uncle you wished you hadn't invited to your party. They would always annoy you.

I leaned forward and was about to light a cigarette, when I heard footsteps coming along the corridor; the sound of heels nearing the office, hesitant, then rapid, as if the woman was looking for the right place. She was probably heading to the Jeevan Sathi travel agency down the corridor. They did package tours around India. The way I felt right now, I could do with taking one.

The footsteps stopped outside the waiting room door, perhaps she was reading the title and having a laugh. I received that reaction often, the few times I'd mentioned it. Private detective, I'd say, and people would give me that knowing look, as if I was a peeping tom, a man who went after the dirty secrets of the city and of the sexual kind. They always wore an astounded look, when I stated that I didn't do that particular line.

The footsteps again. Someone had walked confidently into the waiting room; I might actually have a client. I wanted to welcome them with a garland of flowers as they do on Hawaii. There was a light knock on the door. Before I could say come in, the door opened, and the woman strode inside.

She wore a blue business suit, with a large-collared white shirt; smart black heels, and today I couldn't see an inch of her legs. Her black hair bounced on her shoulders and her eyes took in the office. It didn't take long for her to assess my worth. But that was all right, she wasn't going to propose to me. I stood, behind the desk.

–Please, why don't you come in? Now that you're here, take the load off your feet.

I pointed to a seat.

–Are you sure the chair won't break?

She sat down.

–I hope you haven't come for an argument, Mrs Fernandez. What brings me this honour? You could've sent the stiff MD to tell me I'm fired, and that would've made him a happy man, although I doubt he really does happy.

I lit a cigarette, blew the smoke towards the window and the window blew it back towards me. I offered her one, she took it and lit it with a gold-plated lighter that was worth more than my office. She liked showing it to me and was slow in placing it back inside her purse.

–That's a peace offering, I said, –I'd offer you a pipe like the Native Americans used to do, but I don't happen to have one around. Is MD outside?

–No, he's in the car below. I think we underestimated your talents, Chauhan.

–It happens all the time, I must have that kind of face.

She smiled.

–We started off on the wrong foot yesterday. When you came to see me, I had just finished a stressful call.

I blew out the smoke. I wasn't buying that.

–Is this really your office?

–It really is. You don't make so much money in this racket. I'm seriously thinking about increasing my rates.

She blew out the smoke, weighing me up.

–How did you end up in this nasty racket?

–What first attracted you to the *multi-millionaire*, Joseph Fernandez?

–Oh, she said, and smiled, –let's not start fighting again. I've been trying to call you.

–I was busy talking to Mrs Chatterjee.

–Who?

–It doesn't matter. Did you want to see me about Santana? I said.

Her face tightened a little and her eyes narrowed.

–Poor man, I heard about it and I thought, oh dear God.

–You knew him?

–Yes, because of our little problem.

–Hopefully, that might go away now.

She leaned back in the chair and crossed her right leg onto

her left.

–Do you think so?

–Not really. Who told you about him?

–A friend of a friend. Actually, Joseph told me last night, someone called Gautam phoned him.

–Well, I was about to phone your husband.

–Don't worry, you will be paid. I can pay now if you like, she said, and touched her purse.

–Is that the nice way of saying my services are no longer required?

She tried to smile but it was insincere.

–How much do we owe you for your trouble?

–Let's see, around three thousand so far, plus expenses.

–I spend more on my haircut, she said and brushed her hand through her dark hair. She did this twice, to make sure I noticed.

–You're paying too much.

She stopped smiling. –Okay, I'm feeling generous.

She searched inside her purse and placed a new bundle of hundred-rupee notes on the table; Gandhi was smiling at me and the notes looked real.

–Ten thousand rupees for your trouble. Joseph told me to pay you this.

–It's kind of him. I'd rather be paid directly from Mr Fernandez however as I'm working for him, after all.

She was trying hard to keep a lid on the anger she had displayed yesterday. She kept giving me insincere smiles. I think I preferred her anger.

–Oh I see, you don't trust me, is that it? You really are hard to like, she said.

–To think I've been making an effort.

–Take the money, this place could do with a coat of paint and some new furniture, she said, half turning in her chair and pointing with her right arm in a flourish all around the room.

–What's the rush to get rid of me? I said, –You can drop the act Mrs Fernandez. You didn't come all the way up here to pay me off. What do you really want?

Her cheeks reddened. She blew the smoke out quickly.

–You don't need to be involved anymore. I'll deal with our delicate situation my way, without having a detective snooping around.

–Who's snooping around? I'm on the level.

–I don't want to worry dear Joseph in this silly Anita business. I know how to handle it, so name your price and leave this case alone.

–And why should I do that? I said, and tapped the cigarette in the ashtray.

–Because women can see the dangers coming from a far distance, while you men just walk off the cliff. There's big trouble coming, and you're in way over your head.

I smiled.

–Trouble is my business, Mrs Fernandez.

She narrowed her eyes and stared at me.

–I'm telling you, and that's what counts, she said, and a little ice came into her tone.

–I'd like to hear it from Mr Fernandez all the same. I've never liked working through intermediaries. I find they confuse the message.

–MD was right about you, he said you were a stubborn sonofabitch.

–Nice French, I can think of some choice names for MD too, but that can wait. Your husband is a good judge of character and sense. You don't build that wealth being stupid and unable to handle pressure. Until I hear from him that I'm fired, I'll be sticking around.

She tapped the cigarette into the ashtray. The money lay temptingly on the table. Boy, could I do with that right now. I tried not to look at the smiling face of Gandhi.

–All right, what does he really want you for? she said.

–I told you before. Didn't you ask him?
–I did, but he's being very stubborn and secretive.
–Losing your charms?
She smiled but her eyes didn't.
–This is about Prem Nath isn't it? she asked.
–No.
–I don't believe you, but I'll find out. I usually get what I want.
–I believe you, but this is about Anita and the blackmail, I said.
–Did you find the photos at least?
–No, the poor sap died before I could find him.
She didn't seem to believe that and bit her lower lip.
–Does Anita know what happened to Santana? I asked.
–Yes, and she's very upset. He was a friend of hers, but she'll get over it in two days, that's how she is. She always gets over it.

She thought for a moment, then put her hand inside her purse and pulled out an envelope. She pushed it across the table. I opened it. A new demand, and the price had risen to twenty-five lakhs. The letter this time was addressed to her, at the offices. There was a photo of Anita lying in her underclothes on a bed, with the hand of man on her thigh, probably Santana. She looked high on drugs, had that dreamy look again and her eyes were staring at the camera. I put the photo back in the envelope.

–They want twenty-five lakhs for five such photos and the negatives, and no I haven't showed them to Joseph. It would really hurt him, and she causes him enough stress as it is, she said.

–The demand came how?
–A man telephoned early this morning, and about half an hour later this was delivered.
–Why don't you pay the clowns off, I'm sure you can negotiate. There's something else isn't there?

She blew out the smoke from the side of her nice mouth and held the cigarette in mid-air.

–Does there have to be something else, Chauhan?

–Yes.

She gave me a puzzled look, glanced at the table.

–The man said that Anita was involved in a police case now and that we had better pay quickly or Anita would end up doing time.

–Did you recognise the voice?

–No, but he sounded serious and scary.

I tapped the table, then looked at her to see if she had been unsettled by the new demand. She looked in control but maybe it was a front, and she really was worried.

–These people usually do, they are relying on you becoming scared. They probably killed Santana and mean business. Thought about calling the police? I asked.

–Yes I did, but Joseph wants it this way. Now if you leave the case alone, I'll offer you more money and you can tell Joseph that you've found a better case. I'll call the police to help us. This is police business after all, and not for a one-man band.

–Fired again huh? You don't give up easily.

She shook her head slightly and gave me a sympathetic smile. I almost fell for it.

–Look Chauhan, why place your life in danger for a few measly rupees. It doesn't make sense, you're brighter than that.

–I can get quite far on a few thousand, you'd be surprised.

Her smile disappeared and her eyes were focussed on some other thought. working at some other thought fast.

–Does Joseph know about the new demand? I asked.

–Yes, I told him, but he wants you to stay on the case.

–I guess he must like me then.

–I don't know why, there's nothing to like.

–Tut, tut, let's not start again.

She leaned back in the chair.

–You test my patience, Chauhan. I'm not used to hearing

no.

–We can work on that.

–All right, final offer, fifty thousand in cash right now and you walk away.

We looked at each other for a long minute. She didn't blink, and I believed her offer. She wanted me off the case, but why?

–A nice round figure, can I think about it? I said.

–I want an answer, now.

I leaned back in my chair, tapped the table several times as if I was thinking about the reply.

–Okay, no then. I still work for your husband.

She shook her head and sighed.

–Oh God this is ridiculous, you really are stubborn, she said, and put out the cigarette. –MD was right about you.

–And I know I'm going to be right about him. I also know that you won't go to the police.

–Why not?

–Because you want to protect your good name and the police would dig up all kinds of dirt.

She bit her lower lip again.

–You think you're clever but you're not.

–I never said I was Einstein.

Then she noticed the photo of a boy on my table in a silver frame. The boy was eight years old and his name was Sunil. She narrowed her eyes and then looked back at me.

–I didn't know you were married, is that your son?

–I'm not married. As to the boy, well, let's leave him out of it for now.

–Leading a double life maybe hey, Chauhan? Anyway, last offer, fifty thousand, take it or leave it.

I nodded, then smiled.

–I'm on this case until Mr Fernandez says otherwise, so I'll be seeing you around.

–It's your life. Don't say I didn't warn you later.

She stood, face tight, eyes angry, and headed towards the

door without the photo or the cash. I stood, took the ten thousand bundle and handed it to her. She placed it reluctantly in her purse.

–Hold on Mrs Fernandez, you didn't tell me the name of the person who phoned you with the new demand.

–He didn't leave a name. He told me to leave the money at a drop off point in two days, he'll call me again.

–They know what they're doing this time around. And I think you and your husband are going to need me more than you think. These kinds of criminals attack without warning, I said.

She turned, looked up into my eyes. They were some eyes, and, unexpected, I felt the warmth, and the chemistry.

–I don't like arguing with you, Chauhan. Please accept my offer before this gets out of hand.

She held my hand. And her eyes lingered on my mouth. I wasn't sure what her game was, whether she was testing me or if she really wanted to kiss me just then.

–The answer is no, Mrs Fernandez.

–Oh, go to hell. You think too much of yourself.

She hurried out of the office and I heard her heels clicking down the corridor. I moved to the office window and looked down. MD was standing near her car. She stepped outside shaking her head. MD closed the door.

A nasty feeling turned in my gut. This gang wouldn't stop at twenty-five lakhs. How many more people would die before they were satisfied? Maybe I should have taken the fifty thousand and walked away, that was the smart thing to do. I locked the office and went out.

I drove out of the office car park. At least I hadn't been fired. Fernandez had come through and was having a ball standing up to her. What had started as blackmail had turned into a double homicide. I had no wish to be added to the homicide count. Maybe I should have settled for one lakh and booked myself a nice holiday. Along the pavement, men were standing drinking chai out of plastic cups, near the stall. Some were smoking cigarettes under the tall umbrella. A poster on the wall read, *Laxmi building apartments coming soon.* They were nice looking apartments, but pictures always looked better than reality.

I turned right at the next corner where street traders were selling colourful blankets, piled high against the wall. Why had Maya Fernandez tried to buy me off in person? What was her angle? Maybe she didn't want me to find out about her dealings. I had a few ideas but none of them had any legs. Someone who might know, was probably smashed out at another party. On instinct, I thought I should find her.

9

I DROVE back to South Mumbai, then headed out to Malabar Hill. Tall palm trees stretched along the road in a line to my right, the leaves darkened by the light rain. Seagulls flew above the sea, their wings sullied with dirt. I turned at the lights, a woman in a pink sari with a flower-print design, waited for me to pass, holding a tilted umbrella. The signboard for Eden Gardens showed, and I parked my car. It was a long shot that Miss Trouble was at home and sober. She was holding back, and it would be tricky to prize the information I needed. Maybe she would be prepared to talk now, after learning how Santana had gone to hell.

Her white jeep was parked near the entrance, a good sign, but that didn't mean she was at home. The clean elevator glided up to her floor, the place looked nicer in the daytime. I walked along the corridor and tapped my knuckles on the wood. Then I placed the side of my face on the door. There was movement inside. The door opened. She tried to slam it shut but I had wedged one foot in the doorway. I pushed my way inside.

–It's good to see you too, Anita.
–Get lost!

She stood in a sleeveless red t-shirt and black tracksuit bottoms, radiating hate. Her eyes swollen with dark semi-circles underneath. She folded her arms across her chest.

–Can't keep away from me hey, cutie.
–I guess not.
–What do you want? she said.
–Some honest answers.

–Sure you do, well, you had your chance last night and you blew it.

–Breaks my heart.

–That's your problem Chauhan, you're too much in love with your job. It's all you think about.

–We can discuss my love life later, I'm here on business.

She shook her head and shifted her weight onto her right foot.

–I have no business with you. The door's over there, she said, and pointed her hand back to the door.

–Hold on a minute Anita, I'm here to help you. I need answers.

–You can't help me. None of you can.

–Why don't you give me a shot?

She weighed the question a moment, sat down on the sofa and took a sip from her whisky glass. Sadness appeared in her eyes despite the bluster. Maybe she needed to talk to someone after her friend had been knocked off. I made myself a drink, and she didn't object. The whisky tasted fine.

–I'm sorry about Santana, I said.

–I don't believe you.

–I didn't want him killed. We need to clear up a few things. Otherwise the police are going to be questioning you.

–I'm not scared of them or anyone else.

I waited for her to make up her mind. She took another sip, then some deep breaths and she held her glass tighter. She stared at the table a long time. It was the kind of expression that lonely people made. Perhaps she had exhausted everyone's patience. The sad part was that no one was doing anything about it. Prem Nath could have saved her from the life she was leading. For the first time, I felt sorry for her. I lit a cigarette and offered her one. She refused and stared at me like a wife who had discovered an affair. I stopped feeling sorry and moved towards the window.

–Well, what do you want? I haven't got all day.

–I want to know about Santana.

–He's dead, probably because of you. Someone murdered him in cold blood, poor Sant...

–I had nothing to do with that, trust me, I said.

–Really? You come along and now he's dead. How do I know you didn't shoot him?

I raised my eyebrows and took a stiff drink.

–That's a new angle even for me, but for the record I didn't. Why would I kill him? Whilst you were high in the bedroom, someone shot him from the window. They would have killed me too, if I hadn't dived for cover.

–Liar!

–Ask the police if you want. Before you start your tantrums, I took you out of there remember. Otherwise you'd be sitting in a police cell right now.

–I don't recall, anything.

I looked at her hard then, kept my eyes on her face. She didn't meet my eyes and stared at her glass after a few seconds.

–I'm not buying it. You know something and I know how to make you talk.

Her eyes widened.

–I'm shaking! Will it involve blindfolds? Handcuffs?

–Here, I said, and showed her the photo. She turned it over with her hands, admiringly.

–I bet you enjoyed looking at that, cutie. Isn't that a sexy body?

–What were you up to with Santana? And who has the negatives?

–Go to hell!

My patience was running thin. When she saw I was going nowhere, she stared at her nails.

–You're not easily insulted, are you? she said.

–Actually, I'm rather sensitive.

She looked up at me, her eyes questioning.

–Look, me and Santana were just friends. He made me feel

happy after my husband ran out on me.

–What kind of friend?

She didn't like that question and remained silent.

–What about the ten lakhs, your friend Santana was asking for?

She pulled her mouth to one side and shook her head, as if this was a great trial for her. She took a deep breath and sighed.

–Yes, I knew about it, happy now? He was just trying to help me out of a sticky situation.

–By blackmailing your father? You're really something.

–He wasn't into blackmail. He was helping me.

–Cut the bullshit. If you don't start talking, I'm handing you over to the police. There's a new inspector dealing with this case, Dhanwan. He isn't gentle.

–I've nothing to hide, she said, and touched her nose.

I took a sip of my drink, waited a moment and said,

–Did you ever meet Raja?

Her eyes widened a fraction. She finished her glass and made another. I could tell she was scrambling for a clever answer; her eyes blinked several times in quick succession. She took her time before saying.

–A few times. He hung around at Rubies.

–Was he Santana's partner?

–Why don't you ask him?

I gritted my teeth and narrowed my eyes. She watched my face.

–I have news for you, Anita. He's dead too. They found him in the Sagar inlet, crushed against the steering wheel. He wasn't a pretty sight.

Her eyes widened and she took another sip with a shaking hand. It still shook when she put the glass back down on the table. Something cold seemed to register.

–You need to wake up. What's your involvement? Your life might be in danger, along with your father. If these thugs killed for ten lakhs, they'll kill for more no doubt. So, let's try again, who had a problem with Santana?

Finally, she didn't look so self-assured. She bit her nails. I was firing arrows in the dark, hoping to hit something.

–Last week outside Rubies, Afzal Khan, he's the manager there, well he argued with Santana. They shut up when I approached.

–Who owns Rubies?

–Some big property company, I think.

My instinct said Khan could be something and I needed to find him. My instinct however had sent me into more tight corners than I could remember. We could be getting somewhere at last, or she was a very good liar.

–What were they arguing about?

–Something about money. My name was mentioned. Men always fight over me. They love me so much.

–I wonder why, I said.

–You have no taste, cutie.

I took a sip from my glass. The whisky was strong and tasted good.

–Did Santana tell you what they were arguing about?

–No. Now you can leave, my head hurts and that's all I know.

She took a sip and rubbed her forehead with her left hand.

–Did you ever see this Afzal before?

–Yes, he runs Rubies. He's always nice to me.

–Anita, there's a new demand for your photos. They want twenty-five lakhs now.

She stood uncertainly and blinked several times.

–If my family cared, they would have paid it a long time ago. Santana would still be alive. But Maya the bitch, she won't pay it. She hates me and father can't stand up to her. Let them deal with this for a change, yes let them deal with it.

She folded her arms across her chest, almost as if she was holding herself for comfort. Her temper seemed to be returning as she gritted her teeth, and anger climbed back into her eyes.

–You're really a spoilt little brat.

Something came alive in her, all the frustration, sadness, and anger. She swung a mean slap at my face. I caught her wrist in time, so she tried to bite my hand. I pushed her back, pushed her harder than I wanted to, and she went flying onto the sofa. She fell on the sofa in an un-lady-like pose. She moved fast and grabbed the neck of the whisky bottle. I ducked. It smashed into the back wall.

–Now get out! And stay out!

I moved towards the door.

–I'm going to find Afzal Khan and for your sake, I hope you're not involved. Next time, you'll be talking to the police.

She looked around the table for another object. There was none. She made do with an angry stare. No one wins in a glaring contest. I opened the door.

–So long princess, I'll be seeing you around.

As I closed the door, a glass smashed against it. I smiled and walked down the corridor. Two women in brown faded saris were mopping the floor. They looked up and smiled. I couldn't figure out how much she was involved. She was upset about Santana's death and surprised about Raja. It gave me hope. Next stop, Afzal Khan. I checked the Glock inside my coat pocket, I had a feeling I might need it tonight.

10

AT THE corner of Eden Gardens, I waited in my car. If Anita was involved, she'd be in a hurry to find Khan. Maybe things were out of her hands. I still had to find the negatives and the people behind the new demand. Fernandez wouldn't be happy with my progress. Santana and Raja were dead, and I didn't have many ideas about who killed them. The price had gone up for the photos, and rich men hated that.

The glass entrance doors of the building opened. A woman wearing shades walked out. It wasn't Anita Fernandez. I could be sitting here into the late evening. That didn't feel right. I made a decision to drive to Rubies. It was a nice four-storey hotel behind the mall, with parking to the front and sides, and I found it easier than I thought I would. RUBIES was written in bold red. It looked more like a private club than a hotel, with a thick hedge lining the outer boundary wall.

Parked cars from outside Mumbai, lined one side. The registration plates: GJ, Gujarat, RJ, Rajasthan; people on business or on a holiday break. A family of eight walked out of the entrance and moved towards a large vehicle, as I parked. I pushed the Glock underneath the car seat, stepped out of the car and entered through the main doors; bouncers in cheap black suits gave me the eye without smiles. I seemed to stop a conversation. Maybe they were discussing the political future of the country.

It was cool inside, with AC, a plush lobby, sofas and chairs around small tables. The reception desk was to my left with two women in dark green saris and hair tied behind their smiling heads. I walked over and leaned on the counter.

–Namaste, saab.
–Hi, I'm looking for a room. What are the rates for one night?
–A single room is five thousand, a double seven and half.
–No kidding, for a night?
–No saab, no kidding, she said, smiling.
–Actually, I wanted to see the manager Afzal. Is he in?
The women looked at one another.
–Yes, he's in the office.
She looked at a door to the side of the reception desk.
–Thanks.
Before they could react, I slid over and knocked on the manager's door.
–Come in.
It was a deep voice from behind the door. One of the women hurried towards me.
–Saab, I'm supposed to ask him first. I don't have your name.
–It's all right, I want to surprise him, we go back years.
This didn't convince her.
–Come in, said the voice, louder.
I entered. A large office with photos of film stars lined the walls. It showed people with thumbs up and big smiles with famous celebrities. Khan sat behind a mahogany desk, a man my age, a big man with a sizeable belly. He looked more like a chef than a manager; maybe he had missed his real vocation. He wore a tight grey shirt and his breathing was heavy. He tapped the desk with his chubby fingers adorned with several gold rings. He was clean-shaven except for a moustache, had short black hair, and a small forehead. He looked nervous. Like a man before a keen tax inspector.

He put his pen down on a piece of paper. A side door, slightly ajar, led into another room. The light shone from that room too. I walked across and stood before the desk.
–How did you get inside?

–Through the door.

–Is that supposed to be funny? No one enters without the receptionist informing me first.

–You just can't find the staff these days, I said.

–What do you want? I'm busy.

I placed a hand on the chair.

–I need a few minutes of your precious time, no more.

–Look, what are you selling? Our stocks are good right now, he said.

–Do I look like a salesman to you?

–You look like someone who wants something.

He stood up, and was bigger than I had thought, almost six feet tall. His fat was the fat of a sturdy man who could handle himself if the need arose. There was nothing friendly about his stance either. I stayed behind the chair.

–I've come to talk about your friend, Santana. He met with an unfortunate accident. Maybe you heard about it?

–And who the bloody hell are you?

–I'll come to the introductions. I'm here to help.

–I don't need your help and I don't think I like you very much either. Walking in as if you own the place.

–You should never make snap judgements, that's what stupid people do.

–Are you a cop, *sala*?

–What gives you that idea?

Khan's right hand shook at his side as he glanced towards the side-door. The look meant there was someone inside. He liked to act tough but he wasn't that tough. A man walked out of the room, a man who had 'tough bastard' written all over him. He moved towards the desk, and Khan moved away in a hurry.

–I'll handle this, Afzal. Can you take care of the guests outside?

–Yes, saab.

Khan gave me a dirty glance as he left the office.

The new man lit a cigar and blew the smoke in my direction. He had hard black eyes. I had seen the man before in the papers. It was Dinesh Bakshi. He owned properties and clubs in Mumbai. A dark-skinned man, wearing a black suit, with a diamond pin on the outside breast pocket shaped like a star. Around his mid-forties with flecks of grey hair appearing at the temples. He was of medium height, clean-shaven, short crew cut hair, but the force of his personality was in his eyes. It looked as if he owned this club too.

He blew the smoke from the side of his mouth, sat down without a smile and indicated with his cigar for me to take a seat.

–Excuse Afzal's manners. They're not his strong point.

–I've met worse, probably.

–What can I do for you? I don't think you are here to book a room.

He gave me a sly look, a quick narrowing of his hard eyes.

–I came to discuss photography with Afzal. Before you interrupted us.

–Photography? Afzal doesn't have any such talent.

–That's too bad. Well, I need to speak to him if you don't mind. I guess I'll be on my way.

I stood and nodded at Bakshi. He leaned back in his chair and brought his hands together.

–Not so fast, Mister, I haven't finished yet.

He pointed with his cigar for me to take a seat. It seemed like he was used to pointing his cigar at people. I sat down again but didn't like the feeling.

–Don't give me that look, he said, –I have two boys in the next room and four outside. They do exactly as I tell them, like Rottweilers, and they all carry iron.

–I didn't know dogs could shoot.

He leaned back into the leather chair, put the cigar to his mouth. He had an unpleasant sneer on his face. He was trying to figure me out. He held the cigar between his fingers, and his eyes were working fast.

–I don't like clowns coming into my office without invitation. What's your name and what do you want? If you don't answer correctly, you'll spend six months in hospital wondering what happened.

–I don't like that idea too much. I might start to shake in a minute, I said.

He grinned.

–You think you're tough, hey? Most men who think they're hard, wished they had never tangled with me.

He stood and moved to a cabinet behind him. He took out a bottle of Johnnie Walker whisky and poured a neat half glass. He also took out a pistol from his pocket, as he turned around. The pistol pointed to the floor.

–That's all right, I don't want a drink, I said.

–You're not funny, Mister. Name, and make it quick.

–You said Afzal had bad manners. Name's Chauhan, Abhay Chauhan. I'm a private detective.

–I should have guessed it. Who are you working for?

–You don't need to know right now but he's a respectable client. A man called Santana was blackmailing him with compromising photos of his daughter. Santana however decided to take a bullet to his head and that leaves me back at square one. I need to pay him and collect the negatives, and I think your man Khan is involved.

–Hmm, that's some story, I thought you might be serious but you're whistling in the wind. Khan isn't my man, he works as a manager here and that's all.

–You must own Rubies.

–I have many properties and I'm expanding all the time.

–You might be expanding in the wrong direction.

Bakshi grinned, played with the pistol and tucked it back into his trouser pocket.

–This meeting is over. You're a time waster.

–Not so fast, I know you, Bakshi. You own clubs, gambling

dens for flash and careless people. The local law in your pocket, along with several MLA's. You're a big developer with big protection. What I don't understand however is why your man Khan would bother with this cheap racket. Maybe it's better I inform the police. They won't be so cooperative. My client also carries influence.

–Who's the big shot?

–I'm sure you know him.

I was hoping he would spill Fernandez's name but he was too sharp for that.

–I don't care for you, your client or the police. You're wasting my time. What is it you want with Khan?

I clenched my right fist and opened it slowly.

–I think he's involved in the blackmail racket and they're running it from here, from your place. The police won't like that.

–For a second, I thought you might have something of interest. You're not very good, are you?

–I've often been underestimated, must have that kind of face.

I tapped the desk and looked at him.

–I found an interesting little red book with lots of names and telephone numbers. It went missing from Santana's bungalow, and the police might like to thumb through it.

I'd fired an arrow completely in the dark again, hoping to hit something. He stared a long time.

–You have a book, big deal. Go ahead and read it.

He grinned and placed the cigar in his mouth. He was confident, smooth, I couldn't figure what he was thinking. I tried again.

–Santana kept a record, I'll give him that. If the numbers he left find their way to Khan and this place, then the police are going to be asking questions.

–You're still whistling in the air, Chauhan.

–In that case, I had better leave.

As I stood, Bakshi whistled.

Two large men hurried out of the side room to block my path. They gave Rottweilers a bad name. They wore ill-fitting grey suits and glared the only way such men glare. Maybe I had disturbed their discussion about the political situation of the country.

–Stay still, said Bakshi. –See if this loser is carrying.

The first man frisked me. I turned around like a bored man at airport security with my arms raised.

–No iron, boss.

The man slipped a big hand into my leather jacket and drew out my wallet.

–Abhay Chauhan, Private Dick, down from Boriwali. He's a detective all right, boss. Cheap too, only has a few hundred rupees in his wallet.

–It's more honest money than you'll ever earn.

He put the wallet back and pushed me roughly to face Bakshi again.

–Easy, I said, –I didn't know dogs could read.

The two men didn't like that crack, and if Bakshi wasn't present, they'd happily let me know.

–Okay leave us, said Bakshi.

The thugs walked back to their cage and I didn't see two brain cells rubbing together in their thick skulls.

–Let this be a lesson for you, Chauhan. Next time, you'll be spending time in a hospital.

I adjusted myself and smoothed out my clothes.

–The police will find who killed Santana and Raja. If your man Afzal is involved, I suggest you get good lawyers. And I'd advise you to get some protection because new people are taking over that racket. People who don't think twice about killing people.

–You like to give advice? Let me give you some free advice as well. Maybe it's you who needs the protection.

We looked at one another, as Bakshi blew out smoke.

–I can handle myself. All I want is the photos from your man Afzal. Then I walk away. I suggest you accept my offer, before everything becomes very interesting and you start to have nightmares.

The grin left Bakshi's face.

–You need to see a psychiatrist, Chauhan, you've lost your mind. Take my advice and see a shrink. Stop putting your nose where it doesn't belong and you might live.

The hard look he gave after that sentence, made clear what he meant.

–Okay, have it your way. If the police call, don't say I didn't warn you.

–Let me worry about the police. Don't show your ugly face around here again. You're a time-waster, Chauhan. Find a new profession, because I don't think you will last long in this one.

–Don't worry about me. Start looking over your own shoulder. Time is running out.

I straightened my jacket, turned around and walked towards the door without looking back. If he was going to shoot, he was going to shoot. I doubted he would do it at his workplace. I opened the door, walked out and took a deep breath. The receptionists weren't smiling, and Khan glared at me.

–I think I'll skip staying here, I said, –I've decided the hospitality isn't to my liking.

–Get moving.

–We need to talk, Khan, before it's too late.

Khan gritted his teeth and turned his large hands into fists.

–We have nothing to talk about, now move before we throw you out.

–Customer service isn't what it used to be. Think about what I've said Khan. It's for your benefit.

I left with a nod to the receptionists. They put their heads together in quiet whispers, without smiles. A couple crossed my path, they seemed like honeymooners, all in love and oblivious to the rat-infested hole they were entering. They held hands and smiled at me. I smiled back. It was nice to see happy people for a change. I went outside. Sometimes you have to poke the fire with an iron rod to make sparks fly. I hoped Khan became nervous and made a false move, because Bakshi wouldn't. It was doubtful Bakshi was involved with small fry like this. This had to be Khan's racket or he was working for someone else. I reached my Contessa and opened the door. I had ideas flying around my head, ideas that seemed to be going nowhere fast.

11

I STARTED the engine and reversed. Driving out of the gates, I turned right and wondered how to find the blackmailers. If Khan wasn't involved and this was Santana's racket, then it was a dead end. I turned the car, parked diagonally across from Rubies and smoked a cigarette. Sometimes waiting was the best option, instead of running around like a rabbit and getting shot at.

The wait wasn't long. A black SUV drove out of the gates. Bakshi was sitting in the back. The vehicle turned left and disappeared. Khan wasn't there, yet he was the one I wanted. He had the kind of nervous disposition that gave answers. He would finish his shift by nine tops on a Thursday night. An hour to kill, so I picked up the novel.

The hero loved a young woman but could neither express his love, nor understand whether she had any feelings towards him. A nice scene. I wanted him to be braver. In love, as in life, it was better being bold. Yet the rejection would have crushed him. He mumbled through the scene and got nowhere. It has been said, that if you are waiting for a woman to make up her mind, then you'll be waiting a long time. Khan drove out then, in a white Fiat, looking anxious. I raised the novel to cover my face as he drove past. I was in luck and was able to follow him, keeping three cars behind.

We drove for twenty minutes, over the flyover, past the slums. We drove along and through a concrete jungle that was expanding all the time. Under the bridge, there were families sitting on open blankets and the kids looked hungry. Hundreds of migrants came into the city daily, hoping for a better life. It wasn't easy by a long shot, and the chances were, the family would remain under the bridge for many years to come.

Khan turned into a side road with squat two-storey houses and parked at the end. His large figure hurried out and opened the door to his house. I parked five houses back, then pulled out the pistol and nestled it in the small of my back. It was safer to carry such a piece around a nervous looking big man. They had a bad habit of being trigger happy in tense situations. Cautiously, I moved towards the house. Khan had looked tense back at Rubies. A wrong turn of phrase and I might be in a tough fight.

I waited at the front door, listened for voices: nothing. The smell of chapattis and aloo sabji drifted across from next door, along with a film song. It happened to be the famous one from Sholay, *Mehbooba, mehbooba*. An upbeat folksy dance number, at odds with my present tense situation. If I didn't handle this right, I'd be dancing to a different tune.

I pressed the button. A strange bell that sent the sound of birds chirping fluttering up the hall. I smiled, it didn't fit with the hulking mass of Khan. The door opened slowly. Khan stood there irritated. His big hands were twitching by his side. He said nothing.

–We can stand here all evening, but I have better things to do, Khan.

–You better go and do them then.

He opened and closed his big fists and made sure I noticed. He probably thought he could lick me in a fight. I wasn't in a hurry to find out.

–I need to talk to you about Santana. It's important.

–He's dead. That's all I know.

–You will be too, if you don't listen.

He considered that, looking more nervous than irritated.

–I need five minutes, that's all, then I leave.

He relented and opened his fists.

–All right, come in, you're a persistent bastard, aren't you?
–I've had better compliments.

We entered a lobby, turned left into a square front room with a three-piece sofa suite, a wooden table in the centre and not much else. There were no family photographs. He was single, for there were no feminine touches around the house. We stood facing one another, and he didn't ask me to sit down. He looked at his watch.

–Your time has started. I have nothing to tell you.
–Perhaps you want to talk to the police. There's a new inspector in town and he's a real son-of-a-bitch.

He cracked a knuckle, seemed unimpressed about the police.

–I have nothing to hide. Now what to do you want?

I heard quiet footsteps out in the corridor, and they were moving closer to the lounge door.

–I think you have Anita Fernandez's photos and negatives. I want them back.
–I've never heard of her.

He didn't shift his irritated eyes from my face. The room had no cheer, a bit like Khan. He didn't smile, his vibe spread throughout the room and put me on edge. He leaned towards the table, picked up his cigarettes and lit one with a slight shake in his right hand. That could be one of two things: a nervous disposition or he was hiding something.

–You haven't told me your name.
–Abhay Chauhan, Private Detective.
–Huh, thought you looked like a greasy *policewalla*.
–I'm not one.
–I can't stand any of you.

He reached behind his back and pulled out a pistol. It looked like a lady's gun, and ridiculous in his big hand. It was still powerful enough to blow a hole in my heart.

–I talk politely, and people point guns at me. It's not my day is it? You don't need that, I'm here to help.

–I don't need your help.

People speak more confidently with a gun in their hand, even when their hands shook the way Khan's did. I didn't want him to fire a shot in my chest. He kept pointing the gun at different parts of my upper body.

–Put that down Khan. It might go off.

–Think you're funny, hey? Your jokes might get your head blown off.

–It's a risk you take, comedy isn't easy. You should try smiling. It's good for you.

He narrowed his eyes again.

–You have the photos and I know that you knew Santana because he was a regular at Rubies. A little bird told me you met regularly and something else, I also have Santana's red book.

His eyes were working fast now. They blinked several times.

–The book has important numbers and names. Santana had a growing racket but look where it got him. If you're not careful, you'll be following him to hell as well. So, what I want is answers, and you need to be quick, time is running out for you.

He sat back on the sofa, placing the gun on his lap so that it was pointing at the table. I felt better. My mouth was dry. I sat down on the side sofa. He sighed, as if struggling to keep his emotions in check. He shook his head, and focussed on a blue pencil on the table, and for those few moments, I didn't exist in the room. I heard the footsteps shift outside and saw two small shadows underneath the door.

–You knew Santana, right?

He remained silent.

–Look, I don't know how you're mixed up in this racket but you're better off quitting while you're still alive. Santana and Raja are both dead. I suppose you must have known Raja too. The police pulled him out of the water, yesterday. He didn't look well. Santana had a bullet in the middle of his forehead.

Whoever is doing the killing, means business.

–Chauhan, I told you I'm not involved. Are you stupid or what? Don't get me wrong okay, I'm not a tough guy, I'm just the manager at Rubies. I, I don't need this bullshit. I don't know who you are, or what you're after. You might be about to kill me for all I know.

–What gives you that idea?

He sighed and pointed the gun again.

–All I know is that I have to be careful these days.

–You're not careful enough. Your name was written in the book, initials A.K. with a nice sum of three lakhs against it. Santana was a regular at your club and the police will ask you for the details in their nice police cell. They hang suspects upside down and whack their backsides with canes. Now all I want is the photos and negatives. You drop the twenty-five lakh demand. One more thing, can you ask your partner to step inside? They'll get tired standing behind the door.

–Shanti, step inside.

The door opened and a woman came in with a pistol pointed at my head. It was Ice Baby from the boutique and that didn't surprise me as much as it should have.

–Hello you, another one with a gun. It's not my lucky day is it? Okay, I'll buy the dress from somewhere else.

Ice Baby walked towards the window, checked through the curtains, looked up and down the road and turned to face me.

–Shut up, you talk too much, she said, –I told you he was trouble Afzal.

–I was only looking for a dress. If my sister knew the trouble I've had finding her a dress. She can buy her own in the future.

–You're not funny.

–Take it easy, Shanti, said Khan.

She had cool eyes and her hand wasn't shaking. I figured she'd kill me faster than Khan, and she wouldn't even blink.

–Do you always talk to your customers with a gun in your hand?

–You have a nerve with two guns pointing at you.

–Put that away Shanti. I'll handle this, said Khan.

Ice Baby sat opposite me on another sofa chair and placed her gun inside a white handbag. She continued to give me the evils. I lit a cigarette, blew out the smoke from the side of my mouth. Khan's pistol took a closer interest in me whilst I held the cigarette. I also needed a drink but I doubted they were going to offer me one.

–Now, Santana's red book has a list of names and they're written in code. The police will crack the code once I hand over the book. You, Santana and Raja have been making a nice side income, my guess, several lakhs per month if not more. Santana pulled the girls at Rubies and other nightclubs. He took pictures and blackmailed their parents or boyfriends. The police won't have any difficulty linking you to this dirty racket. You can save yourself trouble by giving me Anita Fernandez's photos.

–He's crazy, said Ice Baby, –Are you going to listen to this nonsense, Afzal?

–Just listen for a change will you, you might learn something.

–I don't know how you're involved with this Ice Baby, I said, –But you quit while you're ahead. The police will be here soon enough. All I want is the photos and I'll leave you two in peace.

Khan's eyes glanced at her, then back at me. I tapped the cigarette; the ash fell on the granite floor tiles. Something had hit home, it looked like Khan was thinking about it harder than she was. She clutched her purse and bit her lower lip.

–It's a good story, said Khan. –You don't have anything on us apart from a red book you keep talking about. You claim my initials are in the book yet there are many people with A.K. as initials. So, that doesn't prove anything, is that all you have? You're not a good detective, Chauhan. Bakshi was right about you, you're a time waster.

Ice Baby smiled, it made her look sinister.

–Suit yourself. My five minutes are up anyway. It's about time I gave the book to the police.

I blew out the smoke. No one said anything. We could have been sat round a poker table.

–Okay, I'll play my hand first, what you did before was small-time, but the murders change everything. You're looking at life and hard labour in jail. Whoever killed your friends isn't going to hesitate to kill you two either. I can help you leave this behind before it becomes too late. Now, it's your turn, who's running this racket?

–You take big chances Chauhan, don't you? said Khan.

He looked beat, worried and his right hand shook again as did the gun. Ice Baby was cool, there was no twitching or shaking of any kind, just a stare, weighing her options, and she looked as if she didn't believe a word I said.

–You're crazy! You sit there and tell us that Santana was running this racket right from his boutique in broad daylight. You're crazier than I thought. Now tell him Afzal. He has nothing on us.

–He might have something, Shanti.

–It's bullshit!

–Pipe down.

Her eyes turned to ice, then she turned away from Khan to look at me. She picked up the pencil from the table and snapped it in two. She kept her mouth shut. If she'd been running this outfit, I'd have had a hard time getting anything.

–Who killed Santana? Don't you want to get even? I asked.

Khan sighed. His hand was shaking again, and I became nervous.

–I'd love to get even...

–Shut your mouth, Khan!

–No Shanti, Santana and Raja were like my brothers, damn him, they were like my brothers.

He wiped tears with his big hands, breathed deeply, heaving

his large frame as he did so. I needed that gun out of his hands.

–The bastard killed them. And for what? For no good reason I can think of. That scary bastard killed them for no reason.

–You're dead now. You should have kept your mouth shut, she said, shaking her head and blowing out her cheeks.

–I'm sick of it, Shanti. I never liked this racket from the start, and now it's all fallen on my head and I can't stand it. Here's the funny thing, I don't even know how to get out of it. I was planning to leave Mumbai tonight, did you know that, Shanti? It has to be better than living in this fear all the time.

–Is this Dinesh Bakshi's racket? I asked.

–No, said Khan. –He wouldn't become involved in this. He's a rich man, this is small fry.

–Then who's behind it? Give me a name and I'll help you out.

–How will you do that?

–I used to be a police inspector, I know how to cut a deal.

Ice Baby didn't look impressed. This however had been a weight on Khan's shoulders that had proved too much. He had decided to come my way.

–Do you have the photos of Anita Fernandez?

He pointed the gun to the floor, opened and closed his left hand. Then he glanced at Ice Baby, as if to decide whether to speak the next sentence. She shook her head. He sighed and turned to face me.

–Yes, they're with me, Chauhan. I never wanted to be involved, it was all Santana's idea. He said we could make easy money. Look where it got him.

–What's her involvement?

I nodded towards her.

–Don't tell the bloody cop!

–No, Shanti. This is too dangerous, look what happened to our friends. She keeps the accounts.

–All right. Who's your boss?

He glanced around, shook a little and looked back at me.

–The man is called Kasim. He's the scariest man I ever met. Santana introduced him to us a few months ago. I never thought he'd kill Santana and Raja.

–You think he did it?

–Who else would it be?

–I don't know yet.

Khan placed the gun inside his trouser pocket and I instantly felt better.

–I want out. How can you help us?

–Don't you worry about that right now. Can you describe Kasim?

–Nearly as tall as you, muscular, a big scar down his left cheek that he doesn't like people looking at. Raja asked him about it once and he beat him to within an inch of his life, in front of us all. He only stopped when Santana intervened. Raja was a bloody mess. But it's the eyes that scare you the most. The deadest grey eyes I ever saw. If he looks at you once, you don't forget. People move out of the way even when he grins, and he doesn't do that very often.

–Where's he from?

–We don't know. But once he joined Santana, our income rocketed. People paid more and on time. You don't cross Kasim.

–He sounds like a bag of laughs all right.

–I'd like to see you crack jokes in front of him, said Ice Baby.

I looked at her with a slight smile.

–He might like them more than you. It can't be any worse.

She didn't smile.

–If he finds out about this, we're all dead, she said.

–Did Kasim make the twenty-five lakh demand?

–Yes, he told us that we didn't know how to blackmail, said Khan.

–He was right about that. This set up suits Kasim just fine.

Anything goes wrong, and he's totally out of the picture. The evidence is all with you guys and there's no question you'll see jail time.

–I told this to Santana, but no one had the nerve to tell Kasim. He gives the orders and you bloody well listen, only I'm not taking it anymore. I can't stand the *bhenchod* to tell the truth…I thought about going to the Police but you beat them to it.

–Well, I'm not, said Shanti, and stood. –It's time I left Mumbai. You had better run too, Khan. You won't live here, not after what you've just said.

We all stood.

An awkward silence followed, as we looked at each other with suspicion. Khan had put his hand on his gun again and pulled it out slowly. She held her purse tight, unsure about the next move. She kept glancing at Khan to check if he'd let her go. He wasn't giving an inch and stayed still looking at her.

–All right, pass me the photos and negatives Khan, then I'll tell you how to leave this. You'll have to hide until the police find and deal with Mr Bag of laughs, you understand?

–They won't ever catch him. He's shrewd. No, I'll get out of this myself. I'm no longer scared of Kasim. You can only scare a man so much before he fights back.

–That's the spirit. Why don't you give me the photos now?

–I'll be glad to be rid of them.

Ice Baby stepped forward towards Khan.

–You can't hand over the photos just like that Afzal, Kasim will kill us. Are you crazy or what?

–No, Shanti, I'm getting out of this right now. I advise you to do the same. We can't trust Kasim anymore, not after what they've done. They had no right to kill Santana or Raja.

–How do you know they did it? I asked.

–It's them all right, he replied.

As he moved towards the door and opened it, the sound of birds chirping rang around the house. She shook her head and widened her eyes. Khan took a deep breath and his hands and the gun were shaking again. I peeked through the curtains and saw the shadow of a man. The birds carried on chirping in an unfriendly way.

12

KHAN TOOK a cautious step towards the front door. He looked back at us and placed the gun to his lips. His face was sharp and mean, but when he held the gun to his side, it shook again. I moved my left hand behind my back and checked the pistol, still hoping I wouldn't need it. The birds kept chirping. If the visitors were Bakshi and his men, then I could kiss goodbye to the photos and a lot more besides. Had someone followed me? Maybe I had concentrated too much in tailing Khan.

Mumbai was full of sharp operators and Kasim's involvement had made me fearful for the first time in a long time. I hoped it wasn't him at the door. This could involve a lot of gunfire. Shanti threw me a glance and pulled out her gun. She looked like she knew how to use it.

Khan opened the door, whilst holding the gun in his right hand. It didn't do him any good. He was too slow. He stepped back from the door. Someone was pointing a big revolver in his face. Khan took quick breaths and sweat ran down his face. He backed up into the room. A squat well-built man with a black moustache and stubble, closed the front door and came inside. The man looked like a thug who snatched purses from grandmothers and enjoyed doing it. He glanced at me, at Shanti. He took Khan's gun and placed it inside his short brown jacket. Khan was holding his big hands in the air. The man pointed his gun at Shanti.

–Drop your piece on the table, slowly, Shanti.

Her gun clattered to the table.

–Stand next to Khan. No. Check him for a gun.

She moved over to me, took my gun and then handed it to the man.

–Who the hell, are you? I asked.

I felt a sharp slap for my trouble. The man hit hard.

–You talk only when I tell you to, you understand? said the man.

He looked a few years older than me.

–Get the photos and negatives right now, he said, looking at Khan.

–I am supposed to keep them until we are paid, Manjit.

Manjit turned his thick neck, left and right. –Is this Chauhan, the useless detective? Has he come to pay?

–You can talk to me, I know how to speak.

He looked as if he was going to slap me again.

–So, you're the smart *bhenchod*. A five-year old girl could follow you, he said with a grin.

–He has a big mouth on him too, Manjit, and he's trouble, said Shanti.

–I'll deal with him. Khan, get the photos. I won't tell you a second time.

–That's not what Kasim said.

–This is his order. He thinks you've lost your bottle, you wimp. I can see why. Has this bastard paid you yet? Does he even have the money with him?

–I have the money, I said, –You will be paid once I know who I'm dealing with.

Manjit pointed the gun at my head.

–Is that right? What have you been talking about all this time?

He looked around at Khan, Shanti and me.

–We were agreeing a time and a place for the swap, I said.

–I don't trust you Chauhan, so we have a problem. I don't like the look of you either.

–That's all right. I won't lose sleep over it, but I wouldn't mind a date with Shanti. What do you say Shanti?

–Shut up! He's not worth trusting, Manjit, she said.

I hoped she wouldn't spill the beans on Khan, because if she did, he'd be dead in no time.

–Khan, do you know what happens to people who get careless? I thought we had made that clear at our last meeting.

–I didn't know about him, he came here by himself, ask Shanti.

She didn't reply but was now composed. She smiled at Manjit.

–Shall I get the photos? she said.

–Yes Baby, you do that.

She hurried out of the front room and returned in less than two minutes with a thick blue envelope. Manjit placed the envelope inside his jacket.

–Now, tell me what these bastards were talking about. Kasim likes to hear bad news immediately.

She grinned at me, then at Khan.

–This fatso went soft.

–Bitch, shut your mouth! spat Khan, eyes wide with panic.

Manjit pursed his lips and shook his head slightly.

–I thought so. For this baby, Kasim will reward you. He said you had more guts than all these clowns put together.

–She's lying, said Khan, with a voice that lacked conviction.

He had lost the trust battle. She had landed the first blow and it could be fatal. Beads of sweat formed on Khan's forehead and rolled down the side of his face.

–Keep quiet or I'll shut you up with this, said Manjit. He pushed the gun towards Khan's face.

–What were they discussing, Baby?

She grinned at me. –What's the matter, Mr Detective? No more jokes, find you're not so funny anymore?

–My jokes would be wasted on dumb people, especially you and your ugly boyfriend here.

I received another slap, harder this time from Manjit.

–He has a mouth on him all right, he said, –Now, what was

he saying, Baby?

She looked up at Khan, then grinned. Khan was shaking his head and his hands were twitching by his sides. She didn't care to take notice. She explained Khan's words, adding a little spice.

–You double crossing bitch, said Khan, he was half dead with nerves and his face looked beat. He wrung his hands in front of him. –Did you double-cross Santana and Raja too?

–No, she didn't, said Manjit, –We saw they were too careless. But what are we going to do about you? I mean this is really bad news Khan, we expected better.

–Tell Kasim to go to hell, said Khan, his voice weak with fear.

His eyes bulged with a hatred I hadn't seen before. If Manjit didn't have the gun, I was sure Khan would have killed him with his bare hands.

–Whilst you have your domestic argument, I think it's best you hand over that envelope, I pay you and leave.

–Chauhan really thinks he's funny, said Manjit, –I'll knock that smart mouth off you in a minute. There's only one place you're going, to Hell.

–Sending me there won't get you the money. Only I know where it is.

He touched the snub of the gun to his small forehead, using it to scratch it. Thinking seemed like trouble to him.

–You're not that important Chauhan. Besides you know too much.

–I know how to keep quiet, unlike Ice Baby over there. She would sell her mother to get away.

–Shut up! she screamed.

–Take it easy Baby, I have this under control.

She flew at me and tried to knee me in the place where it always hurts. She succeeded in pushing me onto the sofa, and her hands tried to scratch my face. I held her wrists as she tried to bite my hands. She had sharp little teeth. I managed to drag her head away by pulling her hair. Manjit laughed.

Khan saw his chance and jumped on him. A shot went off. Khan and Manjit grappled on the floor, punching one another, Khan's eyes were wild with fury. Ice Baby was trying to bite me again. I forced her back and pushed her away. She went flying across the room, missing the two men on the floor, and fell near the door. She didn't look very lady like either.

Meanwhile, Khan had managed to knock the gun out of Manjit's hand and was now pummelling him with heavy hate-filled punches. If I'd let him carry on, he would have killed Manjit, not that I cared too much. I picked up the gun from the floor and tapped Khan on the back of his round shoulders, then pointed the gun. They both came back to their senses, but not before Khan punched Manjit a few more times.

Khan stood breathing heavily, but his wrestling partner lay sprawled out on the floor, looking up with a bloodied face. I took all the guns, it was a nice collection, and then leaned over Manjit and took out the envelope containing the photos and the negatives, and slotted it into my jacket pocket.

Shanti sat up, hair dishevelled. She looked at me like an alley cat sizing up its prey. I smiled at her, for the whole set up had started to amuse me.

–If you want a kiss, all you had to do was ask.

–I wouldn't kiss you if my life depended upon it! she said

–Breaks my heart. People can be so cruel. And I thought we had something going, just goes to show.

I looked at all of them.

–You guys, are real amateurs.

Manjit had blood trickling out of his nose and mouth, and looked up from the floor with menace.

–Kasim isn't going to be happy with you at all, I said.

I noticed the teeth marks on my hand.

–Kasim, the bastard can go to hell, said Khan, slumping down on the sofa with heavy breaths.

–You're dead, said Manjit. –You're dead as well, Chauhan.

–I'd worry about your own state of health. You don't look so good.

–You're a dead man walking, he said, and wiped the blood from his face.

–You could use a different expression, I said, –Then again, I doubt your vocabulary extends too far.

–You're dead!

–Okay, I get it.

I had the blackmail gang busted. Kasim remained out there but that was something the police could figure out. They had to be good for something. One phone call to Dhanwan, and the police would be swarming the place like a rash. I had to get the photos out, weirdly I felt sorry for Khan. I wondered how to play this.

–You can get up now. You look like an angry cat on the floor.

She sprang up, adjusted her hair and clothes and sat in the armchair. Manjit was still lying on the floor looking sore. He had taken an unexpected beating and hadn't been ready. They always hurt the most.

He couldn't believe Khan had beaten him to a pulp. I needed some answers. This was as good a time as any to get them, before I handed these amateurs over to Inspector Dhanwan.

13

I WALKED over to the curtains and pulled them back slightly. The stray bullet had made a neat hole in the window frame. There were no nosy neighbours, and maybe a shot fired at night wasn't such a big deal in Mumbai. More likely the traffic noise had drowned out the sound. I didn't have too much time with these clowns, perhaps ten minutes max before Kasim figured something was wrong.

–What are you going to do now? asked Khan.

–I want some answers.

–Why don't you leave? You have the photos.

–I can never seem to quit while I'm ahead.

–That will get you killed, said Ice Baby, with a slight grin.

–Unless you manage it first with your biting powers. Khan, I'm asking you nicely, is Kasim behind this racket or is it someone else?

He sat up on the sofa and looked more composed now that he had taken his anger out on Manjit.

–What's in it for me? You're going to hand me over to the police.

–I might change my mind. Depends what you say and whether or not I believe you.

I moved away from the window and walked round the sofa to face him.

–It was Santana's idea. He made an easy two lakh about four months ago from the old man.

–Who paid him off?

–Anita's husband. A guy called Prem Nath.

–Where is he now?

He shrugged his heavy shoulders and showed his palms.

–No one knows. He left town, we heard. I don't blame him. Anita Fernandez is too much trouble.

I glanced at Manjit. He had managed to lift himself up on his elbows and was glowering at Khan.

–Whose idea was it to start with again?

–Santana, I told him she was trouble and it was better if we left her alone. Her husband warned him that he would kill us the next time.

–A little weak, but I'll let it pass. When did Kasim and this clown get involved?

–Three months ago and that's when our takings started to rocket.

Manjit lifted his head and grunted. –Shut your big fat mouth!

–You stay quiet Manjit or I will beat you again.

–Take it easy, I said, –you've beaten him enough. Who killed Santana and Raja, was it him?

Khan looked down at Manjit a long time, almost as if he was prepared to confess in a witness stand.

–Yes, either him or Kasim.

–You don't have any proof, said Manjit. –And when I get out, you'll both be dead.

–Wrong answer, I said, –the police are going to have fun talking to you Manjit.

–I'm not scared of the police. But you had better be scared of Kasim. He's going to give you a slow, bloody death.

–You worry about your own situation Manjit. It doesn't look so good.

–Look Chauhan, said Shanti, with something resembling niceness making its way into her tone, –maybe we can cut a deal and you let us go.

–I'm all ears.

–We pay you ten lakhs in cash if you let us go. You won't make that kind of money anywhere, and you have the photos and negatives.

I rubbed the side of my forehead and smiled.

–Who will pay me, you?

–Yes, I have the money.

She fumbled inside her white purse, pulled out a pocket mirror and adjusted her hair. She tried to smile, and it scared me a little.

–We have no quarrel with you.

–Your bite said something else.

–I lost my temper. I'm sorry but you have the talent for provocation.

–I have many talents.

She gave me the insincere smile again. –I think we started on the wrong foot that's all. Well, how about it?

She placed her hand under her chin. –I mean I doubt you earn that much, and ten lakhs in hard cash is a big amount.

–Nice try. I can't decide whether I prefer your anger or your crocodile smile.

She sat up straight and stopped smiling.

–You're too smart for your own good, Chauhan. Kasim won't let you go.

–That's more like it. And I'm the one holding the gun, so that makes me as smart as I want to be.

She shook her head and looked up at the ceiling as if to say, how am I going to convince this guy.

–I doubt you or Khan killed your former partners. That leaves Manjit here and your boss. One more question, do any of you know what happened to Prem Nath?

Manjit grunted and spat on the floor. He was a tough bastard, that Dhanwan would enjoy beating him before he spoke.

–We don't know anything about Prem Nath, said Khan, –I heard he committed suicide, walked into the sea. I read it in the papers, now why don't you let me go?

I rubbed my chin and shook my head slightly.

–No, it's better you cut a deal with the police. You'll get two years max but it's better than running all your life, looking over your shoulder. I'll put in a good word.

He remained silent, wearied perhaps by my advocacy skills.

–I'll never go to jail, never, Shanti said.

–You might like it.

A small hard object crashed through the window. Tear gas hissed into the room. My eyes burned with a fury. I coughed as smoke spread through the room. I saw the glint of a blade as I staggered back and held the gun tight, trying to see. Someone screamed. Doors opened and closed. I staggered out the front door, took deep breaths, pointed the gun in front of me, coughing. The evening air felt good even as my eyes burned. I tried to suck in the fresh air. I leaned back against the wall, I couldn't see anybody there, but that wasn't saying much. My eyesight was blurred.

I was a wide-open target. Tyres screeched. I heard another film song playing from an open window somewhere. It was a happy song, something about a man returning home and finding his love waiting for him.

Gas cleared the door. A few neighbours came outside and looked in my direction. I walked back into the room. Ice Baby and Manjit had gone, but Khan sat on the sofa, eyes wide-open, tears drying on his face. There was a red patch spreading around his chest. There was also a knife stuck in there. He had almost made it.

I moved to the telephone and gave the constable the address and said a murder had taken place. I made a quick check of the rooms. I thought more pictures of Anita Fernandez might be floating around, but there weren't any. Khan had lived alone and there was nothing interesting in the drawers. I walked over to my Contessa, placed the blue envelope underneath the car seat and waited for the police to arrive. They didn't take long to get there.

The sirens rang loud in the night air.

14

DHANWAN MADE me wait in an office at his police station in South Mumbai. It was in a clean compound with neem trees planted around the front walls. The police vehicles were newer. It beat my old station in the north. The light-coloured walls had 'wanted' posters of people who didn't even look like criminals in this part of town. I lit a cigarette. It was ten-thirty and I was getting edgy. The forensics had swarmed all over Khan's house earlier and Dhanwan hadn't believed a word I'd said. I also phoned Gautam to meet me at the station, in case I fell out with the awkward Inspector.

Dhanwan and Gautam entered together. They looked grave, though the inspector had that kind of face anyway. He walked around his desk, sat down in his khaki uniform and placed his hat and baton on the table.

–You find trouble quite easily, said Gautam, pulling up a chair next to me.

–Trouble I can deal with. It's the nice people you meet in this game that are the problem.

Gautam raised his eyebrows whilst contempt flashed across Dhanwan's face.

–Chauhan, you have a bad habit. People end up dead wherever you go. Either you are very unlucky or seriously clumsy.

–They mustn't like my jokes.

–This is funny to you? I have three murders and the killer is on the loose.

–You need to up your game then, Dhanwan.

I leaned back in my chair with a slight grin, but it was

forced.

–I don't like smart answers, not in my office.

–I'm sorry about that, I just don't have any dumb answers, I said, and showed him my palms.

Dhanwan tapped his desk with his hands. He tapped quite hard.

–Do you want to explain what happened?

–Not really, I've had a long day and I'm suffering from trauma. Plus no one has had the good manners to offer me a drink yet.

–Does he ever give a straight answer? said Dhanwan, glancing at Gautam.

–Come on Chauhan, you can do better than that.

–If you're hiding information, said Dhanwan. –Then, I'm warning you, you won't like me when I find out.

–Who said I liked you now?

–Cut it out, said Gautam. –We're all on the same side here and we need to work together. This is going to look bad in tomorrow's papers.

–What were you doing at Khan's house? asked Dhanwan.

–I gave my full statement to your constable.

–I read it. You said a man called Manjit killed Khan in the confusion.

–Yes, I believe so.

–What about the woman?

–She gave me the slip.

Dhanwan shook his head and a smirk appeared on his mouth.

–Looks like you're easy to give the slip to, he said.

–It does seem that way, you can't win all the women, all of the time.

–You haven't answered my question.

I put my hands up in a mock gesture.

–Okay, okay you got me. I went around to meet Khan regarding Santana, they used to know one another.

–Part of the same blackmail gang?

–Yeah, but there's a new problem now. Someone called Kasim controls the gang. They're all scared of him, a nasty piece of work from what I've heard, and it's likely that Kasim and Manjit are your killers. You heard of them?

–Yes, I might have.

That meant he hadn't. He made me repeat my statement. He asked for a description of Ice Baby and Manjit and expressed disappointment that Manjit had killed Khan instead of me. It was all right, I told him many people lived with that disappointment.

I didn't tell him I had the photos; the constables had searched the house but found nothing. According to my little red book, there were over three hundred names, initials and codes. This meant the main files were with Kasim or hidden somewhere else. Kasim hadn't risked leaving them with the amateurs.

I had been close to finding out. If only the tear gas hadn't flown through the window. Manjit hadn't come alone to the house. Kasim was running the gang with an iron hand and on this occasion, it had saved Manjit. I didn't tell any of this to Dhanwan who looked unimpressed with my story. He shook his head and chewed his thumbnail, whilst Gautam nodded at intervals. I didn't give a damn if Dhanwan liked it or not, we were never going to be drinking buddies. You don't like some people and the feeling is mutual, that's just the way it is.

I was concerned about whether Kasim would try to kill Joseph Fernandez and me, if he wasn't paid. An unhinged psycho, who killed people for fun, would enjoy coming after me. Maybe he enjoyed killing more than being paid. There had to be a record on him, and I wondered if Dhanwan would share that information. It didn't seem likely.

–I think you're holding back on me, said Dhanwan at last.

–I'll find out. You're out of your league, Chauhan. You're getting people killed and proving to be a big interference. I don't like it.

–Please, be my guest. You can have the case, but whilst you're lecturing me, your killers are probably on a flight to Dubai.

–Is that right?

–Look, said Gautam. –We are all tired, it's late and we need to work together. Mumbai's a big place.

–Is that why you quit the force Chauhan, found the city too tough, too big?

I clenched my right fist.

–Yeah, that might be it, Dhanwan.

–It's Inspector Dhanwan.

He leaned back, tapped the baton on the table twice.

–You're mixed up with the wrong crowd, Chauhan and it's better if you come clean.

–I'm clean all right. Look, this is a blackmail racket and it has been causing silent misery to many people. You should be glad they're dropping dead.

–Okay, have it your way. Fernandez hired you to find the photos. Do you have them?

I paused a moment. Someone had been talking to Dhanwan. I glanced at Gautam, he had a guilty look and wouldn't meet my eyes.

–Not yet, I said.

–Sure about that? This is going to become a lot worse, Chauhan. It is now a police investigation. These murderers won't stop until they're paid. You know that don't you?

I remained silent.

–And one more thing, I wouldn't have let those people escape so easily, that's really unprofessional and sloppy work. I'll inform Fernandez about your lack of professionalism.

–Are we done? I've had a long day and you haven't even offered me a drink.

Something fired in Dhanwan and he gripped the baton.

–This isn't a bloody bar, you smart bastard, this is my office!

He slammed the baton on the table. The photo frame of his family fell sideways. Gautam jumped and edged back into his chair. I gritted my teeth. Dhanwan held the baton in mid-air, his body was tense.

–Okay, I get it, you're tight with drinks, I said, and stood.

They both followed. Anger darkened Dhanwan's face but right now, he had nothing to hold me with, if he had, I wasn't leaving this station for a few days.

–You're a bloody joke, Chauhan. You couldn't handle the heat as an inspector and you're not handling this either. I'm paying Fernandez a visit tomorrow and, trust me, you'll be off this case. How does that sound Mr Private Detective?

I raised my head and took a short breath.

–I'll believe it when I see it, and listen Dhanwan, everyone talks big standing behind a police desk.

He dropped the baton on the table.

–You just name the day and time.

–I will, I haven't beaten a donkey in a long time...

–Why you ...

–Hey, come on, said Gautam, –This is a police station. I'll report this behaviour to the higher authorities.

Dhanwan wasn't going to receive any help from me, and with his blunt manner, I doubt he'll get it from anyone else either.

–You're protecting Fernandez and his daughter but it's not going to work. I've made enquiries about that family, Chauhan. They are filthy rich and that Anita is sooner or later going to do something that money can't hush up. I'll tell you another thing, the old man believes his son-in-law, Prem Nath, is involved in this nasty business. He happened to disappear at the right time. I'll bet my last rupee that the bastard is mixed up in this. What do you think about that?

–Not bad, but you should stick to finding the killers. You have three dead men on your hands. You'll blow a fuse if you think too much. Prem Nath doesn't sound like a blackmailer to me. He cares for Anita and Fernandez.

Dhanwan clasped his hands together and sneered.

–You look surprised, Chauhan, you thought you could hide that information from me.

–If you have all the information, then you don't need me, Dhanwan. You'd be better off directing your anger at finding the killers.

–Watch your back, and oh, you had better find another job as well. Tomorrow, you'll be fired and that's a promise.

–I'm not going to lose sleep over that.

–Come on guys, said Gautam. –This isn't the way.

I turned and walked out of the office, leaving Gautam inside with a sour face. I knew he wanted me to cooperate with that donkey, but it's impossible. Dhanwan was working fast and could throw me off the case, if he managed to persuade Fernandez. He had a point to prove. True, I'd been surprised at the speed with which Dhanwan had found the information about Fernandez, and about the Prem Nath angle. I walked towards my car with new questions forming and none of them making me feel too great. Whilst they hadn't found his body, Prem Nath was still in the game.

15

IT HAD been a long day and I was beat. I reached home up in Boriwali at midnight and parked the car at the back of my apartment block. There was some traffic noise in the distance, but the car park was dead and most of the lights in the block were off. A cool breeze blew across as I stepped out of the car, and an empty can rolled nearby. I wanted to have a shower, fix myself a glass of Johnnie Walker and have a good night's sleep. Was that too much to ask for? Tomorrow I could check how things stood with the big chief Fernandez.

As I moved away from my car however, a shadow caught my eye, shifting from behind another vehicle. A man was pointing a gun at my stomach. It really had been a day full of guns.

–Remember me?

–What's happened to your face? You look like the elephant man, Manjit.

–Still have time for jokes eh? Well, laugh. A bastard like you should die laughing.

–Where's your side-kick? I said and turned around.

There wasn't a soul in sight, only long shadows adding to my sense of loneliness and unease.

–Don't worry about her. Back up and don't try to be clever.

I moved back slowly, keeping my eyes on his gun.

–That's it keep your hands in front of you where I can see them.

His eyes were filled with hate. He meant to kill me all right, if I made one wrong move I'd be a goner. I'd been in some tight situations before but this was right up there. He would kill me as soon as he had the photos. I hadn't expected him to find me here. He was smarter than I had given him credit for, or maybe Kasim had sent him.

–Where's your boss?

–Funny, he doesn't like you at all.

–We've never met.

–Yeah, but he knows you are a first class *bhenchod*. Now stop stalling, I want those photos.

Shadows spread behind him, a darkness that seemed to say my time was running out. No one came out from the back stairs and no late-night cars came into the car park. It was eerily quiet, I heard a dog bark but even that stray sound came from some distance.

–Do I walk free if I hand them over? I was only doing my job.

–Sure, you walk free. I promise.

He grinned when he said that, a half crazed demonic grin because his face had been altered by the beating Khan had given him.

–The envelope's back at the office in my safe. I went there first. I have a rule, never to take business home.

–Do I look stupid?

–Search me.

He took a step closer, his face was marked and looked pretty bad with swellings and cuts, Khan had given him a good beating.

–I bet Kasim wasn't happy with you?

His eyes widened and he shook a little.

–Shut up. Hand over the photos or you're dead. You have three seconds.

–Why did you kill Khan? There was no need.

–There was a need, but you wouldn't understand.

–Hold on Manjit, I told you they're back at the office. If you kill me and return without the photos, Kasim will beat you. You've already had one beating tonight.

He narrowed his eyes and strained to think about that, scratching his head with his free hand. He wasn't a thinking man. It looked as if it might give him trouble. I noticed an alley cat moving stealthily to my right, behind Manjit. It rushed at something and screeched as only cats can. It was a loud aggressive catcall. It had its victim. The sound forced Manjit to glance round. In that moment, I kicked the gun out of his hand.

It flew and crashed into the car bonnet. He punched me in the stomach, a hard punch that took my breath away. He tried to punch me in the face, but I swayed back, and he missed. I took him down with a left hook to the ribs, then I punched his face. Blood spat out of his mouth. He hurried to his feet and ran across the car park.

I ran after him, the night air cutting into my face. The smell of rotting vegetables hit me. For a squat man he ran powerfully, dodging in and out of cars parked in the car park. He was trying to reach the main road, and the cover of the late-night traffic. A couple hurried out of the way. He ran around two parked motorbikes, glanced back towards me. I caught up with him as he jerked left towards an alleyway. I caught his shoulder with my right hand and spun him around. He fell forward with a groan.

I pinned him to the ground. He struggled to escape. A few hard punches and the fight went out of him. I sat there holding him under my knees. He was breathing hard and looked like a man who knew he had a bad fate awaiting him. He wasn't wrong about that. I thought he'd prefer the police over going back to Kasim empty handed.

I lifted him up and pushed him against the wall. The stench of garbage surrounded us. He looked timid and took deep breaths with difficulty. He spat out some blood.

–It's just not your day is it?

He tried to spit at my face, I moved, and for that I gave him another punch in the ribs. He grimaced.

–Let's go, idiot. An inspector wants to talk to you.
–You're dead.
–You've said that before as well.

I grabbed him by the collar and pushed him forward.

–Now move, you're going on a long holiday, where they take special care of assholes like you.

16

I READ the Mumbai Daily over a late Friday morning breakfast. This year, 1995, was the year Bombay became Mumbai, and there was an article about people coming to terms with the famous city name change. Five more people had died on the railway tracks, trying to cross at places where it was strictly forbidden. There was an advert for a weight-loss pill that was working wonders for both men and women. I smiled, those charlatans were still making money from that angle, and would always continue to do so. Who wants to cut down on food and increase exercise?

I had coffee, toast, two boiled eggs and a glass of orange juice. I had showered, changed into a dark brown shirt, black jeans, and my short black leather jacket was hanging off the chair in my apartment, ready for when I left. I looked out of the window, below a family of three: husband and child in the middle and the wife at the back, riding out on a scooter. No one bothered with safety helmets. It was cool with a breeze picking up. I had a sudden liking for stray cats and decided to buy some special cat food for the one I had seen when I got the chance. That cat was just the kind of break I needed in that tight situation.

The paper had a flattering photo of Dhanwan on page four. The report of the blackmail gang and the way the tenacious Inspector cracked it, made for comic reading. The paper explained that the gang had preyed on vulnerable young women at parties and nightclubs. They took them home and plied them with drink and drugs before taking compromising photos. More women were expected to come forward after the arrests.

It said that an ex-officer - they had kindly left out my name thanks to Dhanwan - had made an accidental citizen's arrest of a man called Manjit. I didn't know how you made accidental arrests. Manjit was a prime suspect to the murders of Santana, Raja and Khan; a dangerous criminal who was going to spend a long time in jail. Manjit said he had been trying to take over the racket and would have succeeded if Inspector Dhanwan hadn't arrested him.

Dhanwan would have enjoyed beating that into Manjit. The report said police were looking for two more accomplices, a dangerous woman by the name of Shanti and a man whose name they had not released. The police advised the public to stay away from them at all costs, and to call if they saw them. Inspector Dhanwan had apparently solved the case whilst brushing his teeth and wiping his face with a nice towel.

I was glad they had left Fernandez, Anita, and me out of the headlines. I wondered what Kasim made of the write-up. Perhaps they hadn't managed to beat Kasim's whereabouts out of Manjit.

As I put the paper down, the phone rang. I thought it might be Gautam, trying to make amends for last night or to tell me that I was off the Fernandez case. It wasn't Gautam, and I was no longer smiling. Too many people were getting hold of my home number. Time for a change. Silence, then hissing sounds as if someone was sucking in the air. It sent a chill up my spine.

–Listen you pervert, I said, –you have the wrong guy. If I get hold of you, you'll wish you were dead.

Silence. Short breaths.

The phone felt cold in my hand. The hissing sound was still there, and I should have slammed the phone down, but I wanted to know who the clown was.

–Nice work, Chauhan.

It was cold, dead, the kind of voice a cobra might have, if

it could speak.

–And you are?

–You know who it is.

–Yes, a low-life killer called Kasim.

–That's right. Manjit said you had a cheap mouth on you. I'm going to enjoy killing you.

–Manjit said that too and look where he is.

–He was careless. Now detective, count the hours before I send you to Hell. And I don't make false promises.

I gripped the phone a little harder.

–It's better if you hand yourself in, before you meet a miserable death. And let me tell you clearly, a violent death is awaiting a scumbag like you.

He cleared his throat.

–I don't like to lose money. And we'll see who suffers a violent death.

–Hand yourself in, if you have any brains.

The phone line went dead. His voice had that cold quality of a killer. The police had their nice write up and photos in the papers, and I was the one being threatened. I stared at the coffee mug, then around the kitchen. It needed a clean. The cold voice still lingered in my mind. I didn't like the way I felt then, I was risking a lot for fifteen hundred rupees a day plus expenses. I took a long sip of orange juice and dialled a number.

–Good morning, this is the Fernandez residence, said a square voice. It was MD.

–Is Mr Fernandez in?

–Yes, who's calling?

–Forgotten me already, hey? It's your favourite detective.

He cleared his throat.

–You can pass me the message if you like, he said, but the tone changed.

–Nope, I'd like to speak directly with the boss, otherwise I'll have to come down in person. I find people confuse my messages.

Silence. I could see MD struggling with his reply and tensing his jawline.

–I will check if Sir is available.

I waited a few minutes.

–Yes, Joseph Fernandez here.

–Good morning, have you read the papers?

–Yes, but there is no mention of your name, Chauhan.

–It figures, I was the ex-officer who made the accidental arrest.

–Why didn't they give you credit?

I shook my head.

–It would be asking too much from Inspector Dhanwan. Anyway, I have the negatives and the photos.

There was a long pause on the line.

–Oh, but that's excellent news. I knew Detective Chauhan you wouldn't disappoint me, he said, and his voice had more cheer.

–I risked my neck for those snaps, for what it's worth.

–Yes, yes, I can imagine, and if you are worried about the payment, don't be. I will make it worth your while. How does three lakhs sound to you?

I tried my best not to sound too happy.

–It sounds about right for what I went through.

–Then you'll hand over the photos.

–It's better if I destroy them Mr Fernandez. They're not nice photos to look at.

Again, a long pause and silence.

–Yes, I can imagine but I need to see the proof, you understand.

–Of course, I said.

–Please meet me at eight tonight. We can have a drink and I can thank you in person for removing this extraordinary worry.

–I like that idea but...

He cut me short as if what I had done wasn't as important as his next question. There was more urgency in his voice.

–Did you find anything on Prem Nath by the way?

–No.

–Oh, no matter, that wasn't part of your job.

His voice sounded disappointed, and I felt his disappointment.

–The missing person's bureau should have some leads by now, I said.

–They have nothing, unfortunately. They think Prem committed suicide. Prem was ex-army, he was tough, he wouldn't commit suicide. Please come this evening, Detective, so that this bad business can be settled.

–Okay, I'll see you tonight.

I thought to mention Kasim. This was nowhere near settled but I held my tongue. He had enough to worry about and maybe I could explain it better in person. I put the phone down. Until I understood Prem Nath's disappearance, the whole case wouldn't satisfy me. How was Bakshi involved? Why had Maya Fernandez tried to buy me off? And what had really happened to Prem Nath anyway? The smart thing to do was to collect my cheque and go on a nice long holiday, put my feet up and drink a cold beer on a beautiful beach. Instead, I decided to check in on someone and try again. That's how smart I could be.

17

NEXT STOP, and against my better judgement, I called at Prem Nath's house. I double-checked my pistol and spare magazine. Then I left my apartment and glanced down the corridor. I had no wish to be shot by the psycho or one of his cronies. It took thirty minutes on this cloudy morning to find the good looking double storied house. There was a park opposite with Neem trees running along the long wooden fence. Children were playing cricket. I got out of my car, opened the small gate and pressed the bell.

The house was quiet, like after a funeral. I pressed the bell again and looked sideways, no cars or bikes on the drive. A top bedroom window curtain twitched, but I couldn't see who it was. I waited and tried not to look like a bailiff. The door opened at last and a woman in a green sari with a light floral design looked up. She was around fifty-six, medium height, with streaks of grey hair. She was a handsome woman with the kind of dignified misery that comes with loss. After all the clowns I had been running into lately, it was good to meet a dignified person. It restored my faith in the human race.

–Namaste, she said.

–Namaste, I've come to see Prem Nath.

I struggled to find words. She had that effect. I thought that if I ever found my mother, I'd be happy if she had half this woman's grace.

–Are you a friend of his? she said and held the seam of her sari.

I finally managed to get some words out.

–Not exactly. My name is Abhay Chauhan, I'm a private

detective. Is it possible to have a word?

I showed my license and hoped. The doorstep wasn't the place for a conversation like this.

–I know Prem has been missing for over five weeks now and you must be...

–Yes, I'm his mother, Mrs Nath. Please come inside.

I entered the house. A Lord Ganesh painting hung in the corridor and a jasmine incense stick was burning by its side. We turned into a lounge. A three-piece sofa suite was the highlight and a cabinet with photos of who I guessed to be Prem. This was the first time I'd seen him, tallish, clean-shaven and holding a tennis racket. I'd imagined him like Santana, as Anita liked that type. Maybe he was too clean-cut for someone like Anita. I scanned the other photos, not a single marriage photo and not one of Anita in the room.

We sat opposite one another across a glass table. She looked at me but her mind seemed preoccupied. I struggled to ask questions in her presence. Dignity combined with genuine sorrow stopped the toughest cops in their tracks. I had experienced that before.

–Mrs Nath, I want to help find your son.

–Why?

She looked at me with a hint of suspicion. I clasped my hands together, my elbows resting on my knees.

–Well, you see I'm on this case and I think, well what I mean is...

–I don't know where he is, it has been five long weeks and not a word. Do you know what that feels like? Do you have any idea what a mother suffers when she has an only child?

She pressed her hands together and sorrow entered her voice.

I looked down at the table.

–Every time I answer the door, I wonder if the police have come with the worst possible news.

I nodded and said, –I know this is a worrying time but I

want to help.

–How can you help? Every two days I visit the police station. They treat me like a nuisance, someone to be rid of as quickly as possible. He's my only son, not yet thirty, full of life, and he disappears from the face of the earth.

Tears formed and she wiped them gently with a pearl coloured handkerchief. She pressed her eyes several times, shook her head slightly. I waited for her to compose herself.

–I want to find him, I said, without thinking.

I was close to walking away from this sorry mess. Her dignity however put all the monetary calculations and concerns of my wellbeing out of the window. Isn't this why I had joined the police in the first place? To help the helpless? Some people have that effect. It wasn't the right way to run a detective agency but many calculations were flying out of my head in front of her.

–I'm sorry, I know it's not your fault and it's very kind of you Detective Chauhan to offer help. Nobody else seems to care, but I don't have anything extra right now to cover your expenses.

She looked down at her hands on her lap.

–I didn't ask for any fees. All I want is information and I'll do the rest.

–What case are you working on?

–I can't explain the details, you understand. Client confidentiality. But I'm working for Mr Fernandez. His daughter Anita is still married to your son.

She fidgeted with her hands, pressing her fingers together and tears sprang into her eyes.

–That wretched woman is behind all our troubles, and she isn't married to my son, she said, speaking suddenly in a torrent, –they were going to be divorced. My poor boy, oh how he suffered. She has no morals, every night out drinking, gambling, dancing, and carrying on with other men. I don't like to speak ill of others, it's not in my nature but that woman would test anyone's patience. I'll tell you honestly, every night shouting and screaming. My poor boy, he didn't deserve that.

–I see.

She shook her head and sighed.

–No, you don't see. Prem is strong but even he couldn't handle someone like her. I had told him not to marry her in the first place. I knew she was a loose woman the moment I saw her. Still, what can one do, young people don't listen to good advice anymore.

She wrung her hands, stood and walked to the cabinet. I rose too, as she pulled out a silver framed photo of Prem. She passed it to me. He didn't look like a sophisticated blackmailer, an idea that had been floating in my head for a while. Whether or not he had been trying to make money from Fernandez, after the quick and difficult divorce, was another matter. I passed the photo back. She stared at it for a long moment, touched his face through the glass frame, before placing it back in the cabinet with care.

–Mr Fernandez said they were not divorced, I said.

–It was in the process. He desperately wanted the marriage to work. He even gave Prem a twenty-five percent stake in that mansion on Malabar Hill, as a wedding gift. It's worth a fortune. He wanted Prem to stay with his wild daughter, but we're not interested in money, they can keep their millions. Prem, poor Prem, he was so in love with Anita, and before he could finalise matters, he just disappears. Oh God, every day I pray he hasn't done something foolish.

The twenty-five percent stake surprised me. New thoughts ran through my mind, and none of them looked good for Prem's health. I even wondered about the honesty of Fernandez himself. Maybe he had regrets about handing over so much money, so quickly. Perhaps Prem had refused to return the stake. I wouldn't blame him about that, twenty-five percent was a fortune. I watched Mrs Nath stifle sobs with her hand and then smooth her greying hair.

–If you don't mind, was there a divorce settlement? I asked.
–No, not that I am aware of, we wanted a clean break.
–What about the share in the mansion?

She could see what I implied, and she narrowed her eyes in slight irritation.

–Prem was willing to sign it back to Fernandez saab, only he wouldn't agree. Fernandez saab wanted him to try to make the marriage work.

–And around this time, Prem disappears?

–From the face of the earth, it's not like Prem. He always told me where he was. I've been to all his friends' houses, but no one knows. I even had to suffer the humiliation of seeing Anita. She laughed and complained that he had run away with her money and she was glad. She never cared about him, all these rich spoilt women are the same. A little difficulty and they run away from the problem. My poor boy, he didn't deserve this.

She lowered her eyes, took a deep breath and seemed to struggle with what she was about to say.

–Do you think, that you can help find him Detective Chauhan? I would be obliged to you for the rest of my life.

She didn't meet my eyes but her simple plea moved me.

–I'll try my best, I said, and gave her my card, –if you hear or remember anything about Prem then please phone me. Did Prem ever say that he was going to run away?

–Never. He would never leave me all alone in the world. And thank you, you have given me some hope.

–Thousands go missing in Mumbai, Mrs Nath, but people are found as well. It's possible Prem wanted time to himself and is staying alone somewhere. I believe he did that once and disappeared for a few weeks, before returning.

–Yes, yes, but Prem told me where he was the whole time. He needed a break from his unhappy marriage. I hope what you say is true.

–Do you know where he stayed the last time?

–He rented a cottage in the hills. I checked there already, he isn't there.

–Let's hope we can find him then.

–I pray you have success Detective Chauhan. This waiting is killing me.

I said goodbye and left the house with my ideas completely changed about the case. People were made to disappear for a few lakhs, this was in crores. From the look of his mother and his photo however, it didn't point in that direction. They didn't seem that kind of money grabbing people. It looked darker and sinister. I wanted to believe Prem was alive, but it seemed unlikely. The divorce was about to go through, and Prem disappears. Whom would that benefit the most, Mr. Fernandez?

There were several other candidates. Anita wouldn't have to pay anything in a settlement. How did Maya Fernandez feel about the share? Then there was Dinesh Bakshi, but he seemed to be keeping his hands clean. It would be difficult to place anything on him.

If I could find Prem Nath, then everything might make more sense. I still had the little red book and if Manjit had told about that, then Dhanwan would haul me to the station before I could blink. Maybe I should hand it over to him now, it wasn't doing me any good. I still couldn't make sense of the codes. The photos were burning a hole in my pocket as well, and I needed to hand them over to Fernandez. He wouldn't be happy to see his naked, high on drugs, daughter. More questions were forming, and the answers seemed to run further away.

I drove out of the quiet road and saw a black Fiat with tinted windows following four cars behind. I turned left and gave the person time to catch up. I felt for my pistol in my jacket, pulled it out, and kept it below the window. The car didn't follow after the second set of lights. I felt better and pointed my car towards the office. To check if I had new clients or messages on the phone. I didn't hold out too much hope on that count either.

18

I ARRIVED at my office in Rising Towers, parked and took the lift up to my business premises. No clients waited in the reception, only a pile of unwanted bills, reminders for rent and taxes. I picked them up, opened the door and placed them on a separate pile in the corner, on top of other reminders and bills. A walking, talking, secretary would have been great; she could deal with those miserable letters, greet me with a smile, and ask how my day was going. I could ask her if everything was fine at her house, boyfriend, or whatever. We could have a conversation. Instead, I opened the window to let a cool breeze into the room.

I sat on the swivel chair, picked up the phone and listened to my secretary. There were several messages, mostly from Gautam. He didn't sound happy and said I had played the wrong hand with Dhanwan. The Inspector was a donkey, so that didn't worry me. He also wanted me to return the phone call immediately. After the excitement of the last few days, he could wait. As I tapped the table, the phone rang and I thought it might be him, so I answered reluctantly.

–Hello, is that Detective Chauhan?

–In person.

–Ah, I spoke to you recently, you might remember, Mrs Chatterjee.

–How could I forget?

Her voice sounded reasonable this time, the high commanding tone gone.

–I want to discuss my delicate problem.

–I thought I had made myself clear.

–Yes, yes, I know, but I'm not having any luck whatsoever, I have fired two very incompetent detectives. They said they could find nothing.

–This might surprise you, Mrs Chatterjee, but your husband might be straight. No skeletons in the cupboard.

–Nonsense, if I can open the right doors, all his horrible mistresses will come tumbling out.

–You suspect that many? What will you do if you discover he has a girlfriend?

–Why, I will divorce him. And he will pay heavily I can tell you. I will take him to the cleaners.

–You wouldn't forgive him?

–Never, no one cheats on me.

I raised my eyebrows.

–What do you want me to do? I mean, I doubt I want to put your husband through all that.

–Find out of course, I will pay generously, you can earn one lakh rupees for a few days work, just imagine.

I tapped the desk. I should consider this line of work. Then I imagined the poor man's face when I caught him red handed, and that sorry taste came back into my mouth.

–I'm sorry Mrs Chatterjee, I'm busy with a murder case right now.

–Murder!

–Yes, they happen in Mumbai.

–I can increase my offer, I need peace of mind. This is killing me.

I leaned back in my chair with a slight smile.

–It'll be cheaper for you to drink a bottle of whisky.

–*Oh really*, I don't know why I phoned you. My friend said you would be useless. Oh well, you just missed out on a lot of money, your bad luck.

–It certainly is.

She put the phone down without saying goodbye.

I hoped her husband wasn't caught with his pants down,

because she would send him straight to hell, no doubt.

I went to the cabinet, poured myself a neat whisky and drank it slowly. Outside, the beautiful billboard of Rekha and her lovely pink lips remained. I hoped they didn't change her any time soon. The whisky washed out the bitter taste after talking to Mrs Chatterjee. I took another sip, the flame burned down my throat and closed around my mouth. I stared at the road below, a man in green kurta pyjamas and a woman in a black hijab, were shouting at one another and pointing fingers.

The man was getting the worst of it, and he bent his head as they walked past a couple of stray dogs. Even the dogs watched them with curiosity. Then a familiar white jeep turned into the car park, and I thought, here comes trouble. I sat back and gave her a few minutes. Sure enough, she came bouncing into my office.

Anita Fernandez wore a bright red blouse, white slacks and a small red coat. She carried a black purse. I rose to meet her.

–You're full of surprises, I said.

She kissed me on the cheek and gave me a nice hug. I smiled and wiped the lipstick off my cheek.

–You're my hero!

I raised my eyebrows and smiled.

–Just doing my job, how did you find me?

–You're difficult to find, I'll say that cutie. Oh God, is this your office?

–It is.

I waved a hand expansively at the pile of junk called my furniture.

–I'll tell Papa to add another few lakhs, you could do with some improvements.

–That's kind of you.

She came around and sat on my side of the desk. Her pleasant perfume was strong with the scent of red roses. I sat in my swivel chair. She had made an effort to smarten up today, with a layer of foundation and pink lipstick. She wore diamond-stud earrings that gleamed in the light every time she turned her head slightly. Her hair was soft and shiny and bounced round her shoulders. I wondered what she wanted.

–I'm sorry. I've not treated you right at all. In fact, I've been mean to you and Anita Fernandez wants to say sorry.

–Apology accepted.

She stroked my arm as if I were a pet.

–No, I mean it cutie, I've been so worried about everything, with this stupid blackmail racket, and so I have decided to go clean. Smell...

She leaned close to my face and breathed out. Her mouth smelled of mint chewing gum.

–No drinks or drugs. I've said sorry to Papa and I've decided to change. He was so sweet about it and had tears in his eyes when he embraced me.

–Yeah, that sounds nice. What brought this sudden and welcome change?

She giggled and I didn't like it, because it was insincere.

–Why silly, you found the photos and Papa said you were going to hand them over tonight, and well, I thought I would save you the trouble. You see cutie, I don't want him to see me like that. I mean it wouldn't be right and it would hurt him a lot.

–I can understand that sentiment.

She smiled brightly.

–Do you have them with you? she said and stroked my arm again. Her eyes were intent upon my face.

–I do and they took a hell of an effort to find.

–Then be a lovely dear and hand them over. I hope never to do such things again. I even promised Papa.

I leaned back in my chair.

–Not so fast, sweetie.

She stopped stroking my arm and a flash of irritation came into her eyes. I moved towards the window, lit a cigarette, blew the smoke out of the window.

–I'd like to know a few things about Prem first.

–What about Prem?

She picked up a pen from the desk and held it tight in her hands.

–Where is he?

–How should I know?

–You don't care that your husband has been missing for over five weeks?

–Oh God, it was a big mistake cutie and we were getting a divorce. This is so tiresome. Why do we have to talk about that loser?

She looked down, scribbled small circles with the pen on the paper, and crossed them out

–I heard he's a good man, I said.

–Good and *sooo* boring! He only married me for the money you know, I realised that too late. He was always asking Papa and me for money. You should marry people from the same class. Prem had never seen so much money, and he tried to take advantage.

I shook my head, tapped the cigarette over the dustbin.

–Good people don't seem to be appreciated these days, I added.

–I need a man to excite me, thrill me, he just spent his spare time talking to Papa or complaining to his mother. God, he was one of those young men who are old before their time. I don't wish to talk about him. I want the photos. Please hand them over, so this horrible business can be finished.

She tried to smile, but the smile was struggling to reach her mouth.

–He cared about you though, I said.

–Yes. He was in love with me, but that shouldn't surprise you. Everyone loves me.

–I wouldn't go that far.

She narrowed her eyes, she was trying hard to keep a lid on that famous little temper. She put the pen down, took out a cigarette and lit it with a silver lighter. It helped her keep the lid on.

–I don't see how this has anything to do with you?

–I'm just a curious kind of guy.

She blew out the smoke.

–Curiosity killed the cat. Give me the photos and you can collect the money from Papa tonight. I'll tell him to give you four lakhs instead of three. God, you could do with it, she said, and pointed her cigarette at the cabinets and the furniture.

–I can always do with the money, I said, and leaned back against the windowsill. –Tell me, why did you marry Prem, if you didn't love him?

She showed her sharp teeth. They would have been neat and as shiny as the billboard woman's if she hadn't been a smoker.

–Papa said he was the first proper young man I'd brought home, satisfied?

–Not so fast.

–Oh, why do you have to upset me cutie? Do you know, Papa likes you too? If we married we could really hit it off.

I smiled.

–I had always imagined a more romantic setting for a marriage proposal.

She tried to smile and looked into my eyes, holding eye contact.

–I doubt you've had any proposals, and certainly not from someone like me.

Her voice had a nice seductive tone.

-You can say that again, but if it's okay, I think we're going too fast.

She tilted her head and looked at me. –Enough fun and games, how about the photos and the negatives?

–Who asked you to come here?

She straightened again, and the playfulness disappeared from her eyes.

–Why, no one!

–You sure?

–I'm sure, I don't know what you're being so difficult about.

She shook her head and tapped the cigarette into the ashtray on my desk.

–Nothing seems right about this sorry mess, I said.

She stood, leaving her cigarette in the ashtray. She took a step forward, her bold eyes intent on my face and held the back of my neck with her cool fingers. She kissed me on the mouth, hard. I tried to pull away, but she held on, and kissed me again, longer this time.

–You don't give up easily, I said, when I caught my breath.

–You're my hero Abhay Chauhan. You found those horrible photos. I like the way you look at me. And I like the way you kiss. If only you stopped asking so many questions.

–I could get used to this flattery.

–I mean it, she said.

–I half believe you.

–Let's go back to my place. I'll thank you in such a way you'll never forget.

–Why didn't I think of that?

She smiled and caressed my arm gently.

–Okay, now can I have the photos? she asked.

I smiled and wiped my mouth with a handkerchief.

–I'll bring them over tonight to your father. I like to do things in person.

–That's not funny. Please give me the photos. You don't want Papa to see me like that do you?

–No, but I can't just hand them over like a box of chocolates. I've had to put my life on the line for your precious photos.

She picked up her cigarette and crushed it in the ashtray. Her eyes widened and she pursed her lips. Her patience had come to an end.

–I hate you! she erupted suddenly. –I absolutely hate you! I knew you wouldn't give them to me. I had you right the first time. You think too much of yourself Chauhan. Marry you, huh! You're not fit to clean my boots. Give me those stupid photos!

I stayed still and looked her straight in the eye.

–You'll have to ask nicer than that.

–Go to hell! You'll be sorry for this, I promise.

She picked up the glass ashtray and threw it across the room. It smashed against the wall and the ash spread over the pile of bills in the corner. I didn't even have a spare one. She rushed out of the office without a backward glance.

I smiled, waited a few moments and looked out of the window. She ran to her jeep. The tyres skidded on the tarmac as the jeep beeped loudly, with people jumping out of the way. She was a mixture of anger, intelligence and recklessness. I thought about her kiss. She was one hell of a kisser. Then, I turned my thoughts to Dinesh Bakshi.

Call it the detective's instinct, but so far, his hands were too clean. People died around him, illegal practices took place at his clubs, yet nothing stuck to him. No doubt he had protection in high places. Before I met him again, I wanted to see someone who might be able to help with Prem Nath. I closed the office door and headed out. I walked towards the car as the grey afternoon light brightened. The clever thing to do was to leave this sorry case behind, collect my nice cheque from Fernandez and kiss it all goodbye. That was the clever thing to do, to stay alive and healthy. I decided instead to poke the iron rod into the fire again. That's how clever I could be.

19

AFTER A long drive through the afternoon traffic, I turned left at a corner. A Parsi Fire Temple came up, a large double storied building with circular pillars running along the front. I had once chased a drug trafficker here in my police days. The thug had ran up the steps before tripping near the two large horse statues that stood to either side of the main door. The horses had upturned wings with the large heads of men with priest like beards. The Parsi's followed Zoroaster, an Iranian speaking prophet from a couple of thousand years ago. The community however had declined, as their birth rate had dropped rapidly. I forgot about their birth rate problems, as I approached the old police station, behind the tax office.

I squeezed my car into a narrow patch of green to one side. Prem's mother came here every other day and I had seen this kind of persistence when I had been an inspector. It was never good for police morale, even though you wanted to be polite, you couldn't help but become irritated.

I went up to the counter and asked for PSI Thankey. He had worked under me on a drugs case some years ago before I'd quit and had since been promoted to this new post that included finding missing persons. The constable nodded, led me past a queue of people holding files and photographs. Everyone looked with an expression that said, it's always who you know in Mumbai that counts. I felt sorry for them, but time was running short.

PSI Thankey sat behind his desk poring over files, behind him, one wall had mug shots of men, women, boys and girls, with names and code references underneath. News clippings were on a separate board. Some photos had big red crosses upon them. To Thankey's left, a constable typed on an electric typewriter with a pile of papers on his desk. There were photos of Nehru and Gandhi on the wall behind the constable, and the ceiling fan was on medium speed. It was entirely ineffective. I didn't miss the police station atmosphere.

Thankey stood and leaned over his desk to shake my hand. He had a large beer belly hanging over his wide leather belt. It hadn't been there before, and it amused me to see it. He'd been a trim officer, six years back. He wore black framed glasses, a slight smile, and waved a hand at a chair. I sat down opposite him.

–This is a surprise, Inspector Chauhan.

–You can drop that, Thankey. I'm a private detective now.

–You will always be our inspector. An honest inspector, if I may say so.

–We all make mistakes.

He smiled, –I mean it Abhay. Why don't you come back? We could do with you here.

–That bad, hey?

–And getting worse, he said, and shook his head slightly with some resignation.

–I won't keep you more than five minutes, thanks for seeing me so quickly.

–Don't embarrass me. How can I help?

–I need information on Prem Nath.

He leaned back in his chair, it creaked as he blew out his cheeks. I looked at the typewriter tapping away to my right. Thankey sighed.

–I live in fear of his mother. She's here without fail every two days. She's such a dignified woman that you can't even get angry. I wish she would leave us alone and let us work on the case. *Arre*, are you working for her? Please take the case off my hands.

I smiled.

–No, I'm working on something else. Erm, can I speak to you in private?

He nodded and turned to look at the constable to his left.

–Patil, take five minutes.

–Yes, Saab.

The man stopped typing with a final flourish of the typewriter keys hitting the paper, and walked out of the room.

–What's the big secret? asked Thankey, with a lowered voice.

–I don't know yet, but people are being killed.

–I heard about it. Inspector Dhanwan came around. He's not easy to get along with. Very strict. Three dead so far. You always had the ability to make sparks fly.

I smiled with my eyes and brought my hands together.

–I don't know if that's a good thing. Any information on Prem Nath?

He sucked air through his closed teeth.

–You think he might be mixed up, in all of this?

–I don't know yet.

He pulled out a file from his drawer. A large dark brown envelope that he placed on the desk.

–I keep this handy in case Mrs Nath breaks down the door.

He thumbed through it, picked out Prem's photo, then held it in his hand.

–Here, take a look.

As I looked, Thankey spoke on.

–He's thirty years old, no criminal record. About six months ago, he married Anita Fernandez. You could say he hit the lottery, but things turned sour. His mother said they were about to become divorced, and she's said that enough times. About five weeks back, he disappears without a trace. No news since.

–Where was he last seen?

–He left Miss Fernandez's apartment in the evening around eight after having a big argument. He drove towards Santa

Cruz and parked his car outside a bar. He had a few drinks on his own and looked miserable according to the bartender. Then he drove out to the beach and drank from beer bottles looking out at the sea. He sat there for a long time on his own. That was the last anyone saw of him. We found the car on the beach. There were no other fingerprints and no other sightings of him after one a.m.

–You think...

–I'm keeping my mind open. We searched the coast in the morning when his mother reported him missing. We found plastic bags and old shoes, but no body.

I bit my lower lip and rubbed my forehead slightly.

–What do you think?

–If you want my honest opinion, Abhay, he walked into the sea, I'm afraid. Everything points that way. He was depressed and young people kill themselves over trifles these days. Even for failing an exam, they hang themselves. But I'm not ruling anything out. The problem is we haven't found the body. Until then the case remains open.

–Do you think he might have run away from it all to find peace?

–The car was still there and there's been no activity in his bank account, no sightings or phone calls. What's he living on? Fresh air. It doesn't look good. His father-in-law is worried. Has he hired you to find him?

–Not quite, but I don't think he'd mind if I did.

–*Arre*, please take the case of my hands, he said, and raised a finger in the vague direction of the backboard. –That board is full of hundreds of people missing every hour and we're understaffed. Many of those cases have better leads, and as you know we have to follow the hot leads first.

I tapped the desk in front of me with my right hand.

–Do you suspect foul play?

Thankey looked up at the ceiling and stared for a few moments.

–I've not ruled it out, he said, –but Prem Nath had no enemies and he hadn't received any threats. We checked. Everyone had a good word for Prem, only his wife had bad words for him, called him too nice, boring and said he was only after her money. She's something isn't she?

Thankey raised his eyebrows.

–She certainly is, I said.

–I mean she didn't care a bloody bean about him. I know plenty of women who'd be happy if their husbands disappeared, he said, with a grin, –she repeated that Prem was after her money and nothing else.

–He doesn't seem to come across as that kind, Thankey.

–Yes, but money turns people's heads, you see it all the time.

I leaned back in the chair and pressed down on the desk with my fingers.

–The money angle doesn't add up. He didn't need to disappear for that, he would have been rich after the divorce settlement, I added.

–Yes, we could retire on a fraction of what Prem would have received. But I'm not ruling out the money angle Abhay. Greed is a deadly thing, I've seen it first-hand. My head says money is behind this, but we have to wait and so far, I've had no luck with this case. And now Dhanwan's on my back along with Prem's mother.

–Who would gain from his disappearance apart from his wife? I asked.

–Motive? It's been troubling me too. If he had enemies, what would be their motive? It all comes back to his wife.

–His wife isn't all bad. She's a spoilt young woman but I'm not giving up on her too quickly.

–It could be that Prem might have received a cash payment from Fernandez and disappeared with that, said Thankey. –But money runs out. And if he's alive, he'll return.

–You asked Fernandez about that?

Thankey nodded, –He said he couldn't remember giving him a large advance. *Arre* he was very careful with his words when it came to his son-in-law. I don't understand that either. Too many dead ends. I've been through the CCTV camera footage. He leaves the bar, then nothing. People saw him on the beach but that's it.

There was a knock on the door, and two constables entered carrying files. They hesitated when they saw me but placed the files on the edge of the desk. The smell of body odour drifted towards me.

–Sorry to disturb you saab, said the taller of the two. –We have a new lead on the two missing girls.

–Okay, I'll speak to you in a few minutes, replied Thankey.

The men hurried out of the office. My time was up. I stood and passed him my card.

–Thanks for seeing me Thankey. Anything turns up, you give me a call.

–Of course.

We stood and shook hands. The ceiling fan was still ineffective. I glanced at the backboard with the missing faces, there were too many to remember. Although Thankey didn't say it, he was waiting for Prem's body to wash up along the coastline. Everything pointed that way. If Prem wasn't Fernandez's son-in-law, this case would have been forgotten a long time ago.

I drove out into the traffic of horns, diesel fumes and impatient drivers. At the large roundabout with the central statue of Shivaji Maharaj on his horse and sword pointing north, I had an idea. I parked in front of a phone booth and dialled the Fernandez's place.

–Hello, the Fernandez residence, said MD, in his bored drawl.

–Put me through to your boss.

The voice livened. –Detective Chauhan?

–You have a good memory.

–Can I take a message?

–Is there no talking to the master without going through you?

–He's busy. He will be free in one hour.

I didn't buy that.

–Okay, tell him I won't be able to see him tonight, I said.

There was a pause on the line. The phone booth had numbers of call girls pinned to the side with a message written in bold red letters, *call me tonight for happiness.*

–You have the photos and negatives, Detective Chauhan? Sir was hoping to settle this unfortunate business and he won't be happy about another delay.

–Don't worry your head about it MD, it might get overheated.

–I don't know why Sir employed you, he said, with growing irritation in his voice, –you have the rudest manners I've ever come across.

–That's all right. I'll get over my manners but what are you going to do about your happy personality?

MD cleared his throat.

–You talk tough hiding behind a telephone line.

–Don't let the phone stop you, MD. Anyway, pass on my message to your boss. I'll see him tomorrow morning. It's always great talking to you, it makes my day so much brighter.

The line went dead. I looked at the receiver in my hand with the dead tone, and he complained I had bad manners. You just can't find the staff these days.

I drove out again around the roundabout and went down Laxmi Avenue with trees to either side. People were strolling along the pavements carrying plastic shopping bags. The road had many women's clothes merchants with displays of bright saris and shalwar kameez in the shop windows. At the next set of lights, I saw the black Fiat following four cars behind. I gripped the steering wheel. Either this was an amateur or it was someone who wanted me to know that they were following.

I couldn't do a u-turn in the heavy traffic, so I turned at the next lights and took a left at the rickshaw stand. The Fiat followed. I slowed down hoping to catch the person as they drove past. No luck, the car slowed too. I wondered if it was the maniac Kasim.

But he wouldn't take chances in broad daylight. As I moved forward, a police jeep pulled up to my side. The black Fiat took a sharp right and disappeared. The police always turn up when you don't want them. I'd been too busy looking at the Fiat to notice the jeep. Dhanwan signalled me to pull over. His face was grim, impatience written all over it. I pulled over and took a deep breath as the jeep parked behind. Dhanwan and a constable stepped out. I met Dhanwan at the side of my Contessa.

–You're not so sharp eh, Chauhan? I've been signalling you to stop for five minutes.

–I can't seem to see police jeeps, not in this traffic. How can I help? Want me to catch some murderers for you?

–You think you're smart, Chauhan, but Manjit's been singing like a canary. You're involved in this more than you said.

–I thought that case was over. I read it in the paper. You solved the blackmail racket whilst brushing your teeth. And some ex-officer made an accidental arrest of the murderer. I don't know how you make accidental arrests. Do you?

Dhanwan grinned, then glared at three men in identical black trousers and grey shirts. They had slowed down to listen to our conversation on the sidewalk next to the chai stall. They hurried away without glancing back.

–No Chauhan, you forgot about the little red book. That's a vital piece of evidence. If it's in your possession, I'm going to haul your sorry behind to the station.

–What red book? I said, trying to look as innocent as I could.

–Don't be too smart. Manjit told me all about it. I'm also looking for Kasim. It's in your interest to help find him. He sounds like a crazy bastard and he won't blink at killing you. Do I have your attention?

I looked him in the eye.

–You certainly do.

Dhanwan nodded, glanced at the constable who was standing to attention near the jeep.

–You handed Manjit to me, so I'm not going to haul you to the station right now. I want that red book by tomorrow evening latest, or I'll forget who you are. You understand?

–I'm getting the picture.

–Try not to get killed, I'd hate to have Kasim knock you off, he said with a grin.

He climbed into his jeep, sitting back as onlookers stared and wondered if I had committed a traffic offence or was a wanted criminal. I let them have their fun. Anything to break the drudgery of daily life. I even smiled at one or two. I waited for the jeep to pull out before I sat back in my car and drove away. So Manjit was singing. If this information reached Kasim, then I didn't want to be in his shoes. I had a bad feeling this could be one of those days again.

The photos and the red book were already placed inside a bank deposit box, and so unless Dhanwan or Kasim had some bank connections, things were safe. I was sure that if I didn't hand over the book by tomorrow, Dhanwan would turn over my offices and apartment with great pleasure. I thought to return to my apartment, wear a nice suit, head for Rubies and find Bakshi. See which way the cards fell. I stopped at a shop and bought a bundle of red firecrackers. I couldn't accept that Bakshi didn't know Khan and Santana ran a blackmail racket out of Rubies. This didn't sit well with me. I could be wrong, but I needed to get tough with that sonofabitch.

I guess I just liked trouble.

20

RUBIES SIGNBOARD was lit-up in red neon lights, as I reached the club just after nine p.m. Lights also shone from the surrounding tower blocks, and from the headlamps of the beeping traffic. Mumbai never seemed to sleep. I parked the car in-between an Ambassador and a blue coloured Jeep. I was in luck, there was barely a free parking space. Maybe I was about to gate-crash a wedding reception or a birthday party. I pulled out the red bundle and stepped out of the car. The bouncers in tight black suits stood at the entrance, checking the club goers, who were dressed in smart suits and shiny saris.

I walked around the vehicles to the far-left side of the car park near a line of bushes and undergrowth. I lit the crackers and threw them behind the bushes. They went off with the loud sound of rapid gun fire. I sauntered back towards the entrance, as the nervous looking bouncers rushed to the sound. Smoke spread through the bushes. People laughed. I moved past the long queue and entered the lobby, adjusting my dark blue tie. Bakshi's security wasn't up to scratch.

The music was in full swing behind some double doors. I pushed them open. It was a 1960s gala evening and an upbeat Dev Anand song played. I tapped my foot to the beat. All the men wore suits, black and white dinner jackets, bowties, and the women wore smart colourful saris with done up hair. Some had long evening dresses that hugged their figures. A seven-piece band played classical music as couples danced. I smiled, I should go out more often.

I looked for Bakshi under the glittering crystal chandeliers, across to the bar to my right and beyond the round tables in-between. No sign. Couples sat around tables, laughing and drinking. Smoke mingled with drink and perfume in the air. A man could forget his purpose on a night like this. It would have been good to dance with Ice Baby, for all her cold stares, it would have been fun. While I imagined holding her, a man came up to my side. A tall well-built man with stubble, in a grey shiny suit.

–Bakshi saab wants a word, he said in a deep voice.

–Now?

–Yes, now.

He didn't smile. I doubted whether he knew how to. I followed him through the smoke, smiling faces, and a couple of women threw me sideways glances. Maybe my black suit looked better than I thought. We walked into a quiet empty corridor. Halfway down, the man knocked and opened a door into an office. It was a square room with several TV monitors to my upper right. Bakshi was there, standing near a drinks cabinet with a fine array of Johnnie Walker whisky and Indian Old Monk rum bottles, with shiny crystal glasses just below. He was in a white dinner jacket, black trousers and a black bowtie. Bakshi signalled the muscle to leave. The man left staring at my face, still no smiles. The office was smaller than the one I had visited earlier, when Khan had been alive. Bakshi lit a cigar and offered me one.

I declined with a slight shake of the head.

–Cigars are too rich for me, I said, and lit a cigarette instead.

–It won't be the nicotine that kills you, Chauhan. How did you get inside? I told the guards ten times to keep you out.

I smiled and blew out the smoke, –They went to play with some firecrackers.

He grinned but it was forced, –It figures. I'm going to change those idiots. What do you want?

–I came to pay my condolences for your manager, Afzal Khan.

Bakshi tapped his cigar into a glass ashtray, the grin was gone.

–Oh really? It was a bad business, unfortunate, and maybe you were right. The police said he was involved in a blackmail racket. I didn't think Khan had it in him.

–You don't seem upset about losing your manager?

He moved around the desk and stood behind it with his cigar. On the wall behind him there was a silver framed picture of him shaking hands with the Police Commissioner.

–Whether I'm upset or not, doesn't concern you. Two hundred people work for me. If I have emotional breakdowns each time one dies, I couldn't run this business.

–You're all heart.

He turned and picked out a Johnnie Walker bottle and poured himself a drink, neat with ice. He swirled the ice around in the glass, then took a sip.

–I'll have the same, thanks, I said.

He grinned but didn't move. I dragged on the cigarette. On the monitors, couples in colour danced in the hall. Slow ballroom dancing, holding one another close. I thought about holding Ice Baby.

Bakshi took another sip, –You haven't said why you came around uninvited, Chauhan?

–A man shouldn't work all the time. All work and no play makes Abhay a dull boy.

–Really? He put the glass down on the table and blew out the strong smell of cigar smoke. –Anyway, thank you for not dragging my name into this sorry business. Inspector Dhanwan visited earlier. He doesn't like you very much. Called you a lying sonofabitch. Do you have that effect on everyone?

I tapped my cigarette over a dustbin to my side and shook my head.

–No, just on miserable people like Dhanwan.

–What's troubling you now, Detective? You solved your case. The so-called blackmailers are dead or in jail.

–Not quite, I found a little red book that belonged to Santana. It had some interesting numbers that are close to you.

I watched him for his reaction. He tried to grin but didn't manage it and took a stiff drink instead. I lied but maybe the numbers were connected to this slippery snake. He watched me with dead eyes, finally he sighed and said.

–You're not still crying about that silly red book, are you? I don't know why you think I'm involved in this cheap blackmail racket. Look around. Do you think I am poor? Do I need money from worried little women?

–It wasn't cheap after Kasim became involved. It was making serious money.

Bakshi tightened his grip around the glass, his eyes narrowed for a fraction of a second. I couldn't be sure however, that he'd heard the name before.

–Kasim who? he said.

–I thought you might have heard of him.

–No, sorry. You're a funny man, Chauhan. I might call Dhanwan here and tell him a useless detective is harassing me. I think he'd like to get hold of you.

–Call him. I'm not scared of a little jail time.

I tapped the cigarette, and my patience with this smooth lying bastard had run out. I didn't like the way he smirked or looked at me either.

–Bakshi, I think you're involved in this blackmail racket. And when I figure it all out, you'll wish you hadn't met me.

He placed a hand on the back of his leather chair.

–Any more jokes, Chauhan?

–Here's another, when I arrested Manjit, he said that you were the boss.

His grin left him and his left eye twitched.

–This is too much, I think you are drunk Chauhan, or you've been taking too many drugs.

–Let me continue, Santana and Khan didn't have the brains

or the balls to ask Joseph Fernandez for twenty-five lakhs. They weren't that smart. But you, the shoe fits. When I find Kasim, you'd better pray that he doesn't spill your name.

He put the glass down on the table, unfinished. The grin returned to his face along with his confidence.

–I can see how twenty-five lakhs would seem a fortune to you. But I deal in crores. You've been running around like a crazy fool, and that's all you can come up with? Sure, I know who Anita Fernandez is. She's a regular here and so is her mother. Nice people, though the daughter's a little wild for my tastes. I had no idea they were being blackmailed, he said, gritting his teeth.

He stared at me a long moment.

–Don't make too many stupid assumptions about me, it won't be good for your health.

Nothing was shaking this bastard. On the camera monitor, couples danced away. Bakshi was getting merrier by the moment. His grin grew wider.

–Since you're here, Chauhan, enjoy the evening on the house, he said, and threw in magnanimity, –no hard feelings. You make me laugh and that doesn't happen often. This meeting is over.

–This isn't over by a long shot, I said.

–Keep up your harassment and you'll be talking to Dhanwan. He told me that he wants to protect good citizens from cheap detectives like you. You shouldn't even be involved because this is police business. Take my advice. This is too big for you, Chauhan. Go quietly before you meet with an accident, you know, like a truck ramming into your car.

I crushed my cigarette into the wall behind me and let it fall to the floor.

–We'll be in touch, I said, –And I don't care about Dhanwan.

The muscle was right outside as I left the office. He glared again. I ignored him and returned to the ballroom music, fine perfume and smoke. I moved around the tables to the bar on the far side and ordered a whisky and soda with ice. A camera would be on me the whole evening. The whisky tasted smooth and I felt good. A lot happens sometimes when you sit still and don't chase every moving shadow. I took another sip, rolled it around in my mouth and turned to watch the dancers.

21

TEN P.M. The women in saris and evening gowns looked lovely. The band took a break and the drummer drank from a water bottle. The guitarist and singers chatted. Waiters drifted between the tables, pouring drinks. I wondered whether Ice Baby was in town or had run off with Kasim. Bakshi entered then and people stood to shake his greasy hand and fawn over him. And why not? He represented power and success. In Mumbai, that counted for more than anything else. He ignored me by staying away from the bar.

The long ballroom was bright with chandeliers and side lamps. Rubies was making good money, and no one cared that the hotel's manager, Khan, had died. It was as if he had never existed. Here, people came to forget their problems. I turned towards the entrance and was glad I did. Maya Fernandez entered in a dark red velvet evening gown, diamonds shining around her neck. I often wondered whether people were born with stardust or was it the clothes that made the star. Whatever the answer, she looked a star tonight. A young man in a black suit, walked behind and to her side, the kind of guy you saw modelling on catwalks. I hadn't seen him before. She made an impression, several heads turned as she strode to a front table. A couple fawned and greeted her by kissing her on both cheeks.

The young man slid back a chair for Maya. He waited for her to sit, before unbuttoning his impeccable dark jacket and sitting next to her. A proper gentleman no doubt. I wondered where MD or Joseph were hiding. The diamonds shone brighter from this distance, an expensive set and it was hard not to look at them. She was too busy talking to her guests to notice me. The bartender in a white shirt and black bowtie, leaned beside me, looking over at her table.

–Have you seen the rocks on her, who needs chandeliers? he said, polishing a glass, eyes fixed upon the diamonds.

–Who is she?

–Mrs Fernandez, very rich, brother. She comes here often but that's the first time I've seen those diamonds.

–They might not be real, I said.

–Are you joking? She wouldn't wear fake.

–Who's the man beside her?

–He's Robby Diaz.

–His real name, come on, I said.

–Ramesh Dillon.

–Is he her partner?

The bartender put the glass down.

–He would like to be her boyfriend but no. She likes to arrive with a good-looking man on her arm. What can the rich not do, brother?

–I see, he's just eye candy. Doesn't Mr Fernandez mind? I asked.

–Which century do you live in? I've heard her husband is a boring old man, who never steps out of his mansion. She's so young and beautiful, I don't blame her, do you?

–I'll remember to attend your lectures on morality.

–That's not bad, he said with a smile.

–Maybe I'll have a dance with her after this drink.

–Now, you're becoming funny and a little drunk. I would stick to the jokes if I were you.

The band played again. A song from a Dilip Kumar film. I tried to remember the film, it came to me, *Dil diya, Dard liya*. I carried on drinking, thinking what a tremendous actor Dilip Kumar was. The bartender seemed to share what I had said with another bartender, and they both laughed. Maya Fernandez glided into the middle of the floor with other couples. She danced with eye candy and they moved nicely together, her in all red and him in all black. I saw no chemistry however, with Robby Diaz. He kept his eyes on her diamond necklace as they danced to a classic upbeat song.

–Wish me luck, this is my dance.

–Go ahead and embarrass yourself, brother.

The bartender shook his head with a laugh. I walked through the couples and came close to Maya Fernandez. Her fine perfume caught my attention. She was about to start the second dance, when I tapped Robby on the shoulder.

–Do you mind if I have the next dance?

He turned, raised his right eyebrow and smirked. He was a model all right, the face was waxed and made up.

–Yes, I do mind actually.

–It's all right Robby, she said, –I know him. What a surprise, Chauhan, you here?

Robby narrowed his grey eyes, shrugged his powerful shoulders and walked away with something like a sulk. I held her in my arms. It had been a long time since I had last danced. I could see why Robby couldn't help looking at the stones around her neck, they dazzled me too. They weren't fake, and neither were her diamond earrings.

–I thought you had forgotten us, she said, in a voice that sounded happy to see me for once.

–Not quite.

–Why are you blinking like that, Chauhan?

–Your rocks dazzle me. What's the occasion, you win the lottery?

We turned around and I tried not to step on her shoes. She was nice to hold, and tonight she looked especially lovely. She held my hand tight and looked into my eyes.

–Hardly, but a woman likes to dress up now and again.

–If I'm not wrong, you look happy to see me.

She glanced at my shoulder with a slight smile.

–I think we just started off on the wrong foot. You're not

such a bad looking man, you know

–Robby will be heart-broken to hear that from your lips.

–Robby, bobby nothing, she said and laughed.

–Look near the bar, he's standing there, throwing daggers.

–He's a nice-looking boy, but I prefer men.

She squeezed my hand a little more with a smile. I was flattered but I wasn't buying her line so quick.

–If you keep this up, I might start to believe you.

–I haven't even started yet, Chauhan.

Her perfume smelt of fine roses, and her eyes held me closer than I wanted. She was my client's wife and tonight she was giving me the works. Maybe she was bored, and I was at the right time and place. It was wishful-thinking, she was too clever for that. We span a few times and then she leaned closer.

–Chauhan, you come and work for me. I'll make it worth your while. You're earning peanuts in your silly detective job.

–You're going to turn my head. What did you have in mind? I said, as I turned her around and past another couple.

–Fifty thousand per month plus expenses. You'll be my secretary with nice bonuses.

She gave me a seductive smile.

–That's the best offer I've had all day, I said.

She touched the side of my cheek with hers and danced slowly. My head started to spin, she was all woman.

–Well?

–I can't seem to think straight, I said with a smile.

–Think then, Chauhan. I might change my mind tomorrow.

–You might, but the glare from your diamonds is distracting me.

–You like diamonds? I will buy you a little diamond bracelet.

–You forget, I'm not Robby, bobby.

She smiled, but it was a little tight. The song finished and I took her to the bar. The bartender looked amazed and I wanted him to close his mouth. He was all yes saab and no saab. No mention any more of brother.

–What will you have, Maya?

–Whisky with soda, just a little ice.

The bartender came back to life.

–Make it two, I said, calling to his back.

Robby Diaz came across and pushed between us with his back turned to me.

–The guests are waiting for us Maya back at the table, he said, with a voice brimming with impatience.

–You entertain them for a while, Robby. I need to speak to my friend here. I haven't seen him for a long while.

–No, we leave together. It doesn't look right, you're with me.

–Beat it Robby, don't be so tiring.

Robby grabbed her wrist.

–You're the one being tiring, we need to return to our guests. Let's go now. It doesn't look good.

–Let go my hand, Robby. Okay, I'll come after this drink. I won't be long.

Robby half turned towards me.

–Look, whatever your name is mister. I want you to get lost, if you know what's good for you.

I took a sip from my glass and put it down on the bar.

–That's the problem with me, I don't know what's good for me. Anyway, I'm having too much of a good time.

He turned fully towards me now and squared up. He was a little taller than me and seemed to spend all his time in the gym.

–Why don't you step outside? I'll wipe that stupid smile off your face, he said.

I looked around him and turned to the cause of his angst.

–Maya, you sure don't pick your friends very carefully. Look, I'm just having a quiet drink. I don't want any trouble.

–Yeah *sala*, just as I thought, said Robby, a little triumphant.

He brushed something off my shoulder. –Your new friend isn't much is he, Maya? Hurry up, I won't wait too long.

He left us with a quick superior smile.

–I'm sorry about that, Chauhan.

–Is he on fifty thousand per month and working as your personal secretary?

–Oh God no, I can buy him for much, much less.

–You haven't bought me yet, Mrs Fernandez.

She straightened, her eyes were sharp as she realised her mistake. She took a sip of her drink.

–I didn't mean it that way. Don't be so touchy, Chauhan.

–You might call it pride.

–Yes, that's why I like you. You have pride and dignity.

–This is my lucky day. What do you want?

She smiled and took a sip from her glass.

–Just your company. I don't meet many honest men, though you are a little crude.

I raised my glass to her.

–I can improve my manners in the right company. How's Anita?

–I haven't seen her at all. She hates me you know. After all I've tried to do for her. No gratitude.

–She met me this morning.

–Oh really, she said, hand tightening around her glass.

I took a sip and watched her. She was curious, her eyes narrowed a fraction, though she pretended otherwise

–She wanted me to hand over the photos, I said, –as if they were a box of chocolates.

–I can understand that. Did you hand them over?

–No.

She smiled.

–She should have known, silly girl. She thinks all she has to do is smile and men will fall over. I'm glad you have more substance.

I took a sip and the whisky was starting to work my nerves.

She had her eyes on my mouth and that was having more of an effect on my nerves.

–Joseph said you are handing over the photos tomorrow.

–Yes, I intend to.

–I'm so glad this sorry business is over. Joseph's going to pay you too much. Three lakhs is too much.

–It's cheap considering I've put my life on the line more than once.

–Oh yes, I forgot about that, but you always managed to stay alive.

–It's a lucky habit.

I glanced over, from his table, Robby's eyes were fixed on us. He looked like a jealous husband. I turned back to Maya.

–I met Bakshi earlier too.

Her hand tightened around the glass as if she didn't like to hear that.

–Oh, you know him?

–You meet all kinds of strange people in my business, Mrs Fernandez.

–But, why would you see him?

–I wanted to know if he had any connections to the blackmail racket.

She laughed.

–I don't think you know who he is. He's only one of the best property developers in Mumbai. Why would he be involved in a cheap racket like that? It doesn't make sense.

–I can't understand that either.

She stopped laughing. The dancefloor filled as the band started up again.

–It's too noisy in here, let's find somewhere quiet. You can tell me what's going on in your wonderful head, she said.

Robby came briskly to her side again. He glanced at me before grabbing her wrist once more.

–Darling, I need a word now.

–Don't hold me so tight, Robby.

–I need a word now, and you don't need to hang around losers like him.

–Lover boy's jealous, I said, –And this happens to be my best suit.

–Why don't you step outside if you're feeling so tough? Yeah, just as I thought, now get lost. I'm telling you for the last time.

–I had better leave Maya, before your boyfriend beats me up.

–No wait, she said, looking irritated with Robby, –I can handle this.

Robby took her out of the side entrance. The bartender came up.

–Another drink, saab?

I finished my whisky and gave him a tip.

–It's all right, you can call me, brother.

–No saab, forgive me.

He shook his head, as I walked towards the side entrance. I hadn't liked the way lover boy had forced Maya outside. The door led into a long corridor filled with cigarette smoke where men leaned against the walls smoking. I headed past them and opened the exit door slowly. The back of Rubies had a large paved patio, then a lawn. A path led through the lawn towards tall trees and bushes. Dim lights lit the path and beyond into the garden. The cool breeze had disappeared, and now it was just cold. At the far end, standing under a tree, Robby was pointing his finger at her face. I walked around the side, on the grass, circling behind them to the far side. I had no interest in hearing the lovers' tiff but I didn't like Robby's pointing. I stopped behind a bush and listened.

–Don't treat me like a bloody fool, Maya. I won't stand for it.

–He's just a friend. What's the matter with you?

–Don't lie. Who is he? And what does he want? I didn't like the way you were laughing either.

–I told you I met him after a long time, that's all.

–I'm not one of your poodles you throw bones to, Maya. I mean it. I care for you, darling. I care more than your boring old husband or anyone else. When will you understand that?

She didn't answer.

–And don't you *ever* insult me like that again, you told me to beat it, remember.

His voice had growing menace and I didn't like the sound of it. I wanted to step in and break it up, but I waited a moment longer.

–Well, you were acting like a jealous child, she said.

–It's because I love you. Don't throw away what we have. I can find a dozen bored housewives with the click of my fingers.

–Why don't you then?

–Shut up! Now, that insult is going to cost you.

He placed a rough hand on her shoulder. When she tried to move back, he held her.

–What do you mean? she asked, and her voice was a little weak.

He looked at her necklace.

–Hand over the diamond set and earrings.

–Are you crazy? This set is worth twenty lakhs. Joseph gave it to me.

He laughed an ugly laugh.

–That loser means nothing to you. I told you from the start. You don't ever cross Robby, not now, not ever. Give it to me. And let this be a lesson.

She tried to step back but he grabbed hold of her and snatched the diamonds from her neck. He placed them in his pocket and grinned.

–I'll call the police, Robby.

Her voice was weak, I hadn't heard it that weak in all this time.

–No, darling. You'll keep your stupid mouth shut. You don't

want me in the papers telling everyone how you're cheating on your rich husband.

–You can't do this. You wouldn't dare to blackmail me.

He pinched her cheek, roughly.

–You need to be kept in line, that's why you like me. I know exactly how to keep you in line.

–Robby, this isn't funny. Now give me back the necklace, I mean it.

He slapped her across the face.

She half fell sideways but managed to remain standing. She looked in shock, tears formed, and she held her cheek with her hand. I moved out from the bushes and walked towards him. He turned around, narrowed his eyes and clenched his fists.

–You're a big tough guy, I said, –Picking on women. Now, hand back the necklace and be quick.

Robby grinned.

–Found some courage at last? Get lost *bhenchod*, before I really lose my temper and you end up in hospital.

–Feeling lucky? You only know how to bully women.

He rushed forward and swung a fierce right fist. I ducked and caught him in the ribs with a left hook. It didn't have much effect. Robby worked out. All I felt was hard muscle. He swung with wild left and rights and caught me in the stomach with strong punches. I staggered back taking a deep intake of breath. He came again with bulging eyes and he was breathing heavily. I stepped forward and smashed an uppercut to his chin. He fell backwards onto his back. He tried to stand again, but I hit him twice more. I leaned back. He was out cold. I crouched down and emptied his pocket of the diamond necklace and placed it in mine.

–You really know how to pick them, Maya.

–He's never behaved like that before, she said, staring at Robby knocked out on the ground.

–I'm sure he hasn't. Though scum like that don't change

overnight.
　She came close and placed a hand on my shoulder.
　–Are you okay? she asked.
　–I'm fine.
　She was shaking in my arms. I held her a moment.

22

WE WALKED along the side of the building and out towards the front. She held my arm tight as we came out into the light. The bouncers were smoking, and it was certain that Bakshi would fire them tomorrow. They didn't look at us as we walked out of the main gate.

–Did you arrive in a car?

–No, Robby drove me here.

–My Contessa isn't exactly a Mercedes.

She didn't say anything as we approached it.

–You weren't kidding, she said.

I opened the door for her and put the Russian novel on the back seat. She slipped inside. I started the car. It saved my blushes by starting first time. We drove out, the headlights showing the way to a place that hadn't yet been decided.

–I'd like to go for a walk on the beach, do you mind? she said and lit a cigarette.

Smoke filled the car. I pulled down the window.

–I know you don't think much of Robby, but he's very attentive. I don't know what came over him tonight.

–Maybe those diamonds turned his head, I said.

I took out the necklace. It was as close as I had ever been to twenty lakhs. I held it in my hand and felt the weight, a fist full of diamonds, they glittered in the dark. I handed it to her. She placed it inside her white purse, with evident relief.

–Oh God, Joseph would have been so upset if I had lost this. It belonged to his first wife.

–But he isn't upset about you roaming around with Robby?

She gave me a sideways glance. –We make allowances in

our marriage. It isn't easy living with him.

–High society marriages, they're something else.

She blew smoke in my direction.

–Don't be small-minded, Chauhan. Joseph understands that I have needs.

She placed a hand on my knee and my knee started to have ideas.

–And there I was, thinking you had married for love.

–Oh, come on Chauhan, you only find that in the movies. Don't be so idealistic, you'll get hurt.

–I'm learning that every day.

After a twenty-minute drive, along a road with a long line of palm trees that swayed gently in the sea breeze, I pulled over. We got out and she held my arm again, as we walked on the pavement. The dark sea lapped ashore, making calm rolling sounds that only the sea can make. There weren't many people out this late, on this stretch of the coast. I wasn't even sure which part we were at. It felt good however to be with her walking with the breeze blowing from the side. I glanced at her face, she didn't have a bruise, only her ego had been hurt. She finished her second cigarette, crushed it under her heel as the large leaves made a rustling sound and the vastness of the sea filled the air.

–Do you understand why I want you as my personal secretary? You know how to protect me.

–I can handle the Robbys of this world Maya, but I like my independence.

–Not interested in money? How strange.

We started to walk again, she kept close to me but didn't take my arm.

–I like money as much as the next guy, but I like my freedom more.

I looked at her sideways.

–Where do you think Prem Nath has gone by the way?

She blinked several times and ran a hand through her hair.

–Must we talk about him on such a night?

–I find it odd that no one seems worried about his whereabouts.

–Joseph's worried. He wants to know. I don't blame poor Prem really. I hope he stays away. I can't imagine being married to Anita. What a nightmare. Maybe he's gone abroad, started a new life, and good luck to him. But I fear, well, I think he actually walked into the sea. He was depressed with his marriage. He told me he had made the biggest mistake of his life.

She held my arm again.

–Your generous husband gave Prem a twenty-five percent stake in your house, did you know that?

Her grip tightened on my arm.

–Well, well, aren't we clever. I suppose Joseph told you, but that's his affair. I warned him against it. I told him to wait and see what Prem's like before handing over such a fortune. It turned out I was right. Anyway, he can give the house to anyone he wants, I don't care anymore. All I dream about is walking away from it all.

–What's stopping you?

–It's not so easy, and this time I would like to marry a man I'm in love with.

–Someone like Robby, perhaps?

She punched my arm lightly.

–Not funny. Before tonight's unfortunate episode, I was starting to have feelings for him.

–Good job they stopped otherwise he would have slapped more feelings into you.

She held my arm to stop me, came around the front. We were under a palm tree.

–You're just a brute, she said thickly, –you hit men, kill them and you don't care at all.

–For your information, I didn't kill Santana or Khan. I haven't actually killed anyone on this case.

–All these men are killed, and you walk away without a scratch.

–I guess I'm lucky, I said.

–You certainly are.

She moved closer, pushing me against the bark of the palm tree. Her hands rested on my shoulders and her face tilted slightly. Her eyes were as alive as her diamonds. Her mouth parted and her breathing deepened.

–Kiss me. Kiss me so that I forget all my troubles.

I didn't move. I could hear the sound of the waves breaking at the shoreline.

She leaned forward and kissed me once, quickly. Her body shook in my arms.

–Well?

–You're my client's wife.

–So?

–So, we keep walking.

She took a hesitant step back and her eyes looked confused.

–I'm so miserable, Chauhan. You have no idea.

–Like a bird stuck in a golden cage. Nothing's stopping you from flying.

–You wouldn't understand.

–Try me.

She grew cold, stepped away and stared into the ocean. She looked a long time, trying to gather her composure.

–You're just like the rest, she said, and her voice sounded disappointed. –I forgot you were a bloody detective for a moment. Come to the house tomorrow like a good little poodle and pick up your cheque. I gave you a big chance Chauhan, but you will always remain a two-rupee detective. You wouldn't know class if it hit you in the face.

–I've seen enough class tonight to last me a lifetime. I hope for everyone's sake, you're not involved in Prem's disappearance.

–What do you mean by that cheap remark?

–I'm going to tell you something else, I'll find Prem Nath and when I do, I hope you, Anita or Bakshi are not involved. If you are, then you're going to wish you hadn't met me.

She looked afraid now. I waited, finally she found her voice.

–I have never heard such nonsense. God, why would I want Prem to disappear? It's not my fault he decided to run into the sea.

–I don't know yet, but I'll find out.

–I don't want to talk to you anymore. My first impression about you was correct. You are a son of a bitch, like MD said you were.

I let her have that and walked towards my car. She hurried behind, her heels clicking loudly on the pavement. I saw a taxi coming up and waved it down. The car pulled over. A man's head leaned out of the window.

–Yes, saab.

–Can you take the madam home?

He nodded.

–I'm not going in a taxi, she said.

–I'm not dropping you home. It's either the taxi or you walk.

The driver smiled to see her discomfort.

–You bastard! she shouted, and hurried into the back of the taxi.

–It was lovely meeting you too. We must do this again sometime.

The taxi pulled away as I checked my watch, eleven-thirty. I had thrown a few things at her but she hadn't seemed too concerned. She was shrewd and had regained her composure quickly after her argument with Robby. She hadn't flinched an eyelid, when I mentioned the twenty-five percent stake. She was tough all right. The questions remained unanswered. How was she involved with Prem's disappearance, if at all? What had she to gain? Someone from the Fernandez family had a hand in Prem's disappearance. I was almost certain, but I felt like I was going round in circles. I thought to have another crack at the little red book and see if it gave up anything. I drove home and looked forward to a quiet drink and the comfort of my bed.

23

MY APARTMENT block car park was deserted. No sign of Kasim or his cronies. As I got out of the car, I noticed that my lucky tomcat wasn't around either, maybe he was out trying his luck with the ladies. I felt my gun in the pocket and was on edge thanks to Manjit, a narrow escape I didn't want to repeat. I looked up at my apartment. The lights were off and most of the block looked asleep. I walked inside. The night manager behind the desk gave me a nod with an odd smile. He never did that. I caught the lift feeling beat.

It had been a long day and I was no closer to finding Prem Nath. Hard yards for few rewards. It happened some days and you had to take it on the chin, slamming into one brick wall after another. The bell rang and the lift doors opened onto my floor. Along the corridor, a wife was shouting at her husband. He had forgotten their wedding anniversary and he was getting hell. You could forget the wife, but not the wedding anniversary. She was still shouting when I opened the door and went inside with a smile.

A good drink would help me calm down. I closed the door, switched on the lights and made for the kitchen. Something was wrong. A familiar scent. Some of my novels were on the table upside down. I never placed them upside down. The curtains were drawn, and the room looked different, things out of place from their usual untidiness. The sofas had been moved too; I pulled out the gun, clicked the safety catch off. No sound. The bedroom door was ajar. Only darkness spread behind it, and it wasn't inviting. I pushed the door open and switched on the lights.

A slow smile flashed from my bed. A black-haired woman was lying on her side, her head held up with her left hand. A bare arm curved up and over a thin bed sheet. My eyes traced the shape of her fine hips. Ice Baby. I glanced around the rearranged bedroom. She had been searching hard for something, and I knew what it was. Her eyes followed me around.

–Hello stranger, I've come to make a peace offering. You can put that gun away.

–I might need it.

She smiled, revealing fine white teeth. I tried hard not to imagine what she looked like under the sheet. I walked around the bed, checked the cupboards, clothes had been turned inside out. I checked the bathroom. Empty.

On my bookshelf, books had been put back in a hurried manner and some lay on the floor. She kept her stiff smile, but it was struggling to keep afloat. How much had she been paid this time? I tried to control my senses, but they were going a little haywire. Fine perfume filled the room. I walked around the bed, sat on the chair, looked at her with my gun resting on my lap. I ran my left hand through my hair and stared at her. She was worth staring at.

–Well how about it, handsome? I know you liked me the moment you saw me in the boutique.

–Did you find what you were looking for?

–I didn't look for anything.

–And I'm Ali Baba and the forty thieves.

Her eyes struggled to focus.

–You can see a lot more than my arm, she said, –I think we could have really hit it off under different circumstances.

–That's the story of my life, I said with a slight smile.

–Well, I know how to change it, tonight.

–It must be my lucky day.

Doubt entered her eyes. She allowed the bed sheet to slip a little, revealing part of her fine figure. She pulled the cover back with a smile. It was a cute trick and something I hadn't expected from her, but sometimes it wasn't good to think too much. I placed the gun inside my coat pocket, lit a cigarette, blew the smoke out the side of my mouth.

–I've seen beautiful women before, I didn't just step out of kindergarten.

She laughed, and her eyes were watching my mouth.

–How did you manage to get inside by the way? I asked.

–Your silly manager let me in. I told him I was your girlfriend. I flashed my eyelashes at him, you see, that normally works.

–I'm going to have a word with him.

–He's an idiot. I could get past him every time, she said, and placed her hand on her hip.

–You haven't answered my question. What were you looking for?

–You know the answer but you're wasting time, detective. Why don't you come over and get warm. I'm sure you've had a very long day.

I smiled.

–I should thank my lucky stars. I thought about you at Rubies.

–Don't think too much on a night like this, Chauhan.

–It keeps me alive. Now if you can get dressed, that would be a start.

Her hand tightened around the bed sheet, lifting it up a little.

–Really?

–Yes really. I know that doesn't help your pride any, but I want you out of the bed. You're here for the same thing that Manjit tried the other night.

She sat up with the bed sheet wrapped around her breasts.

–I thought you were a real man, Chauhan. Maybe I was mistaken.

–Get dressed or I'll help you get dressed.

She straightened, pulled on a white top and a pair of blue jeans. The smile was gone. She was staring at me all the same.

–What were you looking for?

She considered that a moment and looked around the room.

–The photos and the red book. Please give them to me and I'll leave you in peace.

–Just like that, hey? I have a better idea. Why don't you tell me where Kasim is hiding and what he has on you?

Her eyes looked afraid and she bit her lower lip.

–He has nothing on me.

–Manjit, your ugly boyfriend, is singing like a bird and it won't take long for the police to find you.

–I'm not worried about him and he's not my boyfriend, she said and stood.

I rose from the chair too as she came close.

–No tear gas, I hope.

She moved closer, embraced me tight. I felt the warmth of her seductive body. Her fingers pressed my lower back. I tried to keep my senses under control, but they told me to go to hell. If this was an act, I'd give every film award going. I kissed her quick and tight. She broke off and ran her fingers across my face.

–You're a very good kisser for a detective.

–I've had a lot of practice lately. Women keep kissing me.

She smiled.

–Aren't you a lucky boy.

–I guess some days lady luck shines on you.

We kissed again, and I held her tight as her hands ran down my back. She pulled me onto the bed and kissed me some more. I could get used to this kind of persuasion. There was something amiss in her dark eyes. They looked afraid when there was no need to be at this moment.

–Who sent you here? Bakshi?

–No.

–Kasim?

She hesitated.

–What do you think? Look, I've nothing personal against you, Chauhan. If I don't take that red book and photos back, then he'll kill me. Kasim will find me quicker than the police ever will.

I ran my hand through her hair.

–Is that why Manjit tried the other night?

She nodded and looked scared. She was still on the bed and looking up. I didn't want to ask her questions but they kept coming one after another.

–We returned empty handed and Kasim punched Manjit in the face and threatened to kill us both, she said.

–It really wasn't Manjit's day.

She looked around.

–This isn't a laughing matter, Chauhan. You don't know who you're dealing with. You don't want to meet Kasim.

–I think I'd like to meet Scarface. But if you return the photos and the red book, what's stopping him from killing you anyway?

She placed the side of her face on my chest.

–Nothing. That's what I'm worried about, she said.

–Then why don't you leave town and leave this to me?

She turned to look at me.

–Kasim would find me. He's pure evil. The scariest man I ever met and I've met a few.

She turned towards me and placed a hand on my shoulder.

–Did that bastard Kasim ask you to sleep with me?

–He said I'd better not return without the photos. To use all my charms.

–For a minute there I thought you actually liked me.

She ran her hand across my cheek.

–This is the only way I can think of getting the photos.

–You're going to hurt my pride, Shanti.

She smiled and let out a sigh.

–Do you have the photos? she asked.

–I certainly do, just not here.

I stroked her thick black hair. My pride cried out weakly that she had only kissed me because of Kasim.

–I'm only doing this because I want to help you, I said.

A faint smile appeared on her face.

–Let's do a deal Chauhan, if you give me the photos and the book, I'll tell you where Prem Nath is being held.

I held her shoulders with both hands.

–What did you say?

–Oh so, I finally have your attention, Mr Detective.

–You're full of tricks Ice Baby, but I like it.

A shadow flicked across the lounge, I caught it in the corner of my eye. I pulled out my gun, listened again. Nothing. Then I saw a gun appear from behind the door, pointed at us. I grabbed Ice Baby, pulled her off the bed and to the side.

–Oh my God, steady on tiger, she said.

A couple of shots fired into the sidewall. She screamed. I fired back from the bed. Two shots at the door. Shoes scrambled towards the front door. It banged shut. Blood appeared on Shanti's sleeve. I looked, it was a grazing shot on her arm from one of the bullets. –You okay?

She nodded but her eyes were wide with fright and she took quick short breaths. I hurried out of the room and looked along the corridor. A man slipped down the fire escape. I ran after him, glad that I was still fully dressed. The fire escape door was open. A shot fired upwards as I moved through it. The shot missed and made a clanging sound on the steel railings. Another door opened and shut below the flight of stairs. I rushed down and stopped to catch my breath. I opened the door at the bottom. Several shots passed over my head and made loud holes in the door. I hit the ground and crawled along the tarmac. A big black SUV rolled out into the car park, the door banging shut. I pointed my Glock, fired at the vehicle and smashed the back-seat glass. Tyres screeched as it fishtailed out of the car park. Lights went on. People shouted from the windows. Call police! Call police!

The car flew out of sight leaving a trail of exhaust fumes. I hurried to the front of the building and checked at Reception. The idiot manager lay on the floor in a heap holding his head, groaning, with blood trickling out through his fingers. I sat him up.

–What happened? he said.

–Looks like you were hit on the head.

–Oh no!

Blood covered his hands and it scared him.

–Who did it? I asked.

–A man with a scar down his face. Oh no, blood. He took the master key to all the apartments.

There was a sweater on the chair. I passed it to him and told him to press it against his head until help arrived. He placed it over his head.

I took the elevator up to my apartment. My door was open. I entered the front room holding my gun and walked across to the bedroom. Ice Baby was gone. The bathroom was empty as well. I walked to the front room, looked out of the window. She was running across the car park holding her arm, heading towards a black Fiat. She got inside and drove away. In the distance, police sirens grew louder. Apartment block lights turned on, one after another. No one was asleep now. I was having no luck with women, after all. They were either trying to kiss me or kill me.

24

LATE SATURDAY morning, it rained. I woke up feeling beat but happy to be alive. At the front window, I stretched out my arms. A couple was scurrying away under a black umbrella. It was time to change this apartment. Too many people kept wandering in without being invited. When the manager recovered, he had to be warned not to let strange women into my apartment. And it didn't matter how pretty they were. Still, a man who's an idiot, is an idiot and they never fail to surprise you with their idiocy.

The kettle hissed in the kitchen. I made a mug of coffee, drank it and felt more awake. The police had finished at around three a.m., taken a full report and asked me to describe Scarface. They wanted to know why he had been trying to kill me. Why I had a woman in my apartment. And why she was trying to kill me? I answered the clueless Inspector, leaving out the important information. I knew when Dhanwan read this report however, he would be breathing down my neck. Time was short.

I rubbed my forehead, recalled the kisses and smiled. Ice Baby had disappeared but had sent life racing through my bones. She also knew where Prem Nath was being held, though she could be bluffing. Kasim had planned to kill us both and had wanted to find me naked in bed, with her wrapped around me. It was a simple plan, and it nearly worked.

I showered, shaved and pulled on a fresh set of clothes. I took out my short, black leather jacket, placed the gun inside, and thought it was time to hand over the photos to Fernandez. It was time to collect my cheque, before someone finally succeeded in wiping me off the face of Mumbai. I was running late and feeling hungry.

The rain had eased as I walked down to the car. I drove to the bank first and withdrew the red book and the envelope containing the photos from the safety deposit box. Then I drove up to my favourite cafe around the corner, Mohan lal's, and ordered a full breakfast; coffee, orange juice, two boiled eggs, two parathas with side mango pickle, and a banana. The owner Mohan lal, was behind the counter in his regular apron and with his famous large moustache that curled up his chubby cheeks.

The cafe had been modernised recently with a white ceiling and new fans. The wooden chairs had been re-stained in dark brown and varnished. The table cloths were new, a chess board design of white and blue. It wasn't so busy right now; several guys were sitting drinking tea in shirts and ties. Salesmen about to head out on the next round. Two women in pink shalwar kemeez sat in the corner arguing about a bill. It would become busier in half an hour, nearer to lunchtime. I sat at the front and saw the now familiar black Fiat with the tinted glass. It drove past and parked diagonally across the road. No one came out. It seemed like a challenge.

I felt the heat of the coffee through the mug. It could be the psycho or else a cop sent by Dhanwan to keep an eye on me. Either way I was losing patience with this sonofabitch. No one stepped out. Owing to the angle of the light, I couldn't make out who was sitting behind the steering wheel. The person was teasing me.

With breakfast finished, I paid the bill and went outside. I walked in the opposite direction and turned around the corner. Two ragged girls, around ten, pulled at my sleeve. They had pleading faces and sad little smiles.

–Saab *rupiya, rupiya!*

I gave them ten rupees each. The sad smiles grew brighter.

–Look, I'll give you both another ten rupees if you can find out who's sat in that black car.

I pointed around the corner. The grins widened, they peeked around the corner and hurried towards the car. I watched. The girls were as good as their little word. They kept banging on the glass until it wound down and a hand gave them some rupees. They looked delighted as only children can, and ran back across the road to me. I asked and they went shy on me.

–Rupiya!

These were proper hustlers. I smiled and gave them another ten each.

–You two are too smart for me. Who was inside the car?

–Saab, it was a man with a black moustache, and he wore black glasses and a white shirt.

–Anything else? Did he have a scar on his face?

–No, saab.

They shook their heads. –He was reading a paper.

I handed over another ten rupees each. They skipped down the road. If only I could be as happy after receiving so little. Then I decided to walk back around the corner, keeping my hand on the Glock pistol.

The moustached man hadn't moved because my car hadn't moved. I cut diagonally across the road towards his car. A couple of cars beeped, and I gave him a chance to see me. If this clown wanted to kill me, he had his chance. I kept my hand on my gun and tapped on the glass. The window wound down and the man with the shades looked up.

–Yes?

–You said that with a straight face, I said.

The man kept his hands on the paper.

–I'm sorry mister, I don't think I know you.

He turned a page, he was apparently reading the sports section on Indian hockey.

–Cut the bullshit. Chauhan, is my name. You know, the man you've been following around for days.

The man tilted his head towards me.

–I'm sorry, I'm not following you. I'm minding my own business, sorry, but you're mistaken.

–All right, have it your way. I'm going to my office now, it's not far from here. When you make up your mind, come over and tell me what you want. I might even be nice to you. I also carry iron, just in case you have other ideas.

The man stroked his moustache without a care in the world. I left him with that thought and walked back to my car. I drove out and watched through the rear-view mirror. Mr Shades had decided against following. He didn't look like a cop. I wondered who he was working for.

Twenty minutes later, I was inside my plush office in Rising Towers listening to my answering service. There were messages from Gautam and Dhanwan. Both wanted to see me immediately as if I had nothing better to do. There were another two messages but no voice, only deep breathing; either a pervert or somebody unable to speak. For once, no messages from Mrs Chatterjee and I was glad about that.

I put the phone down and opened a reminder for rent from Rising Towers Ltd. I put the letter back in the envelope and tossed it towards the corner chair where the rest of the reminders were gathering dust. There was a knock at the door.

–Come in.

I kept one hand on my gun and pointed it towards the door. It was Mr Shades.

He was of medium height and thin looking, wore a half-sleeved white shirt with dark grey trousers. A couple of cuts were on his forearm, long healed. He looked like a second-hand car salesman, not someone you trusted on first meetings. Perhaps I was being hard on car salesmen. He looked around the office, before sitting down across from me at the desk. He took off his glasses to reveal small dark eyes that moved sharply.

–Changed your mind then?

–Yes. Maybe you've heard of me, I am Hari Singh.

–Sorry, you're just not that famous.

–I keep a low profile, Detective Chauhan. I'm going to make this quick. I have good information that you are looking for. I ask a fair price and I like to be paid in cash. I'm not greedy, brother. When you become greedy, you end up dead.

–I'm all ears.

He leaned back, tapped the desk, happy with himself for gaining my interest.

–Perhaps you don't believe me, he said.

–You haven't told me anything yet. The information you have isn't as important as you think. I also know things, I am a detective after all.

He smiled.

–I came here for that reason. You are persistent and you have the lucky habit of staying alive.

–It might be more than luck, I do have survival skills.

He took out a pen from his breast pocket and played with it between his fingers.

–I saw your skills the other night when you were staggering outside Afzal Khan's house. I was also there last night, when you were busy shooting outside your apartment.

–Do you only enjoy watching people in trouble, Hari Singh? Try helping sometimes.

He showed me his palms.

–I'm not a fighting man myself, brother. I only deal in paid information and that's all.

–I'll remember that when you are in a tight corner. You're in a dangerous game.

–I know. But I'm very good at it. The information is worth a cool one lakh rupees, not a rupee more or less, he said and pointed the silver pen at me.

–In my world, that buys me two sub inspectors and possibly a small-town judge.

He rubbed his nose.

–It's peanuts compared to what I am offering you. I could make five times that amount.

–Then why don't you go to the police, Hari Singh?

–I do sometimes, but for this particular case I would rather trust you.

I leaned back. He wasn't smiling but looked confident about the information he had.

–Let's assume I like what you have. You want paying in cash?

He nodded and grinned again.

I opened another brown envelope. It said I would be evicted from the offices if the four months outstanding rent wasn't paid within ten days. I placed the nice begging and threatening letter back inside. Rising Towers had over half of the floor empty, they needed tenants. Though I doubted I could get away too long without paying them something.

–Hari Singh, you're not a cop and you don't belong to Santana's outfit. So you're either a brave, lonely operator or very stupid.

–I'm not stupid, he said and put the pen back in his pocket.

–All right, I can't handle the suspense. Let's hear your special news.

His sharp eyes slid left and right. There was silence, a light rain tapped the window. Finally, he looked at me.

–I know where they're hiding Prem Nath.

I lit a cigarette, stared to see if he was on the level. Hari Singh had leaned back in the chair and clasped his hands. His eyes were steady and business-like. He seemed to be confident with his statement, because you couldn't make that up and not come through. Yet I had doubts.

–Prem's been missing for over five weeks, I said.

–I know, and it's taken all my skills, brother, to find where he is.

–Is he alive?

Hari Singh grinned. –You haven't agreed to pay me yet.

—You haven't told me anything. I also know someone who knows where Prem is. So, you have competition.

His eyes narrowed, slid left and right again. He took a moment to check whether I was telling the truth.

—I don't think so, he said.

—Okay, let's see what you have, and I might be interested. Is Prem Nath alive?

—I'm not one hundred percent sure, Chauhan. And I'm not going to lie to you. But I know he didn't walk into the sea.

I blew out the smoke and liked what I heard. He could be bluffing, and he could be working for any of Maya Fernandez, Dhanwan or Bakshi. I needed to hear something concrete.

—How can you be sure? I asked.

—What about the one lakh rupees?

I tapped the cigarette into the ashtray.

—Not so fast, if you know where to find Prem Nath, why didn't you see Fernandez?

—I don't trust all those big people. They promise one thing and do another.

—And you trust me?

—Funny as it sounds, I do. Well Detective Chauhan, do we have a deal?

His sharp eyes were concentrated upon my face. I put the cigarette to my mouth again and burned it a little.

—Let's be clear. You know where Prem Nath is being held?
He nodded.

—Who's holding him?

—You have to pay for that part, he said, and gestured with his thumb and forefinger as if counting cash.

—I don't have one lakh in cash right now. Let's meet at seven-thirty tonight and I'll have the cash.

—Okay, but you need to be quick, Chauhan. Don't let me down. It's tonight or never.

He pushed back the chair and stood. I pushed back my chair too, and moved around the desk. He stopped near the door and turned around after he'd put on his shades.

–You have doubts Chauhan, don't you? Let me clear up a few things. I came here to say my piece and I'm going to say it. I knew Prem Nath before he became involved with that Fernandez woman. I knew him like a work colleague, someone you said hi to on your way out of a factory. Don't get me wrong, we didn't meet in any factory. I met him at Rubies, maybe you know the place. He's a man with an easy smile. Then he runs into Anita Fernandez, she sweeps him off his feet and turns his life upside down. I mean, she's a handful.

–She most certainly is.

Hari Singh sighed and placed his hands inside his trouser pockets.

–Well, she's a handful for any man; highly-strung, emotional and temperamental. It was a whirlwind romance and he looked happy and miserable at the same time. We sat drinking at Rubies one night and he says to me, see that woman over there dancing with that man. Well Hari, she's my wife. She'll find someone else tomorrow. She fooled me all right, he said. Then he drank himself out of his head. I helped him into a taxi, while his wife disappeared with the other man through a back entrance.

The next time I ran into Prem, he looked happier, explains he's going to be divorced. I've never seen a man look happier about becoming divorced. I say to him, you will make a handsome profit from the settlement. He narrows his eyes and says he would leave her without one rupee to his name. Only the old man wasn't in agreement and wanted them to work at their failed marriage. You listening, Chauhan?

–Yes, but you could have heard these rumours anywhere.

–True, but Prem told me this. He was worried he wouldn't be able to escape this marriage so easily. Then he disappears. I knew that cheap blackmailer, Santana and about his disgusting little racket. Anita Fernandez was running around with him. I mean, that was no secret, and I felt sorry for Prem. I keep my eyes and ears wide open. I see Santana meeting Afzal Khan, and see him meeting your well-wisher, Kasim.

He had my interest now, because finding that psycho wasn't easy.

–You know what he looks like?

Hari Singh's face pulled up with a slight grin.

–I can follow the best of them, and felt I could make money from this. People are careless in clubs with their loose talk after a few drinks. Santana was arrogant as well as careless. He boasted about the girls he trapped. I suppose a careless mouth is what got him shot between the eyes. I heard him brag that he was going to make a fortune from Anita Fernandez. Anyway, I follow this Kasim. It was my good luck on that evening that I saw Prem Nath being bungled out of a car and taken inside this place.

A slight breeze entered through the window and ruffled a few papers on my desk. We both looked at them. I turned back to face him.

–Which place?

–I tell you the golden information after I receive one lakh rupees in cash. Do you believe me now?

–You tell a good story, Hari Singh. But Prem might have been moved. If I find nothing there, I'm out of pocket. Why is Kasim holding Prem?

–I don't know, maybe a kidnap racket. I'm working on that angle too. I might make more money if I can find that information.

I took a step back. He seemed to have ready answers for all my questions. You only managed that if you were telling the truth or you were one hell of a practiced liar.

–Fernandez hasn't received any ransom demand, and the police are looking for Prem as we speak.

–They're not looking very hard. The missing persons bureau is overstretched. You know that as well as I. They're hoping he committed suicide. Or, and this might not sit easy with you, someone's paid them not to look too hard.

It was an interesting angle, and one I had considered.

–Any ideas?

–I might have, Chauhan. I've told you enough and I've not received a single rupee, yet.

–Okay, Hari Singh, where can I find Shanti? She was working for Santana.

–I have an idea but I'm more interested in the main players.

He moved into the waiting area. I followed him through. He was silent.

–Hari Singh, I'm going to trust my instinct. Where do you want to meet?

He half grinned.

–Do you know the Chetan Building on Shivaji Marg? I have an office at the back, Room 101 on level 12. Seven-thirty sharp, and don't forget the cash. I will help you find Prem Nath.

I took in the information and said, –one more thing, I pay half tonight and the other fifty thousand after I find Prem.

I watched him carefully to see his reaction. He seemed to have expected it, because he shrugged his shoulders. –Hari Singh, don't play me false or I'll find you.

He thought about that and stopped grinning.

–Still don't trust me, eh? That's all right. Okay, we'll play it your way, Chauhan. Don't fail to make it. You won't get a second chance.

He turned and disappeared down the corridor. Ice Baby had said the same thing and knew where Prem was held. Two people, unconnected, or maybe working together to rob me blind. It gave me hope. My only problem was whether Prem was alive or not. A kidnap note would have made me feel easier. I needed to arrange the money fast and there was only one place to go. I dialled the mansion. This time a maid answered and said Fernandez was at home and would see me.

25

SATURDAY AFTERNOON had a monsoon feel, only cooler. A damp dusty smell pervaded the air, trees appeared greener and people hurried along the pavements, black umbrellas tilted over their heads, determined to reach home. Traffic moved slowly and a further delay came up with a diversion sign. A film company had decided to shoot in the middle of the road, like they do. A crowd had gathered. This was going to take at least an hour if not more. City of dreams. No-one was going anywhere. Constables kept the crowd back blowing on their whistles, with half an eye on the hero and heroine, who were practicing dance moves to a loud musical number.

I pulled the Contessa over to one side, stepped out, lit a cigarette and stood under the canopy of a department store. I looked over the dark and excited heads. The heroine's sari was soaking as she danced with the hero, first on the car roof, then on the bonnet, to loud cheers. The director, in his frustration, signalled to the crowd to be quiet by waving his arms up and down. They listened for a while as the couple gyrated some more. It was nice work if you could get it, and the pay wasn't too bad either.

I finally reached Malabar Hill, later than planned, parked the car and rang the bell. The maid answered the door and showed me into the lounge. It felt like déjà vu, but this time an impatient Fernandez entered the room. He came and stood across from me, eyes sharp, hands in his trouser pockets.

–I don't like to be kept waiting, young man.

–I'm sorry Mr Fernandez, there was a dance scene in the middle of the road. There's no stopping artists, they don't value time.

–They're bloody fools. Prancing around the roads, they should be kept inside the studios. You have the photos?

I took out the envelope from inside my leather jacket and felt embarrassed for him.

–I don't know if you want to look at them.

The frown hardened as he rocked back and forth on his heels. I passed the envelope reluctantly. He took it with a shaking hand and walked towards the oil portrait above the mantelpiece. He stared at his first wife, his face blushed with disappointment or anger, as he turned around.

He took out one photo halfway, glanced at it with disgust, pushed it back, and sighed.

–Where did I go wrong? he said, to himself.

He took out a lighter, set fire to the envelope, and threw it into the open log fire. He watched the flames flicker in silence, as the smell of burning spread into the room. So much for all my hard work, though it was the right thing to do.

–Thank you. This means a great deal to me Detective Chauhan. I know you took personal risks to find these photos and I appreciate it. I hope this is the last of it.

He regained some control, though he didn't meet my eyes for a while and rang a bell on the sidewall. A maid arrived with a black briefcase and laid it on the glass table. He clicked it open. It was full of thick, rectangle bundles. I had never seen so much cash at once. He also took out a chequebook.

–I know you said that your rate was fifteen hundred plus expenses, but with the risks you've taken to your life, I'm going to pay you three lakhs. How would you like to be paid?

– A two lakh cheque and one lakh in cash.

He counted out the bundles, wrote out the cheque and passed it to me. It felt good in my hand. I placed the cheque inside my trouser pocket and slid the bundles of cash into my leather jacket.

–Thank you, I said.

–It's the least I can do.

–I suppose Gautam has kept you informed?

–Yes, Detective Chauhan. Him and several other people. Inspector Dhanwan visited and insisted I fire you. People don't seem to like you. Is there any reason for that?

I shrugged and smiled.

–It beats me, Mr Fernandez. I doubt Dhanwan likes many people as it is. As things stand, we're all square. I can leave your case, you have the photos and the blackmail gang is all nearly dead or with the police. I'm hoping you haven't received any more demands.

–No, I haven't, but what do you mean nearly?

–It's a long story, but there's this one man, Kasim. He's a ruthless killer and still at large. If the police arrest him, I'll be able to breathe easier.

–Yes, the Inspector mentioned him too. Is he the ringleader?

I nodded. –We think so yes. Any more news on Prem? The police think he walked into the sea.

–That's what many people think, and I'm glad you've been making inquiries.

He closed the briefcase.

–It came up whilst I was working, I said, –this might not be a surprise but the police aren't getting very far looking for Prem.

–I had expected better, he said, rubbing his temples and looking distracted.

–I met your wife at Rubies last night.

He stopped rubbing his temples and stared at me.

–She likes to socialise. It's the price you pay for marrying someone half your age.

–Oh, don't get me wrong, Mr Fernandez, I don't like to judge people… it's just that some things bother me.

–Like?

–Well, for one, Anita married Prem and she doesn't seem concerned about finding him. And Mrs Fernandez said I should leave finding Prem to the police and drop the case.

–I don't understand what you mean?

–Don't you find it odd that apart from you, no one really wants to find Prem Nath?

–Not really. Anita was going to divorce Prem, they didn't get along, and she is what she is: spoilt. Maya doesn't like outside interference in family matters, and she told me to fire you. She's careful about things and I think that's a good thing, but you see, I liked Prem as a son. He was the son I never had, hard working, honest and decent. I didn't want him to divorce Anita. He could have turned her life around. My own son on the other hand roams around the capitals of European countries drunk; a playboy who has shown zero interest in the business or family. I only hear from him when he wants money every two years or so. He's dead to me, and it gives me no pleasure to tell you these things, Detective Chauhan. People look at me with envy and say I'm a lucky man!

–Every family has problems Mr Fernandez, but you seem to have a few more, no doubt. I want to ask you about Dinesh Bakshi. Do you know him?

He moved around the glass table, keeping one hand on the back of a chair.

–Yes, he wanted to buy this place. He made a decent offer last year. He wants to demolish my house, build one hundred apartments and sell them for three crores each. You can do the maths.

I raised my eyebrows. –Yeah, that's a lot of money. I suppose you said no?

–This place has sentimental value to me. I will only leave it when I die, and even then, I will pass it onto my children.

–And Bakshi isn't prepared to wait?

–No, not at all. He was very good about it. He bought the big plot next to my house. You might have seen the construction going on.

–You can't miss it.

That crushed one idea I had about Bakshi, and my mind began to think about Kasim a little more. A gentle rain tapped the French doors. The trees, lawn and the hedge looked greener. I felt like having a drink, but Fernandez had been business-like today. He hadn't offered a drink because he wasn't satisfied or because I had kept him waiting. Those actors had a lot to answer for, dancing in the middle of the afternoon like that.

–Anyway, I think I might have a lead on Prem.

He raised an eyebrow. –So, you don't think he drowned?

–I wouldn't go that far yet, but that's why I needed the one lakh in cash. It's going to buy information, hopefully. Or I might be taken for a ride. Only thing is, I don't know if I'm still working for you.

Fernandez placed his hands inside his pockets and his eyes came alive.

–You're still working for me and that's the best news I have heard in a long while. I want you to follow your lead.

I took a moment before saying. –I wouldn't like to get your hopes up, Mr Fernandez. Prem might still have drowned.

Fernandez moved his head from side to side. –I don't believe it. Prem is made of sterner stuff. Besides, what reason would he have to commit suicide? He had everything.

–He might have become depressed about his marital affairs.

–He was very unhappy, but he was good for Anita. Prem stopped her excesses, stopped her wildness. I saw my young daughter again briefly and for that I will always be thankful. Then he just disappears. It makes no sense. It hasn't made sense since he disappeared.

I thought about mentioning the twenty-five percent stake in the house that he had given to Prem. That angle worried me but I decided not to bring it up just yet. No one would blame me if I walked away now. My life would be safer. It was the smart thing to do. Quit while you're ahead, count the chips and take the money home. And yet...

–All right Mr Fernandez, I'll follow this new lead. If it's a dead end, then I'll leave it to the police. If not, then I will let you know.

He came forward and shook my hand.

–I had a feeling about you, Chauhan. You would find things others wouldn't. I'm a good judge of character.

–Let's not get carried away with good character. We can all improve on that.

–True. I hope to hear good news soon.

I moved out of the house and was glad that I'd restored hope in Fernandez. My pockets were full for a change, and that restored my hopes, too.

26

MONEY MAKES you happier, whatever the poets say, it's better to have it than being broke. I drove to the closest bank branch and paid the cheque into my account. Some lonely rupees had been hanging out there for a long time and they needed company. Small bills could now be paid off, they'd been snapping at my backside like hyenas. By the time I reached central Mumbai through the slow traffic, it was nearly six-thirty. The rain had been busy, gutters overflowed and large parts of the road were under water. I was early so I parked the car and went to have some food; a coke with vada pav. The green chilli burnt my tongue more than I liked, but it was tasty and good. The simple things often gave the most satisfaction. Then I moved the car to just opposite the Chetan Buildings.

The office was on the twelfth floor. As I crossed the road, splashes of rain wet my ankles. The foyer was empty and dirty. A board with names missing was on my right and there was no Hari Singh listed on it. There were either vacancies or plenty of tenants who wished to remain anonymous. Insurance fraudsters, mail order companies who never delivered any goods but happily took your cash; cheap accountants who made sure you never paid any tax. A forlorn building that had paan spits staining the stairs, a place with the air of disappointment and failure. Every building has a vibe and this one was no different. It could be doing much better if the owners took interest instead of lazily collecting the rent.

A woman in a torn sari swept the floor in a lonely corridor to my right. She didn't look at me and wasn't sweeping the floor properly either. She missed several cigarette ends. Well, it wasn't my building. I entered the elevator, checked my watch and hoped Hari Singh wasn't a stooge for Kasim, luring me into this trap. I patted my pistol and the spare magazine. This place looked good for a shootout, it was quiet enough.

The lift bell didn't work as the lift struggled to the twelfth floor. The doors took their own sweet time in open and for a moment, I thought they wouldn't. I would take the stairs on the way down. The long corridor was dark and narrow, with closed doors all the way along. People had gone home, if there was anyone working here to begin with. The smell of damp dust and stale cigarettes filled the floor, and I could hear the sound of rain dripping into empty offices.

I glanced at the door numbers and continued until I reached Hari Singh's office. The door was open, and the cigarette smell was strong. I entered into another corridor with three or four office doors. As I was about to call his name, a narrow light shone from the last office. A sinister voice froze my blood. It had the same hissing menace that I'd heard before on my telephone line: Kasim. Then I heard Hari Singh speak.

–Yes, I know who you are, but what do you want with me?

I trod gently, opened the next office door and left it ajar. There was another door, connected to Hari Singh's office. It was partially open, the thin light shone into my room, towards the window. I stood behind it and reached for my pistol.

–You're a *ssmall* man, working in a big man's world, Hari Singh, said Kasim.

Chairs scraped on the tiled floor from the office.

–What do you mean? said Hari Singh.

My fingers tightened around my pistol. It didn't make me feel any stronger. I took a deep breath and stayed behind the door.

–You are either *sstupid* or you think I am *sstupid*. Did you think I didn't know you were following me?

–I haven't followed you, Kasim. There's no need.

The chair creaked again, as if Kasim had leaned back into his chair.

–Of course not. I must have imagined it. I want to know two things, and before you answer, think carefully. Where is Shanti? And why did you visit the detective?

Silence.

–I don't know any Shanti, and I went to see the detective on a personal matter.

Raindrops tapped the windows in warning, and the wind rattled the window frame.

–Wrong answer.

Hari Singh laughed nervously. –And what has this to do with you?

–Wrong again. This isn't looking good. Try again.

The damp smell was strong, and it looked like the offices hadn't been rented in years. How could I arrest Scarface without getting Hari Singh killed? I could surprise him, but the door opened the wrong way. By the time I'd pulled it back, Scarface would have shot us both. The other idea was to leave this office and wait for Kasim in the corridor, but that meant moving my tall frame without being heard. –This is none of your business.

Hari Singh's voice was tight, his confidence slipping.

–You're not a brave man, so stop pretending. You know who you are facing now, yes?

–Okay, okay, I thought Shanti was with you. I went to see Chauhan to make a little money.

–So, you know where I stay?

–I have an idea.

–You are not as stupid as I thought, Hari Singh. Why didn't you go to the police? I'm a wanted man.

–I know, but I would make more money for that information from Chauhan. He's working for a rich man. The police would just shake my hand.

–The only problem with your story is that it's not true.

–It's true, I'm telling the truth, said Hari Singh, his voice grew frantic, scared. Maybe Kasim had a gun pointing at his chest.

–No, you're lying, little man. I'll tell you why, before I took over Santana's racket, I checked out all my future partners. I know that Shanti is your friend, and that you two worked in insurance fraud before she became involved with Santana. He had a big mouth, and was a lazy, careless bastard. You know where Shanti is hiding, and the bitch has money and account details I need. Now where do I find her?

–I don't know, we split like you said, after she started working for Santana.

–Wrong answer, Hari Singh. Look at this, you know what this is right?

Silence.

I knew what that meant and the chances of storming the room without Hari Singh being shot were next to zero. Kasim's hand wouldn't shake. He'd had no qualms about trying to shoot Ice Baby and me earlier. I took the pistol out of my pocket. Placed a finger on the trigger.

–I've had a gun pointed at me before, said Hari Singh, but his voice was weak and getting weaker.

–A small-time loser like you probably has. *I'm* holding the gun this time. Last chance, where is your little whore?

–All right, take it easy, don't shoot. I'm not dying for her, I told her not to become involved with Santana, I really did.

The chairs creaked again as if Kasim had moved forward.

–You're too clever to die for a cheap whore like that. Address, and then you disappear for good. Next time I will just kill you, you understand?

–Yes. She has an apartment at the Pratap block, under a false name, Priti D'Souza, apartment 11, level 3. And look, Kasim, anything happens to me and your information goes to the police.

–Hmm, not so stupid eh? I understand. Is she hiding there

now?

–Yes.

Fingers tapped the desk.

–Now, about the detective. Did you see him about Prem Nath? And before you answer, remember that only Shanti knows where he is.

–I don't know anything about that, promise.

–What was he willing to pay you?

–I didn't see Chauhan about Prem Nath, you have to believe me.

–All right, don't shake so much, Hari Singh. No hard feelings. I don't kill people for no reason. You've told me the truth and that's all I wanted.

Thunder echoed across the skies. It was now or never. Kasim was going to kill Hari Singh. I knew that in my bones, even if Hari didn't.

–Let's go for a drive, just you and me, to find Shanti.

–I told you where she is, I...

–Shut up you bastard! You do as you're told.

I edged back to the other door and saw a chance. Chairs moved back, scraping against the tiles. I saw Kasim through the gap in the door, gun pointed and stepping back. He had a scar in the middle of his left cheek. It was a long dark face and he was nearly six foot, lean with eyes that didn't seem to move, fixed on Hari Singh. I tried to move my fingers, but they were frozen against the trigger. I willed a little blood into them.

Kasim slipped out of view and Hari Singh came out, wiping the sweat off his face. The blood returned to my fingers. I pulled the door open and fired a few shots. There was no one there. I fired again, at where I thought Kasim should be. A shot fired back around from the other door. Hari Singh slumped to the floor. A second shot. I rushed to the edge of the door, looked around. Footsteps ran along the dark corridor. I fired. Heard a door bang shut. Kasim was taking the stairs. Hari Singh was on the floor, lying still. He breathed heavily and his hands held his stomach trying to stop the blood and not doing a good job. I leaned over him.

–You'll be all right, try to hold on.

–It's no good Chauhan... I, I don't think I'll make it.

I rushed to the telephone on the desk and told the operator to send an ambulance, gave the address and said a man had been shot. The woman sounded more nervous than I did. I put the phone down and turned to face Hari Singh.

–Was that the right address you gave for Shanti?

–No.

He took deep breaths as if they were his last. I looked around for a towel or a cloth, nothing. There was a small coat on a chair. I grabbed it and told him to place it against his stomach. The blood was making one hell of a mess.

–Does Shanti know where Prem is being held?

He nodded.

–I have your money. I kept my end of the bargain. You know that Kasim was going to kill you, kill you both, I said.

–Yes, I guess so. I wasn't as smart as I thought. Look, you have to help Shanti. Kasim will kill her. She knows where Prem is... tell her I'm sorry.

–Hold on, you're not going anywhere. The ambulance is on its way.

I crouched down and lifted his head. Tears were rolling down his cheeks. He narrowed his eyes, blinking hard. He took a breath and spoke,

–Tell, tell Shanti I loved her... you tell her that.

–Sure, but hold on, you'll make it.

–She's staying in the apartment next to mine. Apartment 6 Oberoi buildings. She needs to leave now. Kasim will find her... look give her the money, she's a good woman, just became involved with the wrong crowd.

–Don't speak, I can hear the ambulance.

–I loved her, you tell her that...

He went limp in my arms, eyes staring at the ceiling. The

ambulance and police sirens were closing in. There wasn't time, I had to leave fast and find Shanti before Kasim did. I checked his pulse, but he was gone. I laid him down, closed his eyes. This was one game he shouldn't have played. Leaving the office, I took the fire escape and ran to my car. As I drove away, police jeeps and ambulances crossed my path, lights flashing, sirens, screeching to a halt outside the office building. They were too late, like they always are in bad movies. Too late for Hari Singh.

27

THE RAIN, rained. Bounced off the road, shone under the streetlight, flowed in the gutters. Hari Singh might have been small-time, peddling information to the highest bidder, but he'd taken a bullet to the stomach for a woman he loved. He hadn't sold her out. That took a different kind of courage. I wasn't sure about their relationship and so I'd have to be careful about breaking the news to her. The money was in my pocket and for once I wished I'd been able to pay it. Street lights cut across the rain, the sound of splashing cars and trucks surrounded me. It took a while but the bold black sign for Oberoi Apartments finally shone on my left, high on a new lit-up board. The building was a recently built tower block, some thirty floors high. Taking the elevator, I kept one hand on my Glock pistol, I didn't wish to run into Kasim unprepared.

She answered the door at the first bell, already packed and expecting Hari Singh with the pay off. She wore a long black rain coat and looked surprised to see me. After a little persuasion, we left the apartment. Fortunately, I had found her before the psycho had. I was in a hurry because I was certain now that Prem Nath hadn't walked into the sea.

We drove in silence around several blocks before I pulled the Contessa in next to a small park, making sure no-one had followed me. The wind blew the trees to the left as we stood under a canopy in the night. She lit a cigarette as she placed her small suitcase at her side. Smoke left her lips, curling up in the night air. Her eyes looked left and right, trying to see people in the distance, across the road, nervous, the cool poise and calmness long gone. The cigarette shook in her hand. I tapped the cigarette, watched the ash blow away from me towards her feet. She looked up, taking the cigarette out of her mouth.

–This is it. I'm leaving this mess for good. God, I should have left a long time ago. Where's Hari then?

–I told you, he's gone into hiding. Kasim found his whereabouts and Hari told me to give you the money.

She weighed my answer as she took a long drag of her cigarette.

–You have the one lakh with you?

–Yes, right here, but not before you tell me where I can find Prem Nath.

–If Kasim has found Hari, then they will move Prem tonight.

–No doubt, I said.

She tapped her cigarette and rubbed her forehead.

–I don't know how Kasim found Hari. We were very careful, I don't understand.

–You underestimated him. It happens.

She glanced around again. Only taxis seemed to be going past on this stretch of road and the occasional bus. The tyres increased the sound of the rain.

–I'd like to see the money first.

With a faint grin, I opened my jacket, pulled out a thick envelope and showed her the cash.

–Fifty thousand in cash. You get the other half when I find Prem. I'm trusting you, Shanti. I might never see you again after I hand over the cash.

I passed it to her reluctantly. She felt the weight, then made the envelope disappear under her long black coat.

–I didn't think it would end up like this, she said, –it had been so easy when Santana was running the outfit. We weren't making a fortune, but we got by nicely. I had never made so much money. I wanted Hari to join the racket as well, but he was always small-time. The problem with Hari is that he never thinks big.

–Was Hari Singh your boyfriend?

–No, I don't mix business with pleasure. And he had become clingy, you know what I mean?

She shrugged her shoulders and burnt the cigarette a little more.

–Yeah, I guess he loved you.

–He wouldn't know what love looked like and anyway he's not my type. We made money. Now look, he's gone into hiding when he should be here making more money. He is always small time.

She made me angry.

–You have the fifty thousand. Now, where do I find Prem?

She looked up. The smile left her face as she blew out the smoke and glanced around again.

–Prem, poor Prem, he was out of his league. There's a road leading out of Mumbai to the east. It heads into the mountain range towards Kolapur. You know it?

–Yes.

–There's a warehouse about twenty miles down that road, opposite the Shirdi Sai temple. You can't miss it. They're holding Prem there.

–You mean Kasim and his men?

–Yes.

–How do you know? The police think Prem drowned, that he walked into the sea.

She looked behind her again as if she expected to find Kasim. Instead she stared at some graffiti on the back wall, and it caught my eye too. It read, Deepa loves Rohit, with a heart shape drawn in red.

–That's the way Kasim planned it. They'd been following Prem for days, and when they saw him on the beach, drunk, they had their chance. Kasim boasted it had been too easy, and he might get into this kidnap racket full time.

I put a cigarette in my mouth, lit it up and took a drag. It didn't make me feel any better. Through the smoke, I could see her thinking quickly on her feet.

—All right, I said, —Let's say I believe your little story and Prem is there. How do you know about it?

She moved her weight onto her right leg and narrowed her eyes. She didn't like my question.

—Remember Manjit? After a few drinks, he became sweet on me. He had the idea that I was in love with him. Drink talks.

I blew out the smoke from the side of my mouth, tapped the cigarette. The ash flew away in the breeze.

—All right, say I accept that Manjit wasn't very bright for a moment, and couldn't keep a secret to save his life. I don't understand why you're turning on Kasim right now?

She held her cigarette in mid-air just in front of her face.

—You don't trust me very much, do you Chauhan? I'm telling the truth. Kasim, the bastard, tried to kill me the other night. If you hadn't pulled me down, I would have been dead. He promised that I was only to lure you into bed, to make you defenceless and he would manage the rest.

—And you believed him?

She looked at the ground.

—Look Chauhan, you don't say no to Kasim. No one does. We're all scared of him. I still am, and well, I want to thank you for saving my life, she said and touched my arm.

She looked vulnerable then and her reply seemed on the level.

—All in a night's work, Shanti.

She pressed my arm. —No, I mean it. That's why I'm helping you now. It's the reason I asked Hari to see you. We've decided to quit this horrible business right now.

—You only help people, when you want something, Shanti.

—Chauhan, I understand you don't trust me after what I've done but I'm telling the truth. You can take it or leave it.

The familiar toughness returned to her eyes. She stood straight, almost ready to leave.

–You can say that again. But I'm prepared to give you a chance, if you tell me the truth. Who's Kasim working for? I mean why would he hold Prem Nath?

–For the money, Chauhan. He's going to make a ransom demand for two crores. He promised us all a share and to make us rich. Only he planned to keep all the money and I saw it too late.

–Yes, but no ransom demand has been sent, Shanti.

–It will be.

I took my time to ask the next question and watched her carefully.

–Is Prem alive?

She raised her eyebrows and shrugged. The cigarette in her hand shook a little.

–I'm not sure. I think he is. He will be kept alive until the ransom demand is met. Then Kasim will kill him for sure.

–Did Dinesh Bakshi know about the blackmail racket?

She took her time, tapped the cigarette and met my eyes.
–Yes, he knew and he's a snake.

–Is Bakshi, a partner?

She took a step back, glanced round. She was still on edge, afraid. I doubted I could keep her here much longer.

–I don't think so. It was too small for him, until Kasim became involved. Look Chauhan, I need to leave now. I'm catching the train to Madras. I'll ring to collect the other fifty, if you're still alive.

I let the cigarette fall from my hand and put it out under my heel.

–Don't you want to find Hari Singh?

–No, I'm finally done with him, I'm done with this life. Believe it or not, I'm going to go straight from now on.

–You wouldn't know straight if it hit you on the head. For what it's worth, Hari told me he loved you.

That statement made no impression, she crushed the cigarette under her heel. She might as well have been crushing

Hari Singh under her shoe.

–Poor romantic fool. He became too possessive. No Chauhan, we're going our separate ways for good. I don't want to see that loser again.

I grabbed her wrist and looked into her eyes.

–That poor man, Shanti, took a bullet in the stomach for you. Didn't sell you out when Kasim pointed the gun at him. Did you hear that?

Her eyes widened, then she blinked quickly several times.

–That's right, poor Hari Singh took a bullet for you. When he lay dying in my arms, his last words were to tell you, he loved you. Though God knows why, because you're not worth his love, not that kind of love.

–Hari. Is he really dead? she said, and quick tears formed in her eyes and rolled out slowly.

–Yes, he preferred dying to selling you out. And when you're on the train counting the cash, you can think about that. Think how a romantic fool, who you didn't care a damn about, died rather than sell you out. It's you, who doesn't understand love Shanti, it's you.

I let go of her hand. She moved back pressing her wrist. The colour had drained from her face.

–I'm sorry. Oh God that's just so horrible. Poor Hari. I never thought they would go after him. I mean, I can't believe it.

She wiped her tears with a handkerchief and stared at me a long time with frightened eyes. She picked up her suitcase, crossed the road and flagged down a taxi. The Mumbai traffic made her disappear as if she had never existed. All I saw was the slanting rain, the back of cars and the exhaust fumes. You can't help the people you love. I hadn't meant to tell her about Hari Singh and how he had died in my arms. The rain, rained. Bouncing off the surface as thunder cleared its throat. I felt no better than before.

My watch showed, eight-thirty. The warehouse was two

hours away. Prem Nath could be dead or moved to another location. I needed a clear head. Kasim might have driven straight to the warehouse too. If that was the case, he had a head start. I hoped he had tried to find Shanti first and was searching for her even now. He would lose time. There were a lot of ifs running around my head. It was a long shot that Prem was even alive. Ice Baby could have told me sweet lies and made a fool out of me. This could be another long wild goose chase.

I had given her the money because Hari Singh wanted me to give it. She could be laughing all the way to Madras. I had to see this through however, for Hari Singh's sake, for Fernandez, for Prem's mother. Four men were dead, Santana, Raja, Khan and now Hari Singh. And Ice Baby walks away without a scratch and a cool fifty thousand rupees. Some people have all the luck.

28

TRAFFIC EASED as I headed east. Mumbai disappeared; noise, buildings, trains, the chaos all left behind. After an hour, I was on the road to the mountain range, and again I wondered whether Prem Nath was alive. Why was Kasim even holding him? There had been no ransom demand. I couldn't figure out what was going on but I knew some kind of dangerous game was being played. Death had brushed me twice where Scarface was concerned, third time I might not be so lucky.

The rain came again, and the wipers could hardly keep the glass clear. Trucks drove past with big headlights, beeping to make sure I stayed on my side of the road. From this point, the road became narrow and lights disappeared. Darkness fell like a damp heavy blanket to both sides of the road. The trees swayed in the breeze. Daytime, this would have been a luscious green cooling to the eyes. In the night, it filled me with foreboding.

I drove slowly and tried not to skid off the potholed road like a new driver and end up in a ditch. My tyres were in need of a change. Headlights flashed in the rain as it fell, slanted into the tarmac. I drove on, if no Sai Baba Temple appeared soon then she had sold me down the river. After another mile however, the rain eased, and the tyres started to grip the road. Thunder echoed across the skies again in a continuous rumbling sound.

Small lights shone to my right. It was the Shirdi Sai temple. A small white stone temple with a courtyard. The doors were closed. Shanti had that information correct and I felt like holding her again. There was no one there, not at this time and not on such a wet night. I parked off the road and got out. My pistol hugged my trouser belt.

The chill in the wind cut across my face with the odd raindrop. I looked at the temple and said,

–Well Sai, you can help me out here if you like.

I didn't receive a reply but there was no harm in asking. You never know, knock and the door might open, isn't that what the Christians claimed. So far, I'd been having doors slammed in my face. Religion was full of nice one-liners.

I looked across the road. The warehouse was set back around one hundred yards from the road. A wide dirt track led to the front, and tall trees and bushes surrounded it. No movement, only a block of darkness. Too quiet for my liking.

It was made of brick and had a slanting tiled roof running from back to front. I crossed the road slowly, came around the front. A dim light flickered underneath the closed wooden doors. There were no cars. It gave me hope that Kasim hadn't made it here yet, though maybe he had already taken Prem somewhere else. If that had happened, I was back to square one.

Instead of walking up to the front, I climbed the wooden fence at the side, which was wet on my fingers. A damp soil smell filled the air. The ground was soft under my shoes and the residue of rain touched my face. Leaves rustled in the breeze, creating a chorus of sound that was unpleasant. It was dark and treacherous. I was a long way from Mumbai.

There had to be at least two guns guarding the prize asset. Maybe they were playing cards or getting drunk. I could hope. The element of surprise was on my side, unless they had been watching my every move from some slit in the wall. I crept around the side, still no talking or movement from inside. No sound, nothing. I gritted my teeth. There was a side door but it was locked.

I moved further along the side of the warehouse stepping

over wet thorny bushes that grazed my legs. My shoes became muddy and would need a polish if I ever got out of this alive. At the back of the warehouse there was a small window, ten feet high and a light flickered from it at a distance. You could miss the dim light if you weren't looking for it. I walked further and tried another door at the back. Finally, it gave way and I entered to a strong smell of cow manure. It was in front of me, piled high in a large mound, but no cows. I cursed Ice Baby and kept my hand on the pistol. Flickering yellow lights cast shadows on the damp walls.

Slowly, I sneaked around the pile of manure. Two men in white turbans, white dhotis and black shawls, were warming their hands in front of a fire. I breathed a sigh of relief. They didn't look from any angle as if they worked for Kasim. These were rabaris, goat and cow herders. I felt I had just kissed goodbye to fifty thousand rupees. Ice Baby was laughing her head off somewhere.

The herders didn't seem to have a care in the world, men keeping warm on a cruel cold night. I came out of the shadows behind them. One of them turned his head. He had a mean look, big black moustache and stubble, then the other turned too. He didn't look so bright. They were both of stocky build and the yellow light of the fire shone on their faces.

–Rama, Rama, I said.

They didn't move at first, then both sprang to their feet, surprised and watchful.

–Rama, Rama, said the taller of the two.

I moved towards them, the pile of manure behind me. To my left there was a wooden door. Maybe it led to interesting places, or knowing my luck, to the cows.

–My car broke down, I said, –I need a place to keep warm for the night.

–Bhaiya, why didn't you knock on the door? You scared us, said the taller of the two before giving his partner a quick glance.

–I did knock. Maybe you didn't hear it. It's very windy outside, so I came around the back.

I moved closer to the fire, keeping my hands out, palms facing the fire, and felt the warmth.

–Yes bhaiya, very much rain. Come sit down, warm yourself.

I sat down on a black cotton blanket. They sat too, watchful, suspicious, which was only natural. They didn't seem to be carrying guns, though large cutting knives and a steel bar were near them.

–Do you mind if I sit here for the night?

–No problem, bhaiya, bad luck to break down on such a night, what's your name?

–Dilip, and yours?

–Bhanu, he said, and pointed an arm to his partner, –he's Ramu, but he doesn't speak much.

Ramu kept his dumb eyes upon me and he looked like trouble.

–Is this place yours? I asked.

–No, it belongs to Patil, we work for him. We tend the cows and pile the manure here as you can see.

–I don't see any cows, I said and smiled, but got no response in kind. They were men who didn't smile easily.

–No, no, we keep them on the farm, bhaiya, here only manure and tools.

–Is the farm far away?

–No, maybe you didn't see it in the dark, but there is a slope leading up to it from here. The farmhouse is some three hundred yards away.

He pointed his arm to his left.

They sat cross-legged. Ramu lit a bidi, smoked it, keeping his eyes upon me the whole time. There were people like him in most villages, they just stared at you as if you were a foreigner, and never said a word. It would be rude in polite society, though I doubted he needed to worry about that. I tried to ignore him.

A gun against these two probably wouldn't get me very far. It would be a physical contest one way or the other. They had the rugged wiry look of men who worked outdoors their whole lives. If I did pull the gun, one or both would pounce on me. I didn't want to have to kill them for no good reason. They had also thrown me off balance. I hadn't expected two cattle herders to be guarding such a rich prize as Prem Nath, if that's what they were doing.

I wanted to check behind the closed door. That was where I'd find Prem if he was even here. Unless he was dead under that pile of manure. If these two give me an evasive answer, then they couldn't be as innocent as they looked.

–Do you have a bathroom here?

–Yes, go through that door and it's to your right.

I smiled, so much for the evasive answer. It sounded too easy and if it was that easy, then Prem Nath wasn't here. I felt foolish and cursed Ice Baby again. I moved towards the door, the two rabaris stayed near the fire and didn't even look up.

The wind made a slow howling sound as it came through the numerous gaps in the front doors. If there was nothing but a bloody bathroom behind that door, then I'd be set for a long miserable drive home. I opened the door and glanced at the men. They were still sitting, palms showing against the fire. The sound of wood cracking and the manure smell filled the air. It was a dark corridor. Some light from the fire brightened it. I tried to adjust my eyes. It seemed like a series of cow stalls, minus the cows. I didn't like it.

–Bhaiya, switch the light on, it's to your right, walk further along.

I nodded and felt the wall with my hand. The light switch protruded against my hand and I switched it on. Low voltage light bulb hung from a dirty ceiling. Shadows reached out from every angle. There were about twenty separate stalls, with bundles of grass and metal chains in each with hooks and pegs in the ground. There were no cows and no bathroom. I moved to the right. In the fourth pen, I saw a man on the floor.

He had a gaunt looking bearded face, his clothes were ripped and stained with blood. His face marked and bruised, and both his hands chained to the metal pegs at either side. He looked up, blinking, as I entered and shook his head. He had seen better days that was for sure. –Help me, for God's sake, help me, he said weakly.

–Prem?

He nodded. His eyes grew wide as if to warn me. I heard a shuffle from behind. Too late. I felt a heavy blow to the back of my head. Pain shot through my skull as I staggered forward and fell to the floor.

29

A THROBBING pain suggested the back of my head was still intact. My head was resting on a big soft cushion, and I had no idea where I was. I tried to move as my brain remembered what to do. My hands, however, were tied behind my back with a thick rope along with my legs. Those tricky rabaris had moved fast and had a lot to answer for. A red light squeezed through my eyelids from a lamp in a corner. A smoke smell lingered. It came from a cigarette placed between fine red lips. I had seen those red lips before, maybe I was dreaming. My eyes tried to focus. I couldn't have reached heaven so quickly, not on my charge sheet. Besides smoking would be banned in heaven, or maybe not.

I was only glad that smoke had replaced the manure smell. I was packed tight like a nice Diwali present. A woman's face looked at me through the swirling smoke. Rain tapped against the windows as my senses scrambled to figure out the danger I faced. Purple curtains were drawn, and they contrasted against the stark white walls. I hadn't expected the woman sitting across the table to be here.

–I thought Sleeping Beauty would never wake.

–Sleeping Beauty wasn't hit on the back of the head. Am I in heaven, Mrs Fernandez?

A smile lit her eyes as she held the cigarette in mid-air.

–You're in the farmhouse, which is about three hundred yards from the warehouse.

I tried to move, but the rope only cut into my skin. It was no use, I was tied good, those rabaris had practice.

–You didn't have to go to all this trouble, you could have

called me.

–Still think this is funny, Chauhan?

–I've had bigger laughs. Where are those goat herders, digging my grave?

–Not a bad guess, she said, with a slight smile, –you're in big trouble this time. I told you to leave this alone, but you didn't listen. Now, I feel sorry for you.

–You can cut these ropes, baby, instead of feeling sorry.

–I have no wish to die, thank you.

She blew the smoke from the side of her mouth and tapped the cigarette into a glass ashtray. I watched her a moment from my horizontal position on the sofa.

–Can I have a drink then?

She thought about that as if I had asked her to sleep with me. She crossed her right leg over her left. She wore grey cotton trousers and a beige coloured half-sleeved shirt. The diamond bracelet on her right wrist shimmered in the evening light. The room's white walls had paintings of hunting scenes, a tiger being shot, a lion eating a deer. The floor had grey granite tiles. Nothing seemed to match. The white ceiling fan wasn't in the centre. It seemed like an afterthought and was fitted carelessly. There was only one door behind her, two windows with the purple curtains drawn.

Then she rose, poured out a neat glass of Johnny Walker whisky. She came over and helped me to sit straight, held my head and let me drink. The whisky revived me. She put the glass on the table and stood looking at me.

–You're too good a man to die like this.

–I was thinking exactly the same thing.

–I'm sorry, Chauhan. We never thought you would get this far.

She moved back across to her sofa chair, as I looked at her nice legs. It wasn't a bad memory to take to heaven.

–I found Prem, I said.

Her eyes narrowed as if it hurt her conscience. She placed

the cigarette to her mouth and looked uncomfortable.

–Yes, I know. Don't worry about Prem. He's fine, well, for now. He turned out to be very stubborn. What is it with you men? You always seem to take the hard road. No sense in being practical. You had the money, you could have walked away but no, you had to find your way here. I told you a dozen times to stay away, Chauhan.

–You did. What time is it?

–Eleven-thirty. Why, do you have somewhere special to go?

–I have some ideas. How long do I have, Maya?

She paced the floor in front of the sofa and looked like she was thinking of something else. She looked at her wristwatch.

–Thirty minutes, at best, she said, and her voice weakened.

–You understand what Scarface will do to me, when he returns?

She was silent, narrowed her eyes and dragged on her cigarette a long time, and blew out the smoke slowly. Before she paced back and forth.

–Yes, I know what he will do, Chauhan.

I'd been in trickier situations, but this was up there in the top ten. Once Scarface returned, it was curtains. He might even torture me before killing me. He was that kind of sadistic bastard. I had to think quick, and I had an idea, but it was a lousy trick to play.

–You really surprised Bakshi. I never heard him so angry on the phone before, she said, moving towards the window, she peeked through the curtains.

–I knew that snake was involved. Does this place belong to him?

She turned around. –Yes. It belongs to him. It hadn't looked so complicated at the start. And everything would have been fine if you hadn't come nosing around. People die, wherever you go Mr Chauhan.

I leaned forward.

–You want to tell me what all this is about?

She moved away from the window, came to the table and poured herself a glass of whisky. She put out her cigarette in the ashtray and took a long sip. Then she stood across from me and looked for long moments, as if undecided about how to answer my question.

–Last wishes of a dying man?

I grinned. –That wouldn't be my last wish.

I tried to loosen the rope around my wrists. She watched me struggle.

–When Kasim arrives here, he's going to kill you. Aren't you afraid?

–No one likes that idea very much. And to think we were starting to get along.

She took her glass to the window again and peeped out. She appeared to be anxious and I searched the room for a sharp object to cut my ropes. There was nothing but the whisky glass on the table. I started thinking about how I could smash the glass. Frantic thoughts rushed around my head and none of them seemed to help. The minutes counted down faster than I could ever remember. –Why didn't you leave this case alone? she said, half-turning, –Bakshi wasn't concerned about you.

–If you feel like that, you can let me go. I promise I'll never return.

To my surprise, she seemed to consider it.

–What would I say to Kasim?

–Say I broke free.

She thought about that too. A glimmer of hope. Twenty minutes, and time was running out to convince her.

–How exactly?

–Release me first Maya. I'll tell you.

She hesitated.

–They wouldn't believe me. They would kill me along with you. No one crosses Kasim, not even Bakshi.

–Maya, they'll kill you after they get what they want, trust me.

–Bakshi isn't a murderer.

–No, he only asks Kasim to do it.

–You have no proof, Chauhan.

I tried to wriggle free with greater effort, but the ropes just grazed my skin.

–What's Bakshi have on you anyway? You don't have to be afraid of him.

She closed the curtain and turned around.

–It's all too late. You should have stayed away, Chauhan.

I didn't like to hear that. I gritted my teeth and looked up at her. Her eyes were thinking things through very quickly, and her breathing was shallow. I tried again.

–The police will catch up soon enough and you'll be spending jail time. Bakshi isn't just a property developer. He's a blackmailer, has connections to the underworld and is a murderer. He won't leave you in peace, after he has everything. You know too much about him.

–Bakshi wouldn't do anything to me. Besides he likes me.

I grinned and looked up into her eyes. –Yes, I forgot, you have a special talent for finding Mr Right.

–I do, don't I? No, you're wrong Chauhan. Bakshi will look after me.

–He has that psycho working for him. Tonight, Scarface killed a harmless man. I saw him shoot him. Who do you think told him to do that?

She blinked several times and anxiety hardened her features.

–Kasim works for himself. He protects Bakshi and that's all I know. Don't place this horrible situation on me, Chauhan.

–Maya, they're going to kill me. My murder will be on your conscience.

It occurred to me then as my life lay in the balance to say something more. To play the idea I had before and to see how it ran.

–One more thing Maya, what about my boy? You know the boy in the photograph back in my office that you asked about. Well, his name's Sunil and he'll be left without anyone to support him if I die.

–You didn't mention you had a son.

–Well, I do. After his mother ran away, the responsibility fell on me.

She stared at me a long time and leaned her weight on her right leg. The eyes lost their cold stare. Ten minutes or so remained. She narrowed her eyes and bit her lower lip again. Such moments decided life and death. Then she rushed to the window and stared out. She looked frantic, came back, took out a penknife from her trouser pocket and cut my ropes. I stood, rubbed my wrists. Blood flowed freely into my hands and feet. I kept the knife. We hurried to the window. I saw the warehouse down the slope drive, a light flickered from the doors. The fire was still burning. I turned around. She moved back, breathing quickly, eyes frantic.

–You don't know what this means. I owe you for this, Maya.

–Thank your boy for this. Now, stop talking and go. Go before it's too late, before Kasim arrives.

I held her by the shoulders. She was shivering.

–Not so fast. Tell me how you're involved.

–Oh, it's no bloody use, you wish to die. Don't blame me in the afterlife.

–Look, time is running out before Mr Smiley returns, so tell me everything.

–You're impossible, Chauhan. Okay, Bakshi wants to buy the mansion. Only Joseph won't sell, says his wife died there. He's still bloody married to her you know, he'll never forget her.

–I know that already.

–Aren't we clever? she said, moving back.

I felt in my pockets. The car keys were there but the pistol was missing. I guess the cattle herders had no use for a car.

–Where's my gun? Do the herders have it down there in the warehouse?

She weighed her reply, and her eyes were wide but a little calmer.

–No, it's here. They gave it to me.

She took it out of a bag near the chair. I checked it. It was full. They had been too trusting of Mrs Maya Fernandez. I placed the gun in my coat pocket, felt the bump on the back of my head. It was sticky with dried blood, but it would hold for now. I felt like shoving the two rabaris up a buffalo's backside. I glanced out of the window. There was no movement, but the rain had eased, even as the breeze picked up.

–Is Prem still down there?

She nodded.

–What's your involvement? I can help you out of this.

She looked up into my eyes and seemed to make a quick final decision.

–All right, when Bakshi discovered that Joseph had given Prem a twenty-five percent stake in the mansion, he went crazy. That's when he planned to kidnap Prem. He wanted Prem to sell his stake and force Joseph to sell the rest, only problem was that Prem preferred dying to signing over the deeds. They tried everything but he's tough, God he's tough. He was in the army you know, and now they're going to kill him. That's when I became afraid. I heard Kasim talking about it. I never agreed to any killing and Bakshi promised me. I don't believe him anymore. When I asked him, he threatened to kill Prem if I didn't go along with his plans. Then you turned up, and everything went out of control.

–Why are you involved in this? You have everything.

She looked at the granite tiled floor with defeat in her eyes.

–People think so. I have very little, Chauhan. I met Bakshi at Rubies and he promised me five crores. If I could convince Joseph to sell the mansion to him. But Joseph is stubborn, and I can't back out now. Kasim would kill me.

She looked very alone then, and I wanted to hold her in a warm embrace, but I held back.

–Yeah, Kasim's a bag of laughs all right. I don't know what made you trust these kind of men.

She sighed.

–I was miserable and looking for a way out. Anita hates me, Joseph's indifferent. I'm entitled to some happiness. Joseph made me sign a prenup before I married him. Only one and a half crores if I ever divorced him. You do the maths.

The shadows in the room seemed to grow. The wind seeped through the gaps under the front and back doors. I felt it on my skin. It was gloomy and I wanted to move, but I still had a few questions left.

–I didn't think he had it in him, I said, –One and a half is still a lot of money, Maya. You should've taken it.

–It's peanuts. Joseph made a fool out of me, she said, and a little fire ignited in her eyes.

I took a moment to let her anger cool.

–You mean you became greedy, I said.

–I should have let you die!

She breathed quickly.

–You should control that temper, I said.

–Go to hell!

I placed a hand on her shoulder. She shrugged it away.

–Why didn't you go to the police, Maya?

–Bakshi owns the police. Besides he transferred one crore into my account as a gesture of good will.

I smiled with my eyes. –And you're having a hard time returning it?

–You don't go back on a deal with Bakshi.

I shook my head.

–We lead interesting lives, Maya.

She stepped back and raised her nose in the air.

–You won't find yours interesting when Kasim returns.

–Let me deal with Mr Smiley.

She placed a hand on my shoulder.
–Please go and never come back. I don't want you to die.
I took hold of her hand.
–That's the nicest thing you've said, Mrs Fernandez.

I moved her to the sofa and sat her down. I picked up the ropes from the floor, tied her hands and feet and put her horizontally on the sofa.

–When Kasim returns, you'll explain that I had a hidden penknife, and became free. You keep him here as long as you can.

I tied a cloth around her mouth.

–Stay still, beauty. I'll be back for you shortly once I free Prem and hopefully before Kasim returns. Remember to tell the story straight.

Her eyes stared compellingly in the room light, a mixture of fear and hope. They were pretty eyes, but time had run out. I heard a car on the gravel drive. Headlights were dimmed. Maybe we'd talked for too long. I hurried out the back of the house, took a route along the far side of the hedge until I had the cover of trees. The wind drove rain into my face and made the tree leaves shimmer and drip. I watched Kasim park the car next to the tractor and step out. He was alone. Maybe Bakshi was in another car following behind.

Kasim looked taller in the dark, an imposing figure in his black coat. There was no hurry in his movements. He stared down at the warehouse. As the rain eased, Kasim walked to the front door, opened it and disappeared inside. I worked my way down to the warehouse, keeping off the gravel. The wet grass covered my shoes. Kasim would come after me shortly. There was no time left for mistakes.

30

THE WAREHOUSE stood tall, dark and threatening. The fire light flicked through the half open doors. Wind hit the back of my head as I pulled out the pistol. Kasim would have warned the herders to be on extra alert. I'd try not to shoot both these rabari clowns. They were pawns. I reached the doors. Agitated voices could be heard. My two friends were having a disagreement.

–I'm going, *sala*.

–You can't. Kasim will kill us.

–I don't care. We hit an inspector. The *policewallas* won't be far behind. We'd better run. Kasim's paying us peanuts anyway.

–No, Kasim doesn't forget. Remember he warned us. He'll come after us and kill our children too if we cross him.

–We can deal with him later. Let's go now!

–We can't.

–Die here then, Bhanu.

The doors swung open, and the man in all white looked a moment at the main house. He darted out over the gravel drive to the front of the warehouse and ran across the road, with his white dhoti flying in the air...

–Wait, *sala*! shouted his partner.

No luck, the man was gone. Lights in the farmhouse were switching on, one by one. Kasim had started a careful search. I came round the door, saw the back of Bhanu warming his big hands on the fire. I swung my pistol onto the back of his thick head. He grunted and fell to his knees. I moved around to face him.

–What goes around, comes around, asshole.

He stared at me with a painful grimace and fell near the fire, out cold. I shoved the gun back into my pocket, searched his pockets. I found a key and hurried towards the side door. I pushed it open and switched on the lights. Prem Nath looked up with blinking eyes. He looked pale and took short breaths. I used the key to release his chains. He coughed as I walked him back towards the fire. I sat him down next to it. The warmth revived him a little but not by much. –I'm Detective Chauhan. Can you hear me Prem? I'm here to get you out.

He nodded. –Water...water.

A half-filled bottle of cheap desi daru was to my left. I put it to his lips. Prem gulped it down and coughed.

–Take is easy. Can you walk?

He nodded but he struggled to balance sitting down and pushed out his arms to either side. I would have to carry him to the car. I placed my head around the door. All the lights were off in the main house and a warning bell sounded in my ear. There was no movement from there. For all I knew Kasim could be squeezing Maya's little neck.

I turned back inside. Prem looked up, dark beard and cut marks on his face and gaunt looking. They had starved him and he had held out. I couldn't carry him to the car, not without becoming a sitting duck. And I had to think about Maya. I stood behind the heavy doors, the Glock in my right hand, and looked up the slope again at the dark farmhouse. Only one thing would work. I'd have to go after Kasim.

Kasim however beat me to the first move. Two figures finally left the front door and slid to the car. I was glad Mrs Fernandez was alive. I didn't think he would suspect collusion. She could talk clever. Wind hurried down the slope and pushed against the doors as if to warn me. Trees swayed in the dark and the leaves rustled. Kasim was coming for me now, coming for Prem. There wouldn't be any more chances. I heard the car engine start and my stomach shifted slightly. Mr Smiley had managed to get under my skin.

Those dim headlights came on and the black hulking SUV trundled down the gravel slope like a hearse. The heavy tyres grinding into the drive. I kept my gun pointed. The SUV stopped at forty yards. Two figures were still behind the glass and I wondered whether Kasim was waiting for back up. Kasim switched on the headlights to full, forcing me to place my arm across my face. A door opened and she stepped out. Kasim slid out from the same side and stood behind her. The way Maya Fernandez hesitated and moved told me that a gun was nestling in the small of her back. That's why Kasim had kept her alive, I got it now.

–Chauhan! she shouted. –Give up, it's no good!

Prem fell sideways onto the ground with a slight groan and closed his eyes. I didn't know how long he would last without urgent medical attention.

–Give up, Chauhan, said Kasim. –Hold your hands up and no one gets hurt.

–Leave the jokes to me! I shouted back. –I tell them better.

–Your choice. Walk out towards me or Mrs Fernandez gets shot.

–Kill her you coward and I kill you.

I glanced back at Prem. He was breathing but otherwise quite still. I crouched down and peeked round the door again. Kasim kept Maya in front of him like a shield, as they moved closer to the car. The breeze blew across the ground and a couple of empty cans rattled in the distance. It was a standoff. He wouldn't shoot her without first getting a clean shot at me. And I didn't want to shoot Maya or have her catch a bullet in the cross fire. Sweat formed on my forehead.

–*Please* Chauhan, she called out with desperation in her voice. –Give us Prem and we will leave. No shooting. No one gets hurt.

–Your offer is politely declined. I just can't stand the psycho by your side.

–Keep up the jokes, Chauhan, shouted Kasim. –They're

going to be your last.

Kasim ducked his head down and two bullets splintered the heavy doors above my head. Maya screamed, and it carried along the breeze and out into the night. I squatted down, peeked round the door, then set my Glock to work. I took out both the headlamps. I watched them crouch down to the side of the car. With a groan, the rabari shifted on the ground. He was tough but there was no way he should be waking so quickly. Rain started to dart down again, a flash of lightning, then thunder. The light lit everything up for a moment. They were by the side of the car.

–Chauhan, let it go, she shouted. –This doesn't concern you. Release Prem and we leave. We only want Prem.

–Okay, I said, –I'll bring him out. Don't shoot.

–I won't shoot, said Kasim.

I saw them stand again, but he still had her in front of him. The rain cut into them from the side, and the water flowed in small channels down towards me.

–Is that your word Kasim? I shouted.

–My word.

I glanced back. The herder was on his knees and feeling the back of his head. He really did have a thick skull. I helped him up. He didn't know where he was. I pushed him in front and I stood behind him. Then I opened the door. We moved out slowly as the wind and rain hit our faces. The two shadowy figures stepped away from the car and walked ten yards towards us.

Kasim pushed Maya Fernandez ahead. I held the groggy goat herder. They came down the slope. At twenty yards or so, Kasim shoved Maya to one side. She fell sideways with a shout. His gun flared. The herder groaned and slumped back against me. I fired three shots. Kasim fired again, but the bullet went over my head. Then the gun dropped from his hand and his fingers grasped his stomach. He fell to his knees. I let the rabari slide to the ground. He was covered in blood. I moved towards Kasim, with the rain in my face, and the wind howling through the trees.

Kasim was staring up at my face. Anguish and pain on his miserable face. His hands couldn't stop the blood.

–I knew you were a bastard, I said.

Those were the last words he heard. Kasim fell face first into the mud.

The rain ran down my face and over my coat. I sucked in the air. I looked at the dark clouds above. It had been a long time since I had killed a man, and the feeling wasn't much better this time either. I was glad that I was alive and Kasim dead, though. It was definitely better this way around. Maya Fernandez touched my arm.

–Is Prem dead?

–No. That was one of Kasim's men.

–Oh God, you're the Devil incarnate, Chauhan. But I'm so glad you are.

She came close and rested her head on my shoulder. The rain grew louder, and the wind rushed down the slope, passing over Scarface's dead body.

31

MONDAY WAS a clear, sunny day, but there was a chill in the air keeping me on edge. Sparrows twittered outside PSI Thankey's office. They always sounded the same. Maybe they only had two songs on their album. Thankey walked inside carrying a file and sat behind the desk. He looked like a man who'd been awarded a big pay rise. He placed the file on the desk and grinned.

–I don't know how to thank you, Detective Chauhan.

–A favour for a friend. You can return it in the future if you feel like it.

I glanced around the office, there were fewer missing persons on the board. They were making progress at last.

–I'd bet a million that Prem Nath had walked into the sea. Shooting Kasim in self-defence was fine too. Though I doubt Dhanwan and the homicide boys gave you any credit.

I leaned back in the chair and showed him my palms.

–Dhanwan doesn't share credit. That's why I called you first to the farm house. So you can bask in the limelight for a while.

Thankey's grin widened.

–I appreciate it. The bosses will stop breathing down my neck for a few years. By the way, I had to hand over the little red book to Dhanwan. He insisted on that.

Thankey lifted his plump shoulders and dropped them.

–No worries. I couldn't crack too many codes in there anyway. Perhaps the homicide boys can work it.

–There are bright young officers in Homicide now. Very computer savvy.

–Yeah, but they haven't got our experience, Thankey.

Thankey nodded slowly and played with a silver pen.

–Any information about Bakshi? I asked.

–He's on the run. Dhanwan raided his business premises. Dhanwan wants that glory so bad.

–Yeah it figures. Bakshi's a big scalp.

–Dhanwan is a first-class donkey, said Thankey, in a lowered voice. –He tramples over people's feelings to get ahead. You should return to the force. We could really do with you here.

–I'm fine working for myself.

An assistant brought in two cups of chai on a plastic tray and placed it on the desk. The sweet smell entered my nostrils. I took a sip from the white cup, not bad. Thankey took a sip after blowing over the rim. Then he leaned back in his chair.

–I'm just an ordinary PSI. Reasonably honest. As honest as you can expect in a city where it went out of fashion a long time ago, he said and narrowed his eyes. –Prem's recovering in hospital. He's one tough young man. The army training helped him through that ordeal. It wasn't easy facing Kasim. But the thing is I like the law to win. I know I won't rise up the ranks like Dhanwan, I'm not smart or devious enough for that.

–You're all right, Thankey, I said. –Don't be too hard on yourself. You'll be fine, if you keep your head down and work honestly. It's when you become arrogant that you get your head blown off.

Thankey nodded again with pursed lips.

–True, very true. But I don't understand what they had on Mrs Fernandez. How was she involved?

–It's a long story. In short Bakshi threatened to kill her if she didn't cooperate.

Thankey stared at me as if he half believed me. The phone rang with that sense of urgency it seems to take on when there's hot news travelling down the line. He picked up the receiver and leaned forward on the desk.

–Yes, PSI Thankey here. What's that you say, Gopal?

Excellent. Just the news for a Monday morning. Yes I understand.

He put the phone down with a big wide grin.

—Surprise me, I said.

—Dhanwan's arrested Bakshi at the domestic airport. He was wearing a false beard. We have our man.

I leaned back in my chair and felt a quiet satisfaction.

—Good news, I said, —But it won't be easy to nail him down. Bakshi will employ the best lawyers - or should I say the best liars.

—No, Bakshi's doing jail time. We have stacks of evidence against him and a living witness in Prem, who won't be intimidated, said Thankey, and then rubbed his forehead with the pen. —Chauhan, you stuck your neck out for this. I hope the fees are worth it.

I shook my head and grinned.

—I'll probably receive my usual fee of fifteen hundred plus expenses.

Thankey laughed.

—I don't know why we bother. Call centre advisors make more money with their sales bonuses *sala*, and they don't put their lives on the line.

—It's a crazy world.

I stood up and looked at the missing persons board again. New faces were on it, one or two young women. It seemed like an endless game. People disappeared and we had to go find them. Sometimes we were lucky but most of the time, people just dropped out of the system, or should I say life.

Thankey had stood too. Now he leaned over the desk and shook my hand.

—I owe you, Chauhan. Where are you heading now?

—Hopefully to get paid by Mr Fernandez.

—Rich people are tight with their money.

—That's why they have it. Take care, Thankey.

I walked out of the station with a light step. The sparrows

continued singing their morning song. It sounded nice but still didn't make sense. The tall Neem tree in the front compound had spread its branches over the wall, and two squirrels ran up the bark. Bakshi had been arrested and that was a relief. The fresh breeze touched my face as I reached my car. It was the kind of day where you were glad to be alive, and out in the open. I placed a hand on top of the car, it was cool to the touch.

I stood a moment thinking about Saturday night. The mayhem at the farmhouse seemed like a distant memory. Some things stayed with me. Like the final crazed look on Kasim's face. I shuddered. He was dead now and that was all that mattered. I lit a cigarette and recalled the surprise in Thankey's voice when I called him from the farmhouse. How the local force arrived first and the whole place swarmed with police, forensics, ambulances and photographers. How we rushed to the local hospital with the sound of sirens going off around us.

Then later, the arrival in the night of Dhanwan with his angry face, because I hadn't called him first. His angry words when I told him I'd killed Kasim in self-defence.

'Chauhan, you think you're smart but you're not. You risked Mrs Fernandez and Prem Nath's life, and you could have all died. You should have phoned me first instead of coming out here like a bloody hero! The next time you pull a stunt like that, I will put you behind bars!'

That was how Dhanwan railed. No congratulations or well done for solving the case. Not that I cared for his compliments. I recalled the look on the constables and Thankey's faces. All of them thinking one thing, Dhanwan was a donkey. They congratulated me after Dhanwan left. It all played out in my mind's eye, as I slept late into Sunday, even when I drank in quiet celebration. I wondered if I hadn't overlooked some angle in the case. And the big question, what was I going to do with Mrs Fernandez? She had looked nervous when I'd given my statement to the police. A few words from me and she'd be behind bars. I still had to decide about that.

I finished the cigarette and crushed it under my heel.

Then I recalled how Prem's mother had embraced me at the hospital, tears streaming down her cheeks. She hadn't said a word, yet that had been the most satisfactory moment of the case. Santana, Raja, Khan and Hari Singh, had died. Singh a small-time peddler of information, finally caught out in a big man's world. And of course, Ice Baby. She was probably sitting happily in South India drinking a cocktail. She might phone me for the remaining cash, but I doubted it now. What I did know was, she would stay as far away from the police and this case as possible.

I tapped the top of the car. Kasim had been dealt with but I had made a powerful enemy in Bakshi. He wouldn't forget me in a hurry. There was no point in worrying about it now.

At last, I sat inside and drove to Malabar Hill. I hoped there were no film dances in the middle of the road, I didn't want to keep Joseph Fernandez waiting a second time. I wasn't sure how much he was going to pay, as he had already paid three lakhs. He had insisted however that I see him before starting another case.

32

IT WAS mid-day by the time I drove up to the white gates. Sun gleamed off the smooth walls, palm trees swayed in the cool breeze. A woman in an elegant pink sari walked a small dog across the road. It was fresher down here, closer to the calm sea than back in the city. I parked the car and stepped out. I always seemed to be returning to the Fernandez mansion, and I hoped this was the final time. I'd thought that a few times already, and here I was again. I skipped that thought and entered through the open gates.

Gardeners smiled as they trimmed hedges. The chauffeur acknowledged me with a nod as he leaned against the Mercedes. There was also a large van with the back doors open. Two men placed boxes inside and I wondered what they were doing here. I knocked on the door. To my surprise, Anita Fernandez welcomed me. She wrapped her arms around me and held me tight with a bright smile. She led me into the lounge, her eyes were alive, and not dreamy or sad. She wore a red shalwar kameez with a white flowery design on it. A change. It was the first time I'd seen her in Indian clothes. They suited her very well. She held my hand firmly.

–You don't know how happy I am to see you! Now before you open your mouth Abhay Chauhan, I want to say something. I know you have an appointment with Papa, but just give me five minutes.

–Have ten, Anita, I said, with a slight smile.

–First of all, I want to say a big sorry. I mean that. My word for the next few months is sorry. I said sorry to Papa, to Prem and oh, to just about everyone I can think of.

–Okay, so you're sorry.

The sunlight streamed through the French doors and spread light on the marble floor.

–When I heard you had found Prem, well I just couldn't believe it. I felt so happy and laughed like a lunatic. Can you imagine that?

I can.

She let go of my hand and twirled in the middle of the room. The sunlight brightened her shalwar kameez and flying dupatta. She looked lovely then and carefree. Someone who was stepping into the light. I felt a gladness in my heart I hadn't felt for a while. She did several turns, stopped and smiled.

–I thought you didn't care about Prem, I said.

–I used to think that but when I saw him in hospital, lying on the bed, full of bandages and tubes sticking out of his arm; I realised how much he loved Papa and me. They had tortured, starved and beat him and Prem still didn't sign over the house. I thought Prem was like all the rest but he's different. He loves me.

–Don't put the poor fellow through any more tests, you might end up killing him.

She tilted her head. –Now cutie, I know you liked me...but my husband has returned.

I leaned back on my heels with a smile. –Oh, you heart breaker.

We shared a smile.

–I'm going to miss you, Abhay Chauhan. I mean that, she said, and punched my arm gently.

–Did you say, your husband?

–Yes my husband. We're starting a fresh and I'm going to be nice. I have you to thank for this, she said and gazed down at her shoes.

–I think you actually mean that, Anita.

She smiled again and clasped her hands in front of her. –I like you, okay. You haven't heard the best news yet.

She came close and I could feel her breath in my ear as she whispered.

–The best news of all, Maya is leaving the house. She asked for a divorce and for once Papa stood up to her and said yes. She's finally out of our house.

She stood back trying hard to suppress a smile.

–And oh, my brother is returning back from Europe as well. I haven't been this happy in a long time.

I thought she was going to do another twirl. The divorce news surprised me, at the suddenness of it, and although I didn't like to hear it, it was the right thing to do. Why go on living a lie?

My face must have darkened a shade because she said,

–Don't look too happy for us, Chauhan.

She came forward and kissed me on the left cheek.

–Wait here and I'll send Papa. I have so much to organise. I'm preparing a big welcome home party for Prem and my brother.

–Not so fast, Anita. Are you on the level? You're really going to keep away from the Santana types?

–I promise.

She placed her hands comically on her heart. I shook my head slightly and narrowed my eyes.

–If you're not, then let Prem walk away free now.

–Don't be like that. I promise to go straight. Happy now?

I didn't know if I believed her, but I wanted to. I doubted the marriage would last six months, still, I wasn't going to rain on her parade. She looked good for once and it was nice to see her happy and sober. She twirled out of the room like a fresh spring breeze and left me standing there once more gathering my senses. Anita Fernandez was one hell of a young woman and I wished her all the best for the future. She wasn't perfect, but how many people are?

I looked at the large oil portrait. Mrs Fernandez was still trying to find my flaws but the man behind her, seemed to have relaxed. Had so much happened in such a short time? It seemed like only yesterday that I was standing here and about to go looking for Santana. A few days can be a long time. Now, once again I was waiting for Joseph Fernandez. Rich people. They always make you wait.

The side door opened but it wasn't Anita or her father. Instead MD appeared. His dark grey eyes looked colder than the first time. It took me a moment to adjust. He sucked out all the happiness of meeting Anita. He moved towards me with a peculiar gait and I became wary of him. We were never going to be beer buddies, he just didn't have the personality.

–You should try and smile sometimes MD, it's good for your health.

All I received was a hard stare. –Life seems funny to you, doesn't it?

–Life is what you make it. I don't like seeing miserable people, that's all.

–I don't find you funny at all, Chauhan.

–I'll live. We could talk all day but I'd like to see Mr Fernandez.

He stood like a bouncer and looked as if he wanted to throw a right fist. There was no getting along with some people. Before he could punch me, the door opened, and Fernandez entered. He was wearing a white suit with a beige, open collared shirt. He looked like one of those distinguished English gentlemen you see on the TV at the Lords cricket ground. Meanwhile MD stared at me and the word hate came to my mind. I couldn't understand how I had ruffled his feathers so much. He turned and gave a short nod to Fernandez.

–Sir, I will be in the hall if you need me.

–No listening behind closed doors, I said.

He walked out and closed the door. Fernandez shook my hand and we sat down near the far end where a new desk and a couple of chairs had been arranged.

–I don't know where to begin, Abhay Chauhan. You have

exceeded my expectations.

–I guess I got lucky along the way. How's Prem?

Fernandez took a moment to think, looked down first, then raised his head slowly.

–He's doing fine, considering what the poor boy has been through. This calls for a celebration.

He pressed a button at the side of the desk. Fernandez moved towards the chair and pulled it out. I couldn't figure out what he was thinking. He didn't look happy, unlike Anita. Maybe the strain of the whole event had finally worn him down a little. A butler hurried inside with a tray and two glasses of whisky and soda. The man passed a glass to Fernandez first, then to me.

–To your health, Detective Chauhan.

–I won't argue with that.

We raised our glasses. The whisky tasted smooth and I felt better.

–I met Anita just now and she said you had made some decisions.

His expression didn't change as he held his glass in mid-air.

–Ah yes, I have won back my freedom. I'm afraid it's for the best. Maya is packing her suitcase as we speak.

–I'm sorry to hear that.

Fernandez shook his head and took a stiff drink.

–I've lost an unhappy wife but gained a happy daughter and Prem. Life could be a lot worse.

–That's a good way to look at it, I said, and took a sip.

–Under the circumstances, it's the only way to look at it. Maya explained her involvement and apologised. She actually asked me to forgive her, after what she had done. I can't do that so easily, so I decided upon a divorce. I should have done it years ago to be honest.

I watched Fernandez as creases formed on his forehead. I wondered what she had left out of her explanation.

–It's all done and dusted now, he continued, –I'm still

young, but the next time I'll watch the age gap more carefully. Now do you wish to tell me how you found Prem?

I had no particular wish to go through the whole story again, so I explained it briefly.

–You see Mr Fernandez, Kasim had decided to take over the racket from Santana. He found them too careless, which they were. When Manjit shot Santana, he hadn't expected me to be there and he panicked and ran. I took a little red book from Santana, a piece of luck that helped me. It opened doors that otherwise would have remained shut. The police will find more connections to Bakshi from that book, although Prem will provide the main evidence against him.

–I never thought Bakshi would stoop so low. All this scheming, just for a plot of land.

I held my glass in mid-air.

–Greed should never be underestimated. A hundred new apartments at three crores each. It's a lot of money Mr Fernandez, as you said.

–No doubt. And it turned my dear wife's head. No wonder she was constantly nagging me to sell the house.

I took a long sip and put the glass down on the table.

–Well, that was a part of it. Bakshi hired Kasim from the north, a fierce, ruthless thug that Bakshi found useful to scare people. When Bakshi discovered that you'd given a stake to Prem, he went crazy. He decided to kidnap Prem and force him to sell his share. When Prem refused, he tortured him. Prem however, held out. He preferred death to betraying you, Mr Fernandez. You don't find many guys like that nowadays, trust me.

He nodded in agreement.

–I will see Prem right, I assure you. What a fine young man, the only thing Anita has done right in her whole life is marrying him.

–They hadn't counted on Prem being so stubborn so kept him out at the farmhouse. Once he'd signed the papers, they would have killed him. And thrown him into the sea to make it look like a suicide. Then I came along and upset the picture and Kasim blew up. The psycho couldn't leave me alone. He came after me. Luckily, I managed to outmanoeuvre him.

I took a sip and let the whisky linger in my mouth before swallowing it.

–You see, Bakshi set up an elaborate scheme to force you to sell the mansion. He wasn't concerned about the house but the land. First, he seduced Maya with a good offer, but really it was peanuts. He wouldn't have paid her the remainder once he had the house signed over to him. Then your wife didn't want to be involved but she was scared of Kasim. They threatened to kill Prem if she didn't play along. She found herself in a difficult situation. Greed does that all the time. It catches people.

Fernandez pursed his lips and shook his head slightly.

–Yes, I know, she told me. It's partly the reason I'm not sending her to the police. Now you've confirmed what she's said, I feel a little better, though not by much. She almost had us all killed.

–She made a big mistake, and she realises it.

He sighed and stared at the table a long moment.

–You can't trust anyone these days. There's no fool like an old fool.

–Don't be too hard on yourself Mr Fernandez. There was a lot of money involved. When Bakshi found Anita was wild, he used Santana's gang to add to your problems. Kasim took over the gang and the blackmail rose to twenty-five lakhs. All this to make you lose your peace of mind, so that you would sell and maybe leave India for good.

He ran a finger over the rim of his whiskey glass.

–I was close, especially after they took Prem. That hurt the most. I think I would have left for Portugal if Prem had been discovered dead. How do you know all these things?

I shrugged with a slight smile.

–Good old-fashioned detective work. The parts I didn't understand I found out later through different people, but I'm not going to bore you with all the details. I always thought the blackmail angle was wrong, not for that amount, they were using it to pressure you. And would have succeeded but for Prem holding out. Do you know, they've decided to give their marriage a second chance?

His face brightened for the first time.

–I heard. I hope they have more success this time around.

I finished my glass and nodded at him. I placed the glass on the table.

–Do you mind if I say goodbye to Mrs Fernandez?

–Not at all. She's in her bedroom. On the first floor as you go up the stairs.

We shook hands.

–I'd like to see you at my office tomorrow, Chauhan. I've had enough of gardening, I'm taking back control again. I'd like you to work for me full time.

–What would I do?

–I want you to become my personal secretary. The pay will be very good.

–What about MD?

–Oh, I've decided you were right about him. He's too miserable to have around, and I don't trust him either. I'm going to fire him today. Well, how about it?

–It's kind of you Mr Fernandez but I'm going to pass.

–You mean you actually like working for fifteen hundred rupees and expenses? Risking your life for such a small amount?

–Not particularly, but I like my freedom. I like working for myself.

–You are strange. People would jump at the opportunity to work for me. It doesn't matter, I want you to come to my office so that I can show you my gratitude for saving Prem. I'm going to pay you another three lakhs. I hope you're not going to pass on that too.

—Not likely, I said, with a smile.

Fernandez shook my hand and walked back through the side door, as I made my way to the spacious hallway. There was no sign of MD. Maybe he had overheard that he was about to get fired. A maid came down the stairs with a box and walked out the front door. The sun shined through, warming my neck. I decided Fernandez wasn't tight with his money, just careful. He'd earned it the hard way, through enterprise and courage. I watched the maid give the box to the men near the van. They helped her and joked as she stood to chat. I looked up the wide marble stairs that curved up to the first floor and wondered what I was going to say to Mrs Fernandez.

33

THE MANSION was spacious and clean. Maybe I could get used to this place if I had a family. On my own, I was better off in my one-bedroom apartment in Boriwali. There was a strange, sad silence. I had expected more noise when someone is leaving; then again this wasn't a happy circumstance.

Along the wide corridor, there were ornate chairs placed along one side with paintings of green landscape in-between. Only one bedroom door was open in the middle. Inside, a couple of suitcases lay on a large king size bed, and Maya Fernandez packed her clothes without enthusiasm. I hadn't seen her since Saturday night and perhaps I had upset all her plans. I felt sorry for her then, she had been seduced by the promise of riches just like everyone else. Still, when the crucial moment had come, she had helped me escape. I wasn't a man to forget favours. She wore a sky-blue blouse over blue cotton trousers and a white silk scarf.

She had her back turned, the doors leading to the balcony were open and the cool breeze blew peach coloured curtains either side of the doors. It felt like a summer's morning. I knocked, and she turned around with a slight smile.

–When did you start to knock on doors?

–Oh, I always knock when a lady's present.

–You caught me at the right time Chauhan, I'm finally leaving. Please come inside.

I stepped inside and leaned against the wall.

–Yes I heard, your ex just told me.

–Did he say anything else?

–He said it's for the best.

She didn't reply and folded a couple of saris inside her suitcase.

–He would say that and before you ask, he has reduced my settlement to only fifty lakhs. He said I don't even deserve that, and if anything, I should be in jail with Bakshi.

I didn't reply but saw the frustration and disappointment on her face.

–A tight man, always was. Do you know, Chauhan, he never spent an extra rupee on me. I always had to persuade him to buy me nice gifts. Good riddance to all of them. Especially to Anita, I'll have some peace at last.

I left the wall and took two steps towards her.

–I'm sure you'll find someone nicer and richer.

–Oh go to hell, Chauhan. But she said it with a smile. –I'm glad to see you though. It's funny how you don't like someone on first meeting and grow fond of them later.

I nodded with a slight smile. –Steady with the compliments, I might start to believe you. I heard you were leaving so I thought I'd say goodbye, although I'm sure our paths will cross in the future.

–I hope so, she said and stopped packing. –Why didn't you turn me in to Inspector Dhanwan?

I looked at her a long moment.

–You know what I think of Dhanwan. And you saved my life by cutting me loose before Mr Smiley returned. So I guess I owed you. Now we're even.

She fiddled with the sari in her hands.

–Thank you all the same, Chauhan, she said in a voice filled with gratitude. –I only let you go because you mentioned your son, Sunil. How is he?

I raised my eyebrows then scratched the back of my head. She saw my reaction and half smiled.

–He's not your son, is he?

–No Maya, he's not. I'm sorry I lied to you but I was in a very tight spot.

She smiled with a slight shake of the head.

–I should have known, Chauhan. Who is he?

–A friend from my younger days. He went missing from the orphanage I used to stay in. Never saw him again but he was the first person who really looked out for me. Maybe I'll find him one day.

She came close and punched my arm lightly.

–You're something else, Chauhan. I still don't know how I fell in with Bakshi. I thought I was a smart woman.

–You're one of the smartest I've met in a while, Maya. And your seductive smile isn't too bad either.

She laughed and placed the sari in the suitcase. –That's what I like about you. You make people feel good about themselves. I haven't smiled in a long time.

–I've had no success with MD.

She half-turned.

–He was born miserable. Anyway, I have to find a job now. Me. Mrs Maya Fernandez. I don't think I'll miss any of this though.

–You might find Robby.

She tried to suppress a smile.

–Robby can go to hell. You were right. I should have left this marriage a long time ago. Then I might have left with my head held high.

She moved across the bed towards a cream coloured cupboard to the far side with mirrors and took out a light grey business suit.

–We all have regrets, Maya. I'm certain you'll land on your feet. I'm going to see Bakshi. Any messages?

She paused a moment and narrowed her eyes.

–The police won't find him. He's far too crafty. I bet you fifty thousand rupees, he's in America by now.

–Here's some breaking news. Dhanwan arrested him at the Santa Cruz airport. Bakshi was trying to fly out under a false passport and name.

She raised her eyebrows and shook her head.

–And I'm Santa Claus, she said.

I raised my shoulders and dropped them.

–I speak the truth, Maya. He's in the police station as we speak. Bakshi wasn't as smart as he thought.

She looked serious and a frown appeared.

–I never thought they'd find him. He had so much influence and connections. He isn't going to forget you, Chauhan.

–I'll take that as a compliment. By the way, Anita and Prem are going to make a fresh start as well.

She lit a cigarette, pressed down her blue blouse and looked at me with cool eyes.

–I give it three months, tops. Do you know Chauhan, there's one thing I never understood. Bakshi always knew my movements, even what I had said sometimes.

I glanced around the room for fitted devices or secret cameras. Nothing caught my eye.

–Maybe he had your phones tapped.

–No, I checked. There was nothing.

–Devious people shouldn't be underestimated.

She hardly heard me and blew the smoke out the side of her mouth.

–Even now when I look out from the balcony, I feel someone's watching me.

Maybe her mood was contagious. I felt a chill on the back of my neck. I half turned. MD was standing there with a black suitcase in his hand. He placed it on the edge of the bed.

–Did you hear MD? she said. –The police have arrested Bakshi. Isn't that good news? We can all breathe easier now.

The suitcase fell to the floor. MD looked vulnerable. The first time I'd seen that look on him. He pulled his lips tight against his teeth and sucked in air. He picked up the suitcase and placed it firmly onto the bed. Then he was back to being MD.

–I'm sorry Madam, that is good news.

It sounded false in his mouth. He gave me a pall-bearer stare. I was a dead body. Perhaps Fernandez had told him that he'd been fired. And not before time too. I half turned to face Maya again, and was about to light a cigarette, when she pushed an arm out with alarm.

–Look out!

I ducked and swayed left on instinct. A hand passed my right shoulder. In the hand was a large flashing blade. I grabbed his right arm but he twisted and swung the knife up to my stomach. I jumped back. Maya scrambled onto the bed. He shifted his weight, kicked, then leapt and thrust the knife at my heart. I jerked left and hit his wrist with the side of my foot. The knife fell, but he kept coming. He grabbed me around the waist and hurled me onto the floor. I felt his hands on my neck, his grip tightening. I wrestled left then right, and swung a fist into his kidneys. It had no effect. I punched him in the face. He had a hard face and my knuckles hurt. I pushed him off and kicked him in the groin. He cried. At last.

When he tried standing, I punched down on his nose, twice. Blood ran out of his nose and spotted the floor. I punched him once more to the side of the head, just so that I felt better. He went down, the fight had left him.

He crawled back against the wall coughing, sat up on his elbows and wiped the blood off his face. He glared at me, taking heavy jerky breaths.

I glanced at Maya, she had got off the bed and moved to the far side of the room. Now, she came forward and stared at MD, stunned. I picked up the knife, opening and closing my hands.

–What's the idea? I asked him.

–Go rot in hell.

MD levered himself up slowly against the wall. Eyes dull and dead.

–You work for Bakshi, is that it? Speak up or I'll...

I moved towards him.

He wiped his bloody nose with his sleeve. He grunted.

–Everything was fine until you showed up. You're going to die for this, Chauhan.

–MD? she said, clasping her hand. –I trusted you.

He ignored her, stared at me and muttered curses under his breath. I watched him, then half turned to Maya.

–Now, you know how Bakshi got hold of a crystal ball for all your movements. He had this gorilla spying on you all the time. Probably had a few other informers too.

MD rushed at me, arms flailing, emitting a piercing grunt of rage. He half caught me, but I parried him off. He tripped over Maya's Gucci handbag and crashed through the room and toppled over the balcony. He screamed as he fell. We rushed over and looked down. He had fallen into a large thorn bush head first. He was strangely silent, then suddenly cried for help. People hurried around him. For once I appreciated a designer bag.

–Hold him, I shouted.

Several heads looked up, puzzled. I turned to Maya as she moved back into the bedroom. A cool breeze followed us inside shifting the curtains slightly. She came close and held onto to my shoulders.

–You just can't find the staff these days, I said.

She smiled. I could smell her perfume. She was a fine woman.

–What can I say, Chauhan?

–If you ever need me, Maya Fernandez, I'll be at the end of a telephone line. Call, okay?

–I will.

We shared a warm look as we caught one another's eye. I saw wisdom, beauty and an insubordinate spirit. I wonder what she saw in me. Then the moment was gone. She pulled away a fraction, but it was a clue, and I stepped back too. I kissed her on the cheek, then headed downstairs.

34

MY TRUSTY Contessa started first time. I reversed the car and looked at the gleaming mansion, hopefully for the last time. I was in no hurry to return. I drove away from that rich and sinister world. There might be some new cases from this success, at least I hoped so. Sunlight reflected off the tall buildings, casting shadows around corners.

There wasn't a cloud in the sky. A clear blue day that spread in all directions. Ahead, the Arabian Sea stretched out, a shimmering blue surface with liners floating on the horizon. I almost felt like stopping a moment, but instead joined the afternoon traffic. I drove to the new Malabar Hill police station. I had no desire to run into Dhanwan, but maybe I'd have to in order to meet Bakshi. He was the sonofabitch who had ordered Kasim to kill me. I wanted to see him face to face.

Police jeeps were parked in the large courtyard to the right. I drove inside and pulled up beside one. I watched from under the shade of a spreading banyan tree. Constables in khaki uniforms walked inside the station. There was no urgency in their steps, it was that kind of warm day. A couple of Alsatians barked from inside a van. I was about to light a cigarette when two constables strode out followed by Bakshi in handcuffs. He was unshaven and wore a creased, dark suit. Dark circles had formed under his blood shot eyes. I was in luck and got out of the car.

A lawyer in white shirt, black jacket and trousers walked sheepishly behind, as if Bakshi had just fired him. They crossed the dusty courtyard squinting their eyes, and moved towards the back of a police van. Two constables waited with the doors open. There was no sign of Dhanwan and that suited me fine. I moved out from the shade towards them. Bakshi saw me and spat in front of me. I was a couple of steps away from him when I spoke.

–Remember me, Bakshi?

He looked up sullenly.

–Detective Chauhan. I won't forget you.

Up close, Bakshi looked worse. A haggard face, and the smell of body odour around him. There was, however, still a fire glowing in his eyes.

–You had everything and lost it all because... I said, and closed the gap so that we were almost touching. I whispered these words in his ear: –Because you're one greedy bastard.

Bakshi tried to head butt me, but I swayed to my right. The constables grabbed him and held him firmly.

–Let's go, said the head constable.

Bakshi ground his teeth and stood still.

–Wait. I want to speak to the detective. I'll never forget you, Chauhan. No jail can hold Dinesh Bakshi for long. And the day I get out, I'll destroy you. I'll destroy everything you hold dear. That's my promise to you.

The constables exchanged nervous glances and fidgeted, unsure what to do. The lawyer stared at his shoes. The menace in the words affected me a little too, but I recovered. I looked him in the eye.

–Bakshi, listen to me. When you leave jail, you'll be well past your prime. At that age, you'll be wetting your pants, dribbling out of your mouth and staring at blank walls. You've lost half your mind as it is. You'll lose the rest in jail. If you do get out, make sure you bring a gun. Next time, I won't hand you over to the police. That's my promise to you. Oh, on the upside, MD will be joining you to keep you company as well. I arrested him today.

Bakshi looked like he'd passed from disbelief to fear to denial. He spat on the ground and stumbled into the back of the van. His face framed by the rear door van glass. The police van drove out of the gates in a trail of exhaust fumes. I walked back to my car and reversed out.

I wasn't sure where I wanted to go after meeting him, but I needed a drink. I drove to a fancy bar that had opened recently. It was half full with office types. I ordered a scotch with soda. The barman looked around twenty and didn't know how to start a conversation. That was all right. A humdrum Hindi song played in the background. I couldn't follow the words, something about a man falling in love and being rejected. The drink didn't make me feel any better. Too many people had died on this case for my liking, but for lady luck, I would have joined the body count.

I had the strange urge to find Ice Baby and celebrate with her. I left the drink and headed out of the bar. The sun hit my face. I had no idea where Ice Baby was now, and I doubted she'd ever be in touch again.

I decided to drive to my office at Rising Towers. Forty minutes later, I parked the car and was riding up the lift to my floor. I flicked the lights on. No one waited in the reception room, but some brown envelopes had arrived on the floor. They always gave me company. I picked up the pile and placed them on top of all the other bill reminders.

In my office, I lit a cigarette and threw open the window. A cool breeze touched my face. Rekha pouted from across the road on the bill board, and I nodded a hello. I sat down on my chair. The whisky bottle was in the bottom drawer as usual, so I made myself a drink. It tasted better than the one at the fancy bar. For one, it wasn't watered down.

I took a sip and watched out of the window at the slow-moving traffic below. Would I ever see Anita, Maya Fernandez or Ice Baby again? Mumbai was a big city and people were swallowed here. I picked up the phone and listened to my secretary. There were congratulatory messages from Gautam, one from Thankey. The next message was from Mrs

Chatterjee. It was one long irritated flow of words and it raised my eyebrows.

–Hello, Detective Chauhan? Why don't you ever employ a secretary? I absolutely hate leaving messages. Is this any way to run an agency? I will phone you later again. My husband has run away and left me. He complained he couldn't deal with my suspicious mind. Imagine!

I put the phone down and finished the drink. I tried to wrestle a smile from my face but didn't quite manage it.

About the author

Vijay Medtia is a novelist and short story writer based in Manchester, U.K. His regular trips to India, inspire much of his writing, along with the great past writers. His debut novel, The House of Subadar, was short-listed for The Glen Dimplex Literary Prize, Dublin.

He has had several short stories published in the U.K. and in literary magazines in India. His short story, English Babu, has been set as an exam question for students in Denmark.

He likes John Steinbeck's quote, 'The profession of book writing makes horse racing seem like a solid stable business.'

For further information please visit:

vijaymedtia.com
vmedtia@blogspot.co.uk
vijaymedtia@twitter.com